SUPER TRASH CLASH

WRITTEN AND DRAWN BY
EDGAR CAMACHO

TRANSLATION BY
EVA IBARZABAL

W9-CJG-033

SUPER TRASH CLASH © 2022 EDGAR CAMACHO

PUBLISHED BY TOP SHELF PRODUCTIONS, AN IMPRINT OF IDW PUBLISHING, A DIVISION OF IDEA AND DESIGN WORKS, LLC. OFFICES: TOP SHELF PRODUCTIONS, C/O IDEA & DESIGN WORKS, LLC, 2765 TRUXTUN ROAD, SAN DIEGO, CA 92106. TOP SHELF PRODUCTIONS®, THE TOP SHELF LOGO, IDEA AND DESIGN WORKS®, AND THE IDW LOGO ARE REGISTERED TRADEMARKS OF IDEA AND DESIGN WORKS, LLC. ALL RIGHTS RESERVED. WITH THE EXCEPTION OF SMALL EXCERPTS OF ARTWORK USED FOR REVIEW PURPOSES, NONE OF THE CONTENTS OF THIS PUBLICATION MAY BE REPRINTED WITHOUT THE PERMISSION OF IDW PUBLISHING.

IDW PUBLISHING DOES NOT READ OR ACCEPT UNSOLICITED SUBMISSIONS OF IDEAS, STORIES, OR ARTWORK.

TRANSLATION BY EVA IBARZABAL

EDITED BY LEIGH WALTON

EDITOR-IN-CHIEF: CHRIS STAROS

ISBN: 978-1-60309-516-7   25 24 23 22   4 3 2 1

VISIT OUR ONLINE CATALOG AT TOPSHELFCOMIX.COM.

PRINTED IN KOREA.

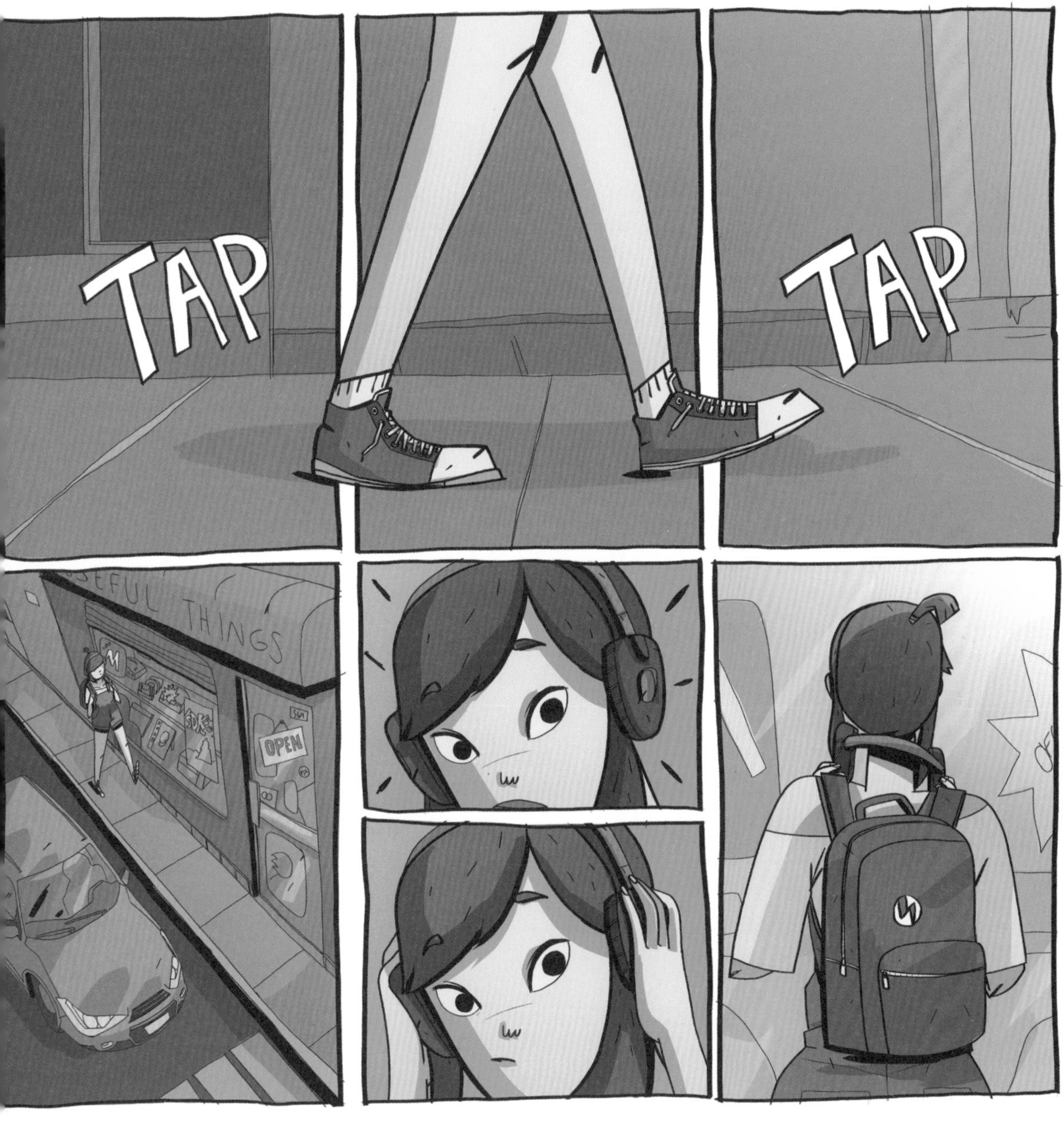
TAP
TAP
OPEN

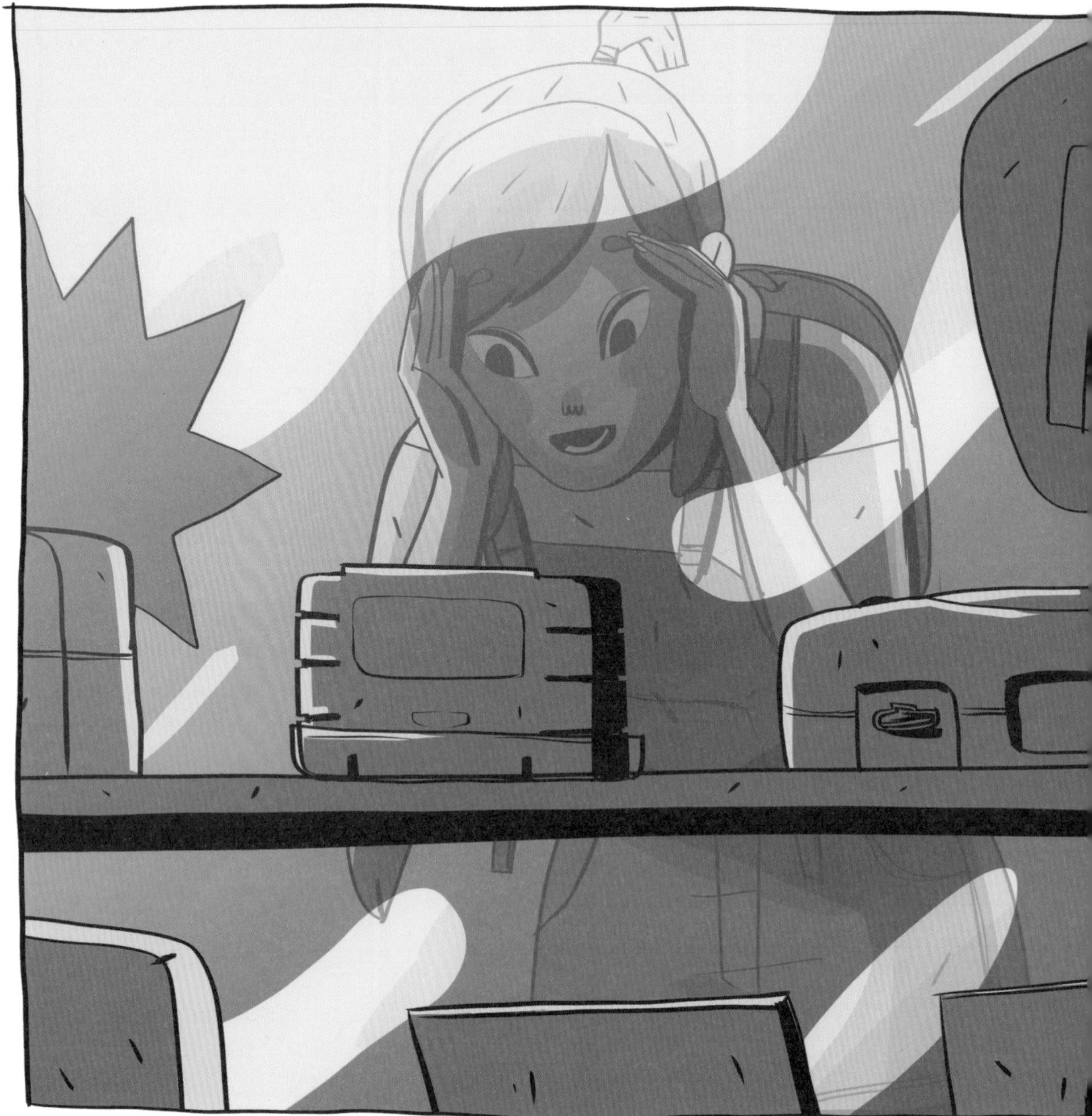

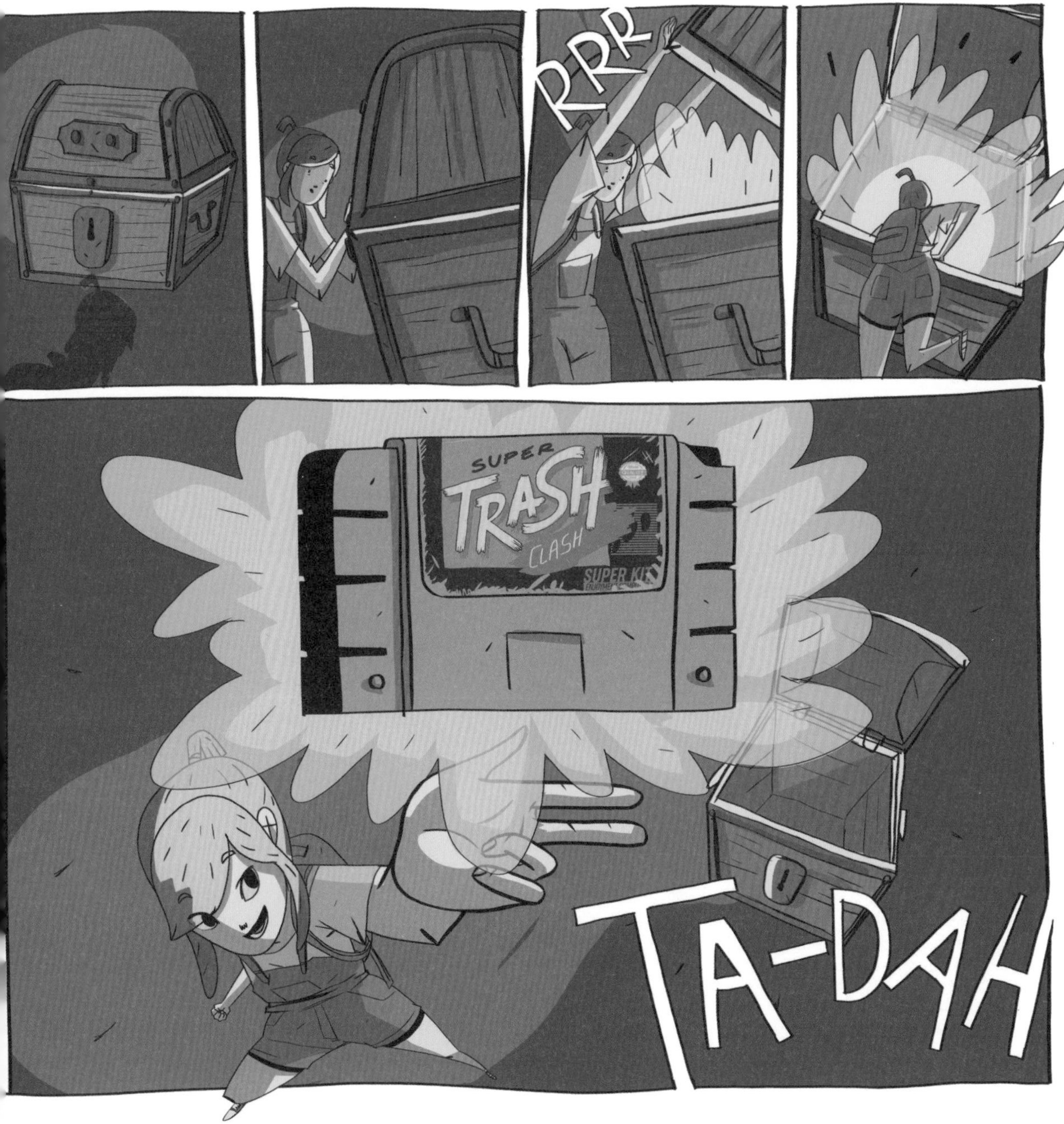
RRR
SUPER TRASH CLASH
SUPER KITS
TA-DAH

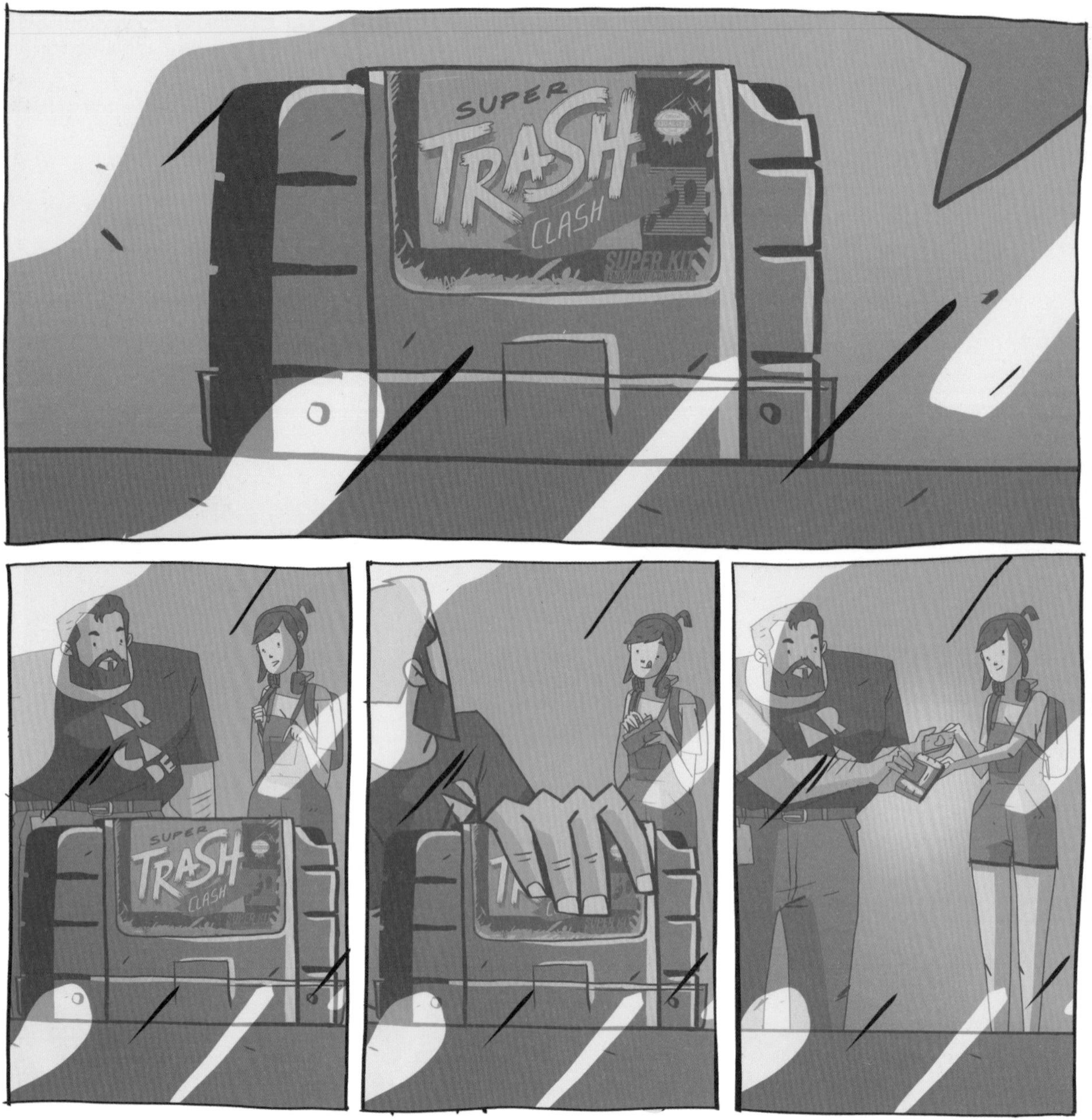
SUPER
TRASH
CLASH
SUPER KIT
SUPER
TRASH
CLASH

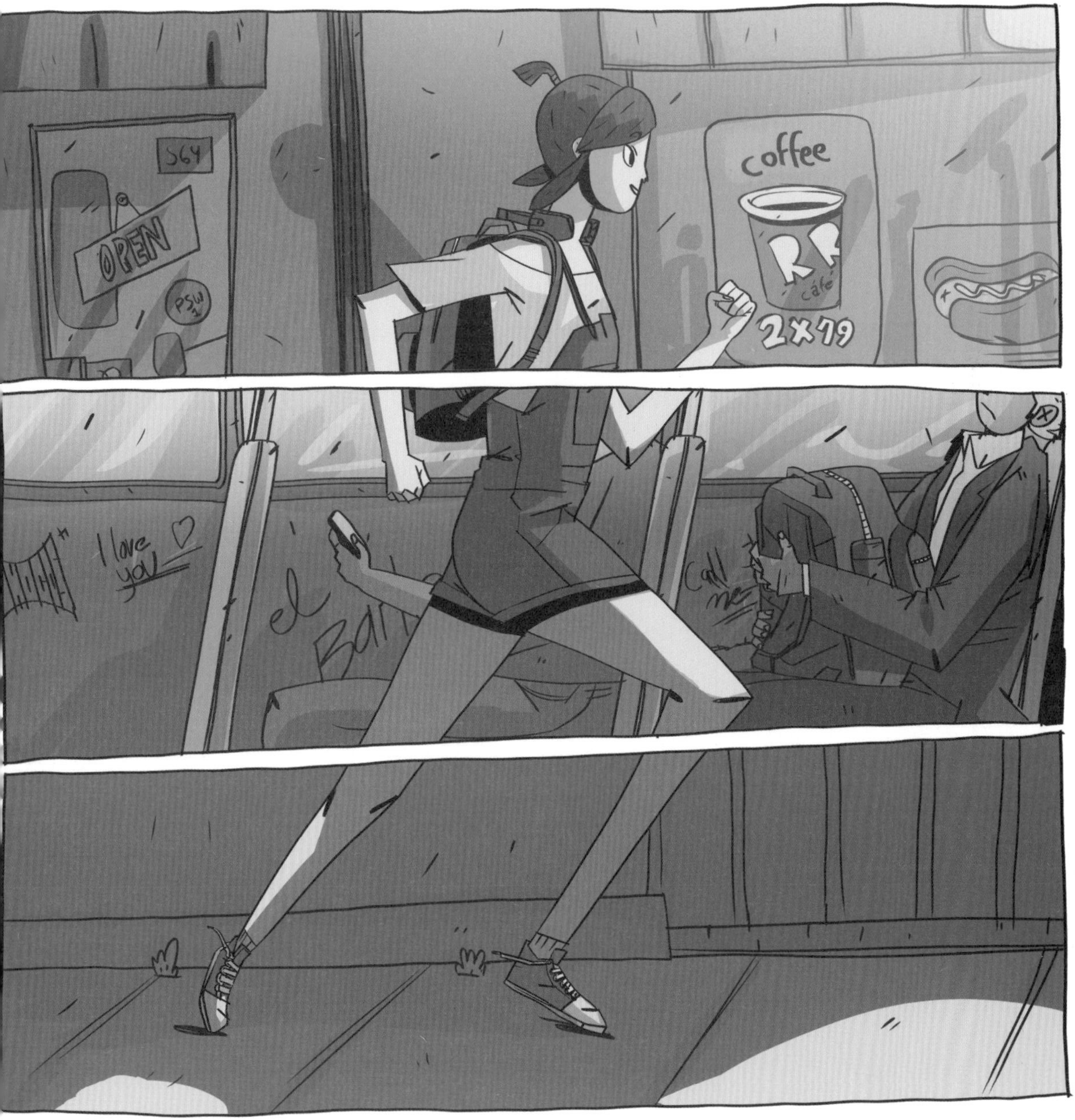
564
OPEN
PSW 1
coffee
RR café
2x79
I love you
el Barr
Call me

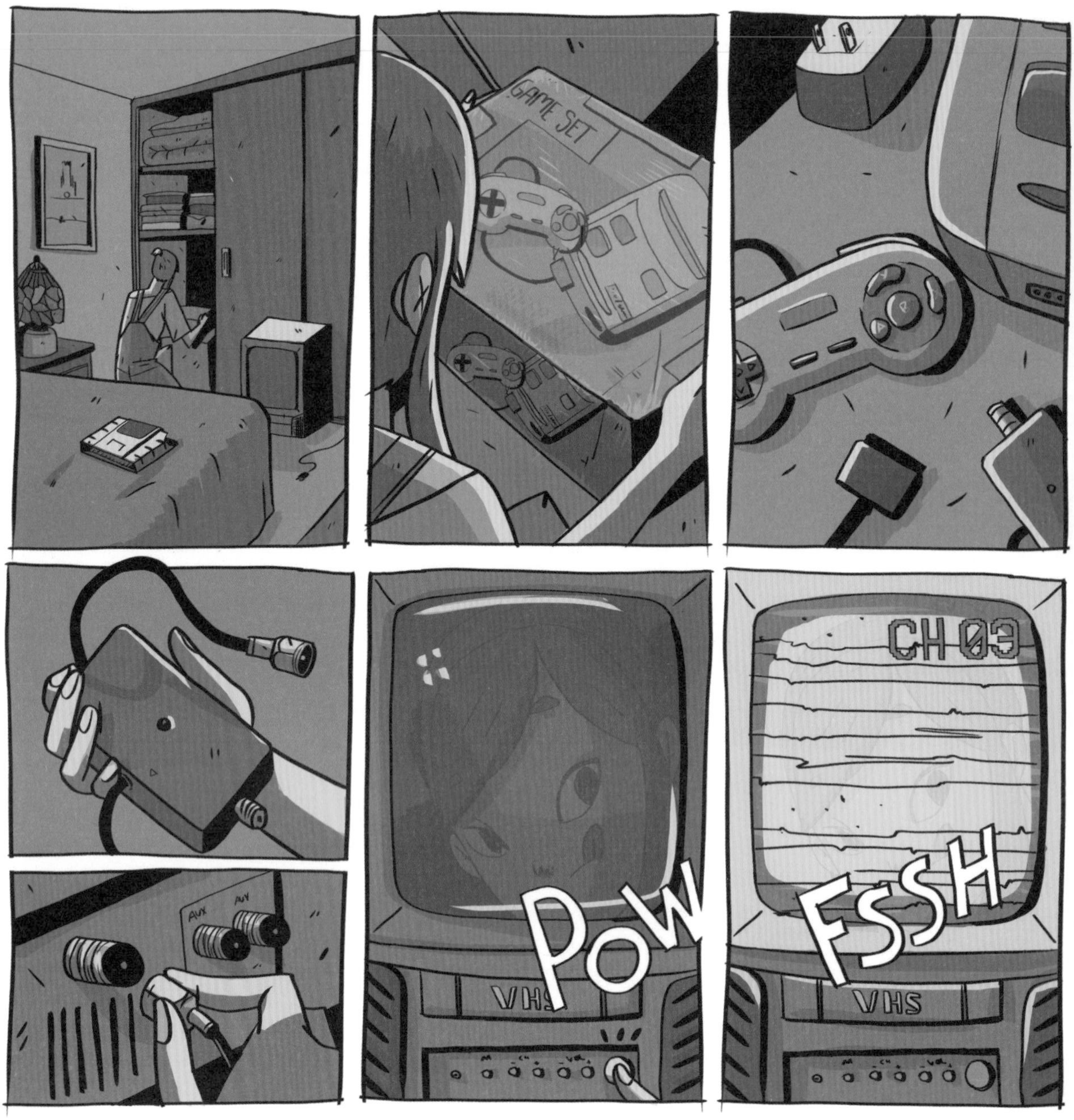
GAME SET
AUX
AUX
VHS
POW
CH 03
FSSH
VHS

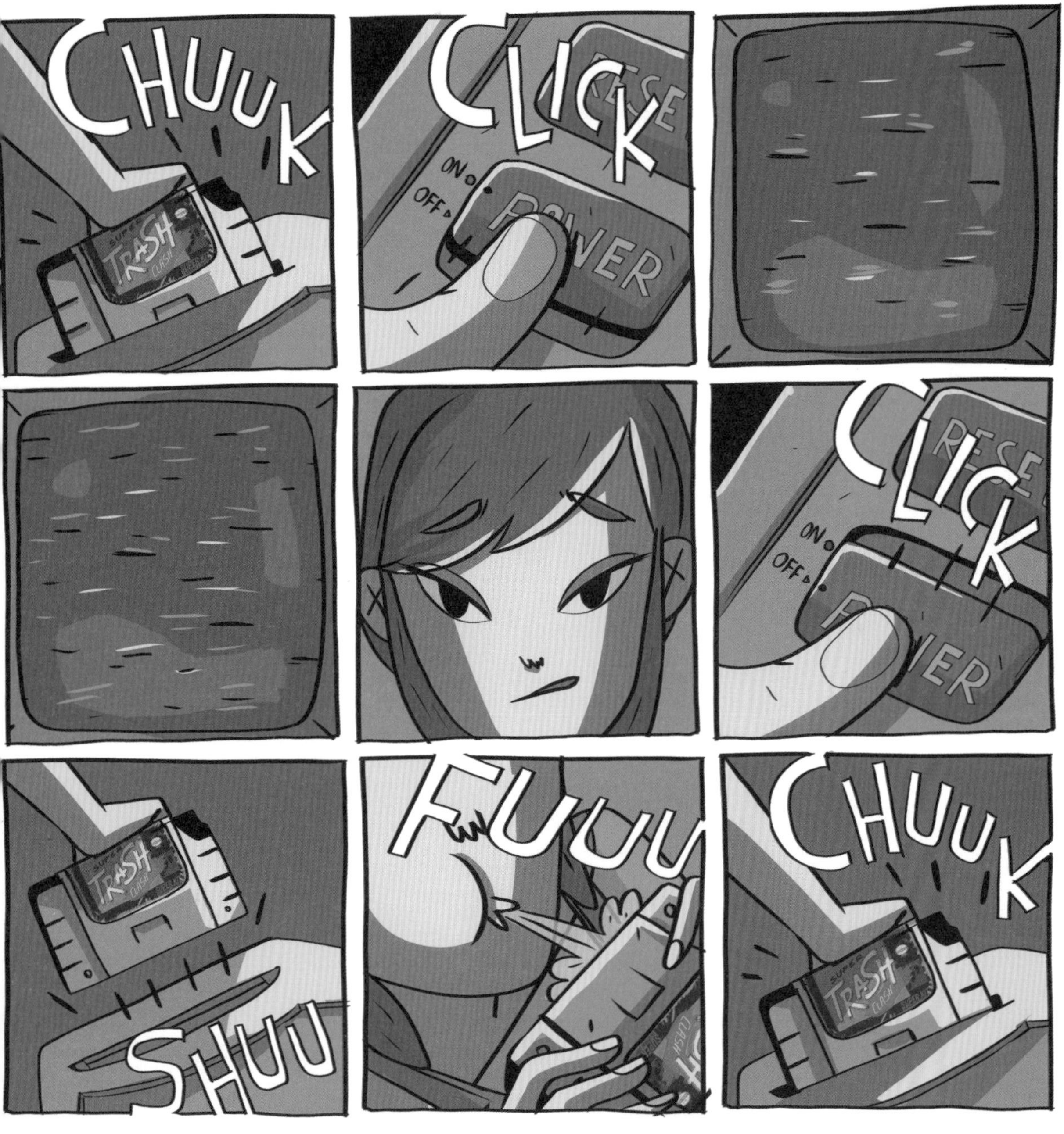
CHUUK
TRASH
CLASH
CLICK
ON
OFF
CLICK
ON
OFF
TRASH
CLASH
SHUU
FUUU
CHUUK
TRASH
CLASH

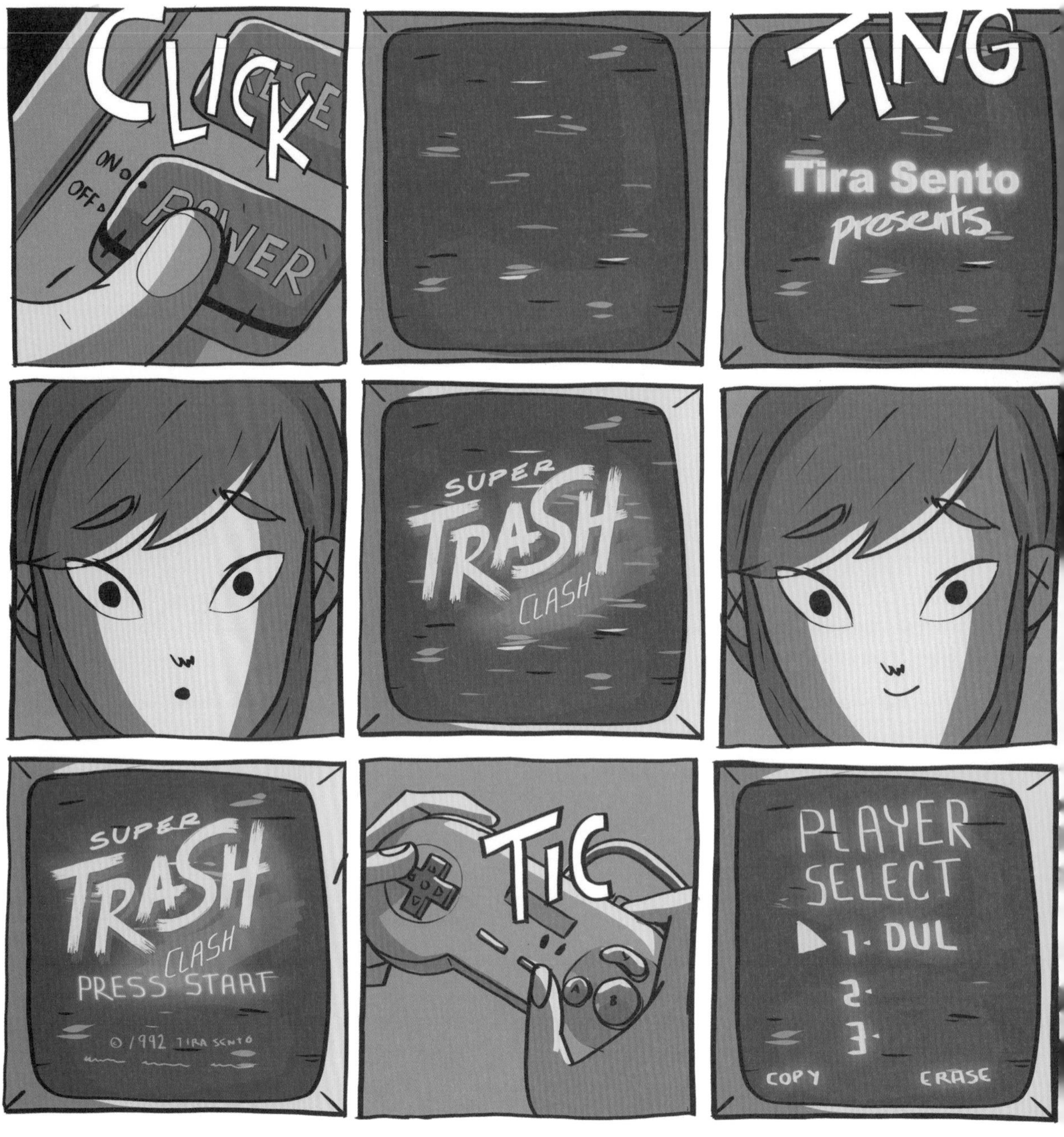
CLICK
RESET
ON
OFF
POWER
TING
Tira Sento
presents
SUPER
TRASH
CLASH
SUPER
TRASH
CLASH
PRESS START
© 1992 TIRA SENTO
TIC
A
B
PLAYER
SELECT
1- DUL
2-
3-
COPY
ERASE

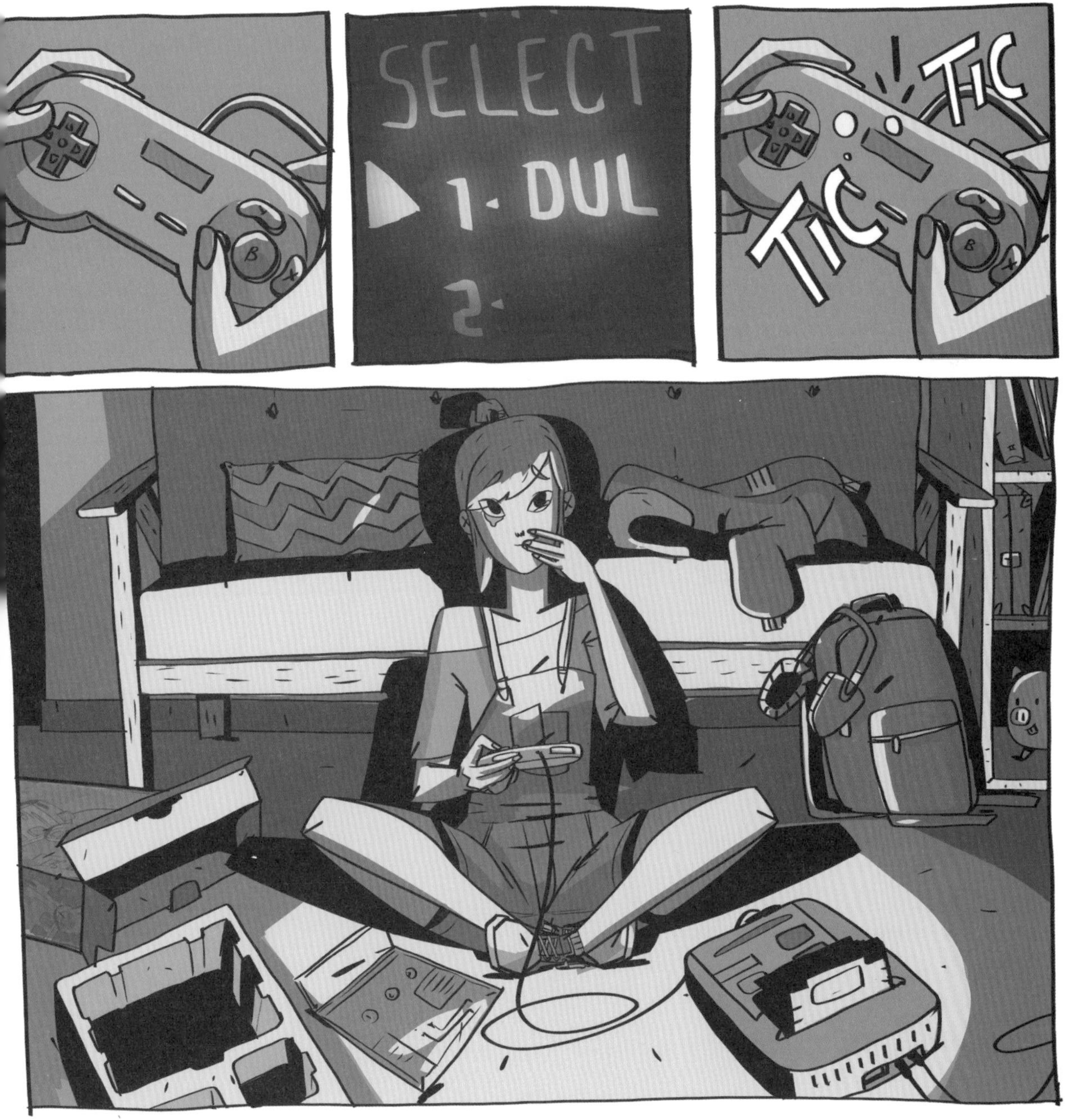
SELECT
1- DUL
2-
TIC
TIC

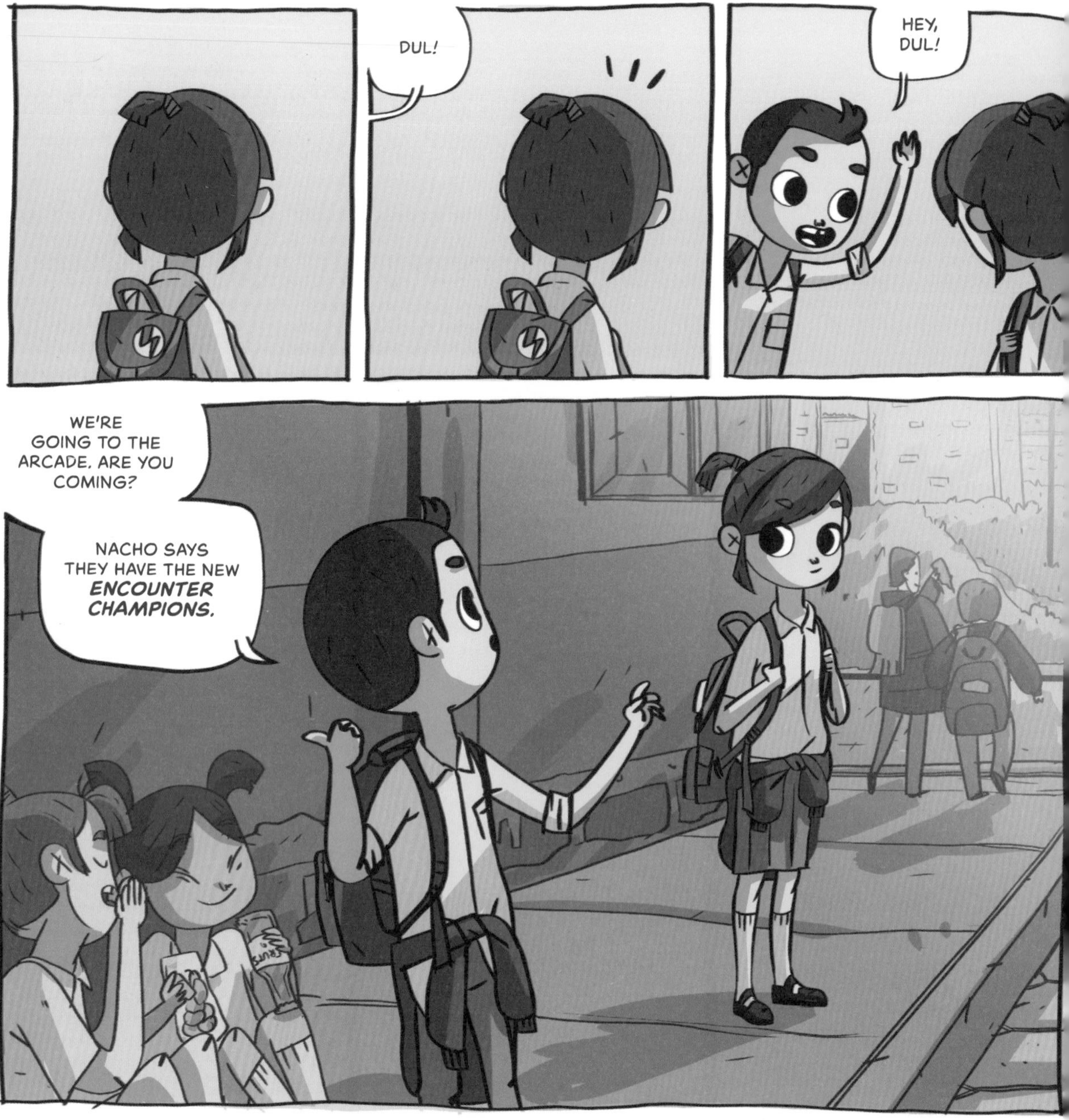
DUL!
HEY, DUL!
WE'RE GOING TO THE ARCADE. ARE YOU COMING?
NACHO SAYS THEY HAVE THE NEW ENCOUNTER CHAMPIONS.

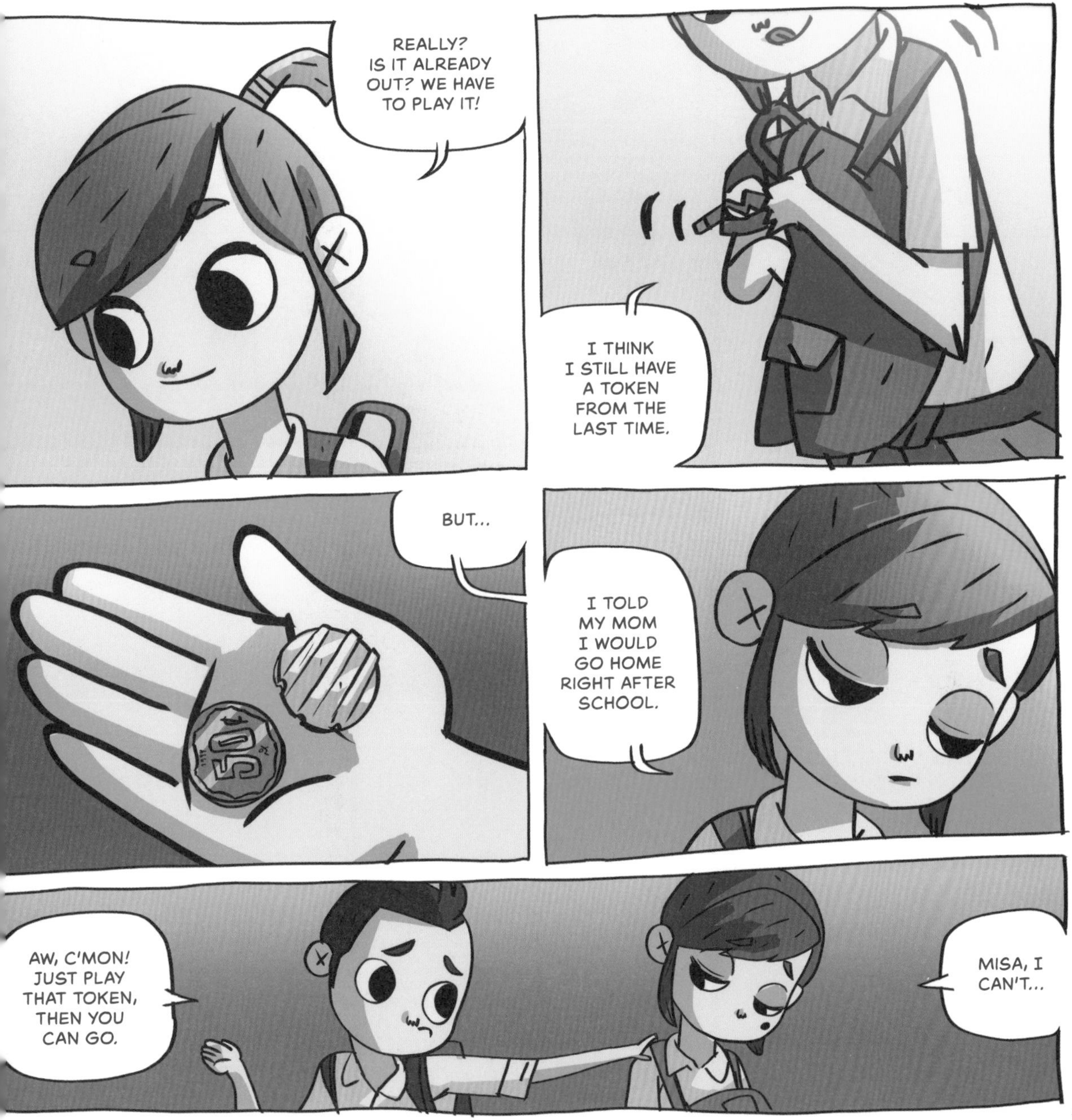
REALLY? IS IT ALREADY OUT? WE HAVE TO PLAY IT!
I THINK I STILL HAVE A TOKEN FROM THE LAST TIME.
BUT...
I TOLD MY MOM I WOULD GO HOME RIGHT AFTER SCHOOL.
AW, C'MON! JUST PLAY THAT TOKEN, THEN YOU CAN GO.
MISA, I CAN'T...

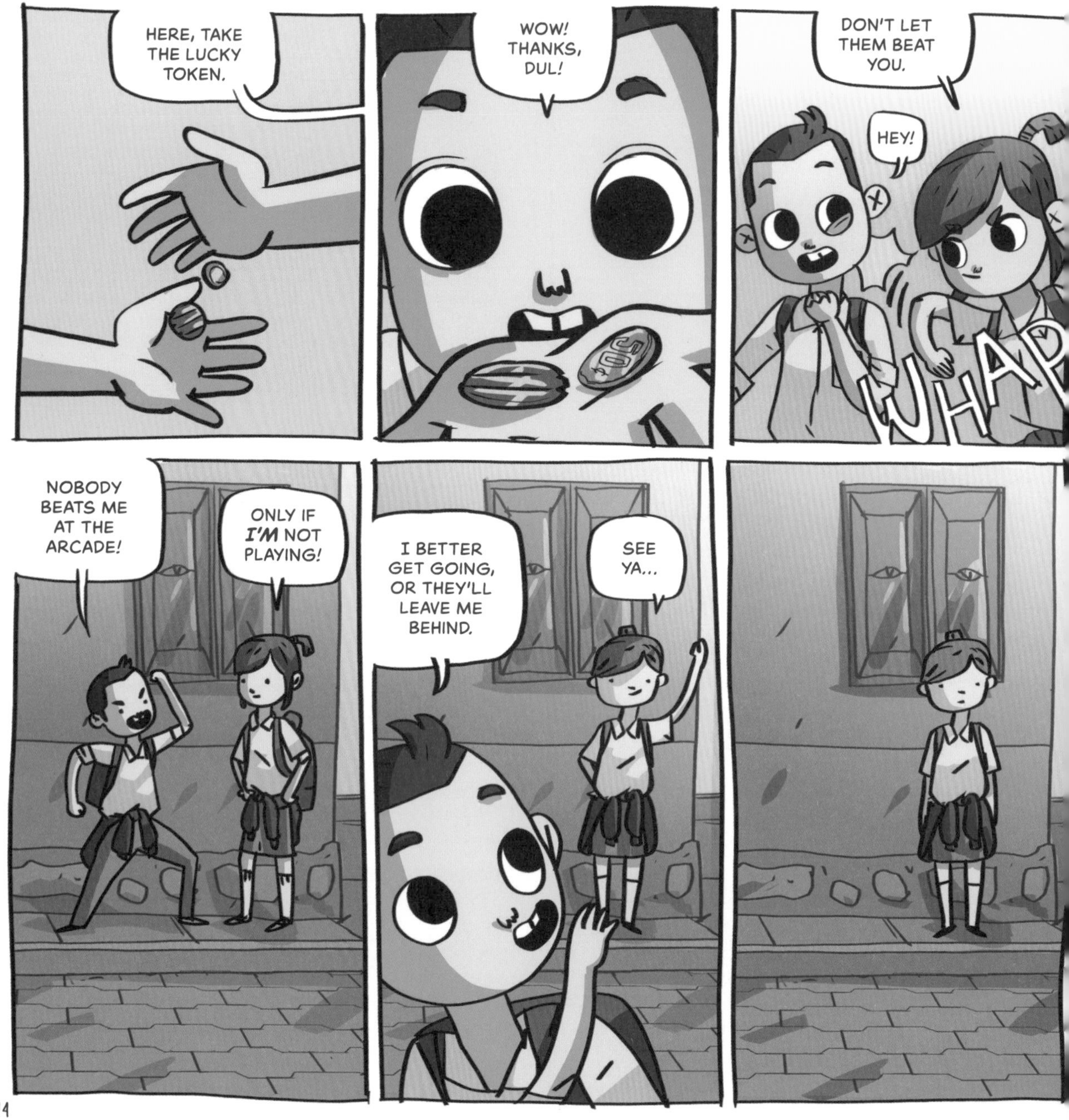
HERE, TAKE THE LUCKY TOKEN.
WOW! THANKS, DUL!
DON'T LET THEM BEAT YOU.
HEY!
WHAP
NOBODY BEATS ME AT THE ARCADE!
ONLY IF *I'M* NOT PLAYING!
I BETTER GET GOING, OR THEY'LL LEAVE ME BEHIND.
SEE YA...

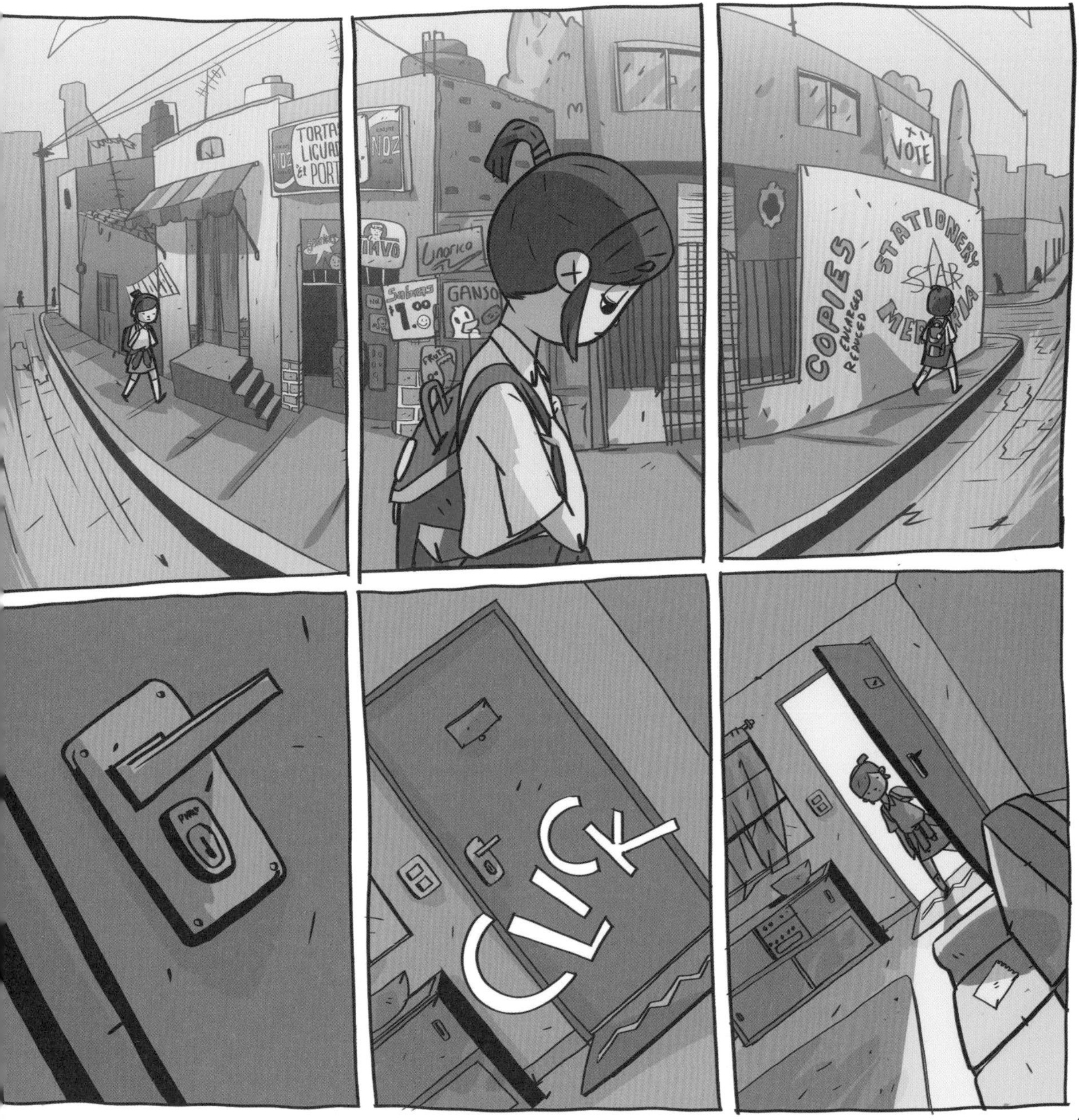
VOTE
STATIONERY
STAR
COPIES
ENLARGED
REDUCED
Sabores $1.00
GANSO
CLICK

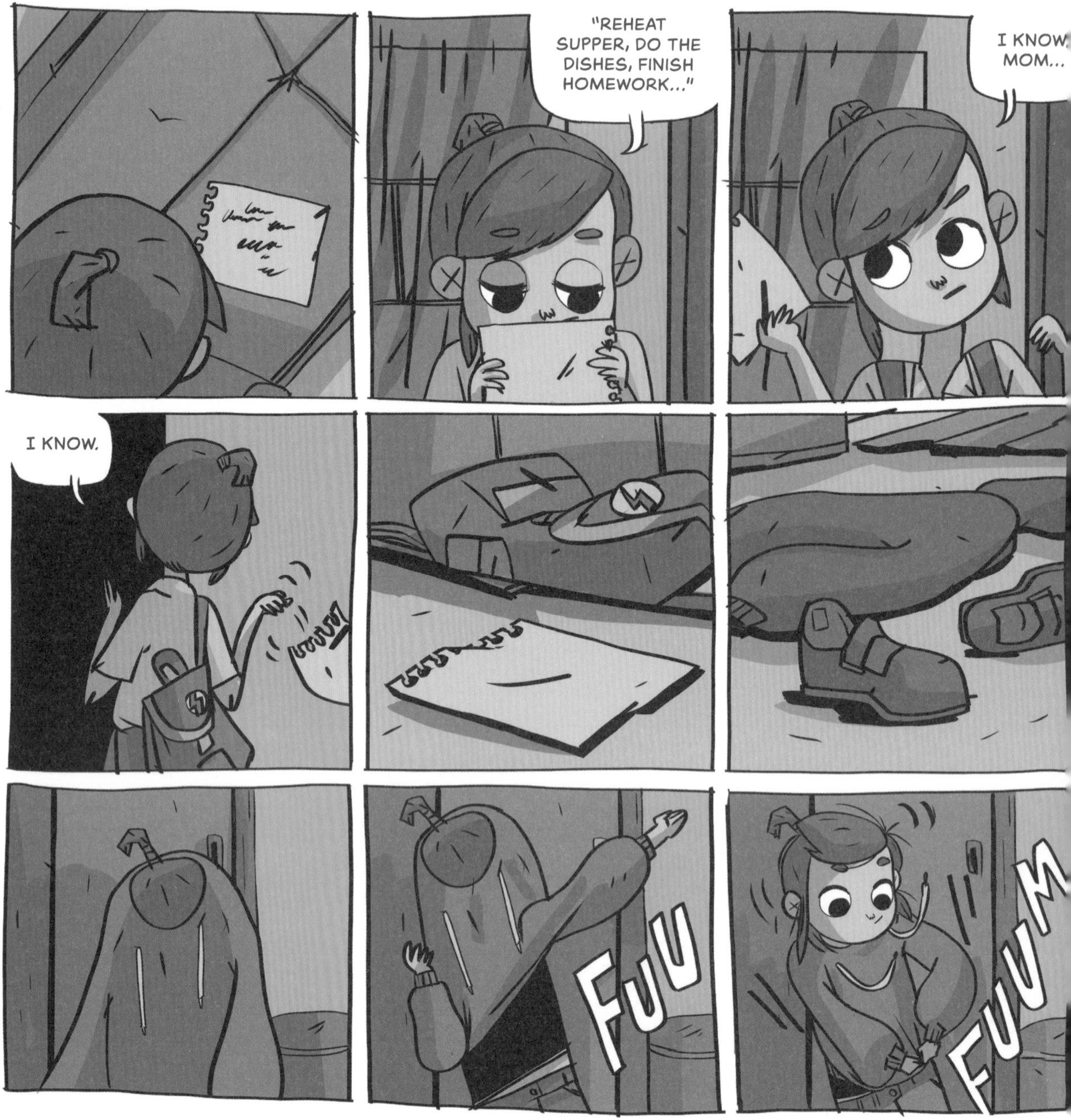
"REHEAT SUPPER, DO THE DISHES, FINISH HOMEWORK..."
I KNOW. MOM...
I KNOW.
FUU
FUUM

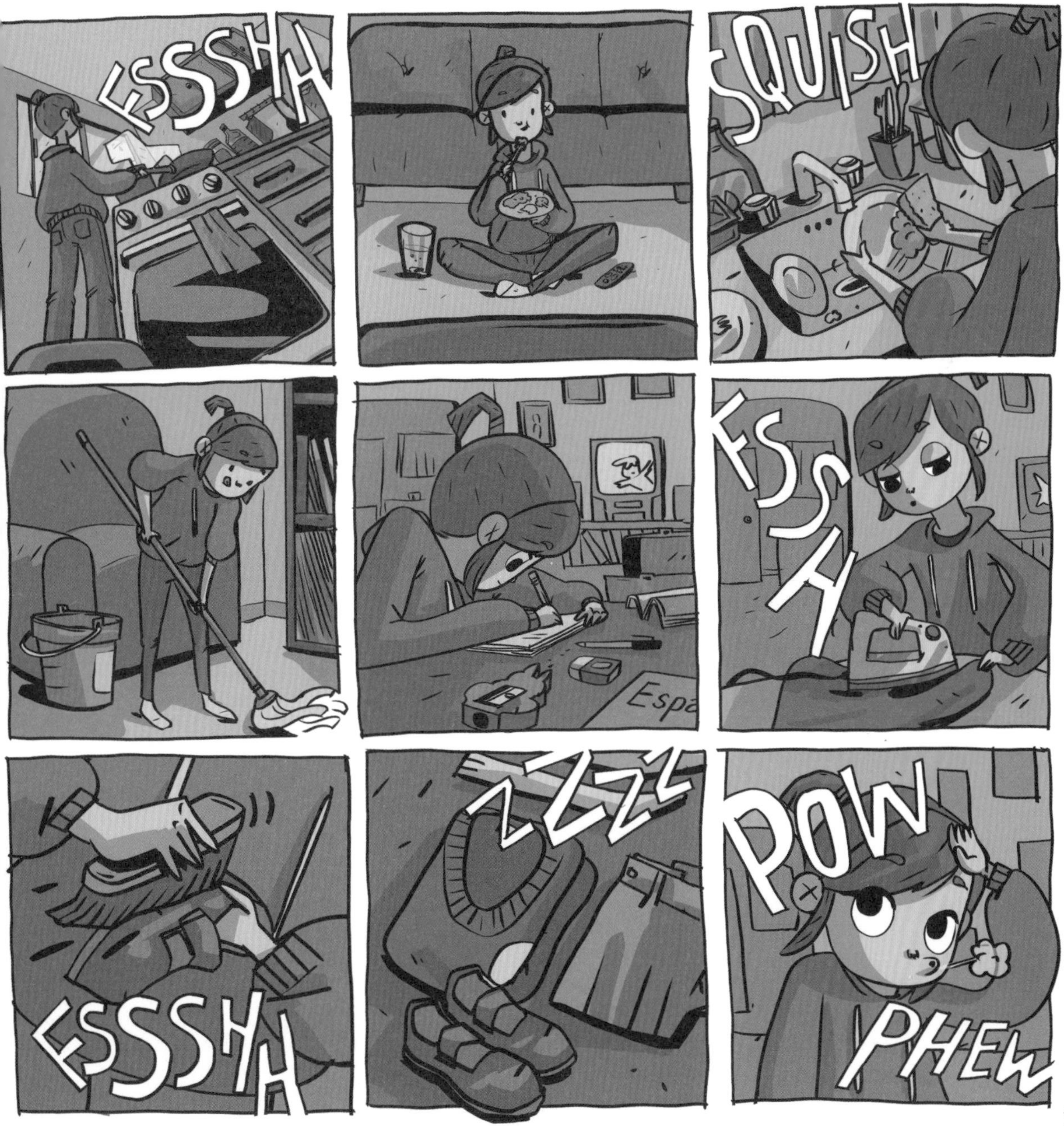
ESSSHH
SQUISH
FSSSH
Espa
ESSSHHH
ZZZZ
POW
PHEW

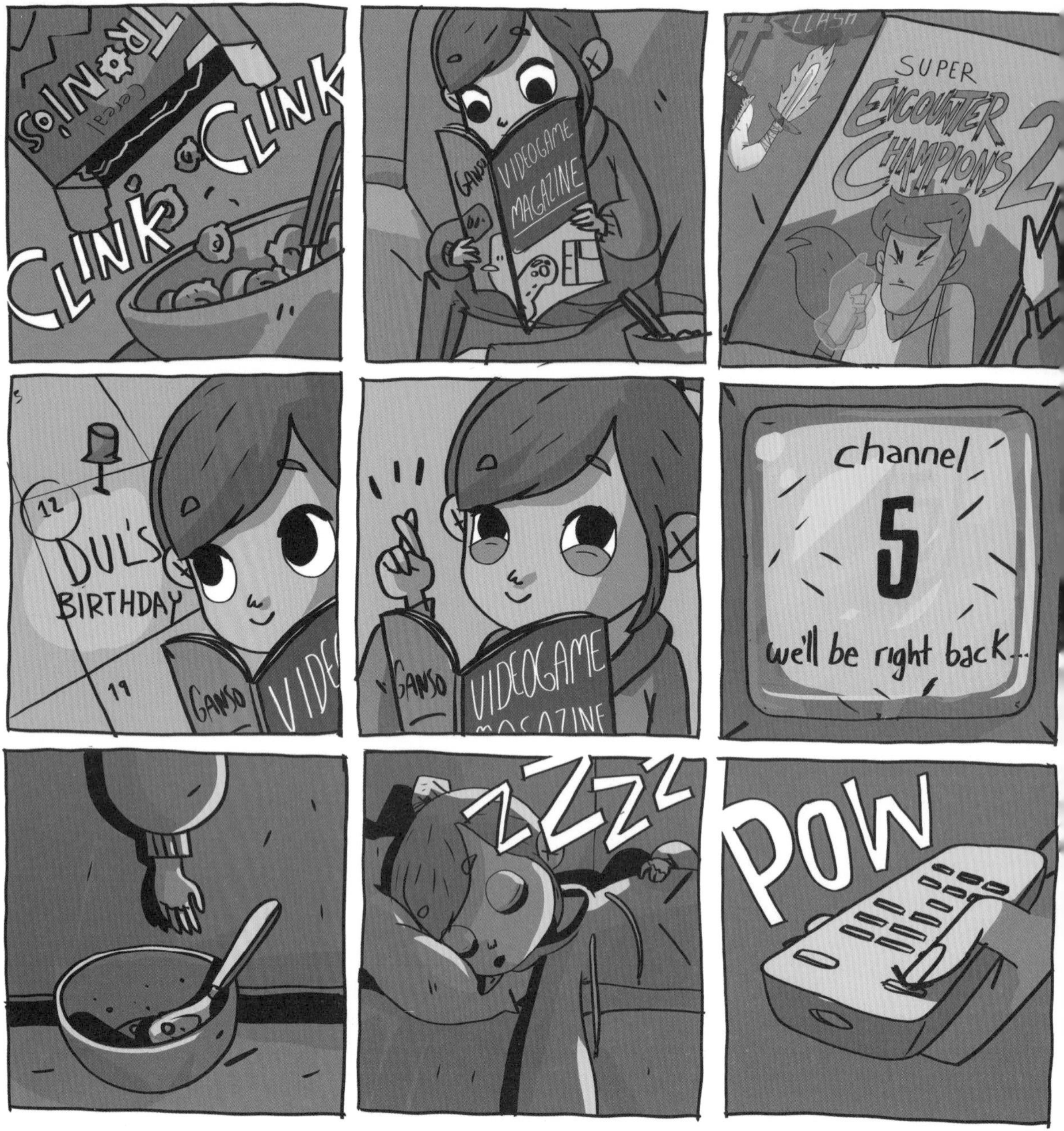
TRONIC'S
Cereal
CLINK
CLINK
CLINK
GANSO
VIDEOGAME MAGAZINE
SUPER
ENCOUNTER CHAMPIONS 2
12
DUL'S BIRTHDAY
19
GANSO
VIDEOGAME
channel
5
we'll be right back...
ZZZZ
POW

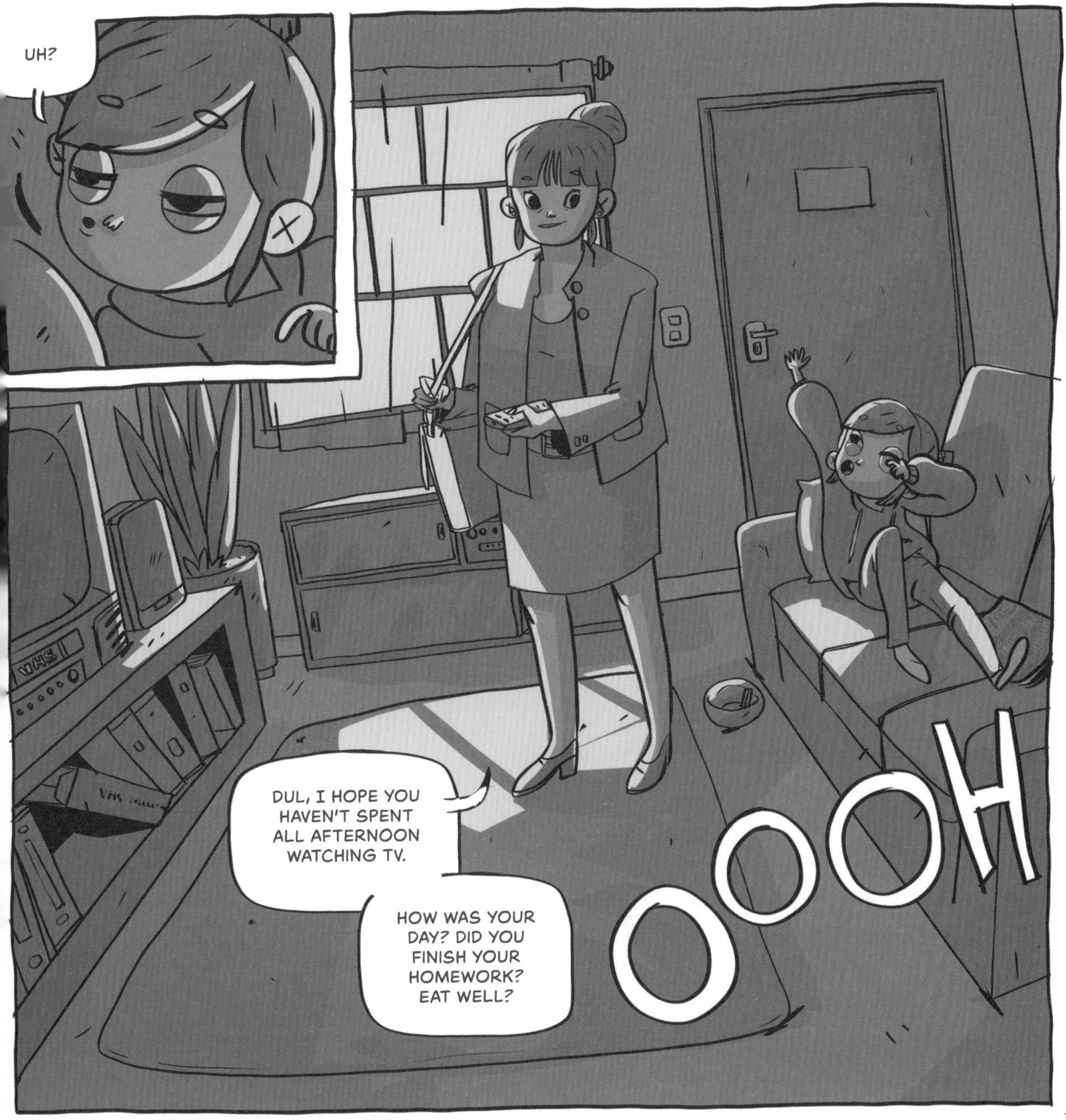
UH?
DUL, I HOPE YOU HAVEN'T SPENT ALL AFTERNOON WATCHING TV.
HOW WAS YOUR DAY? DID YOU FINISH YOUR HOMEWORK? EAT WELL?
OOOH

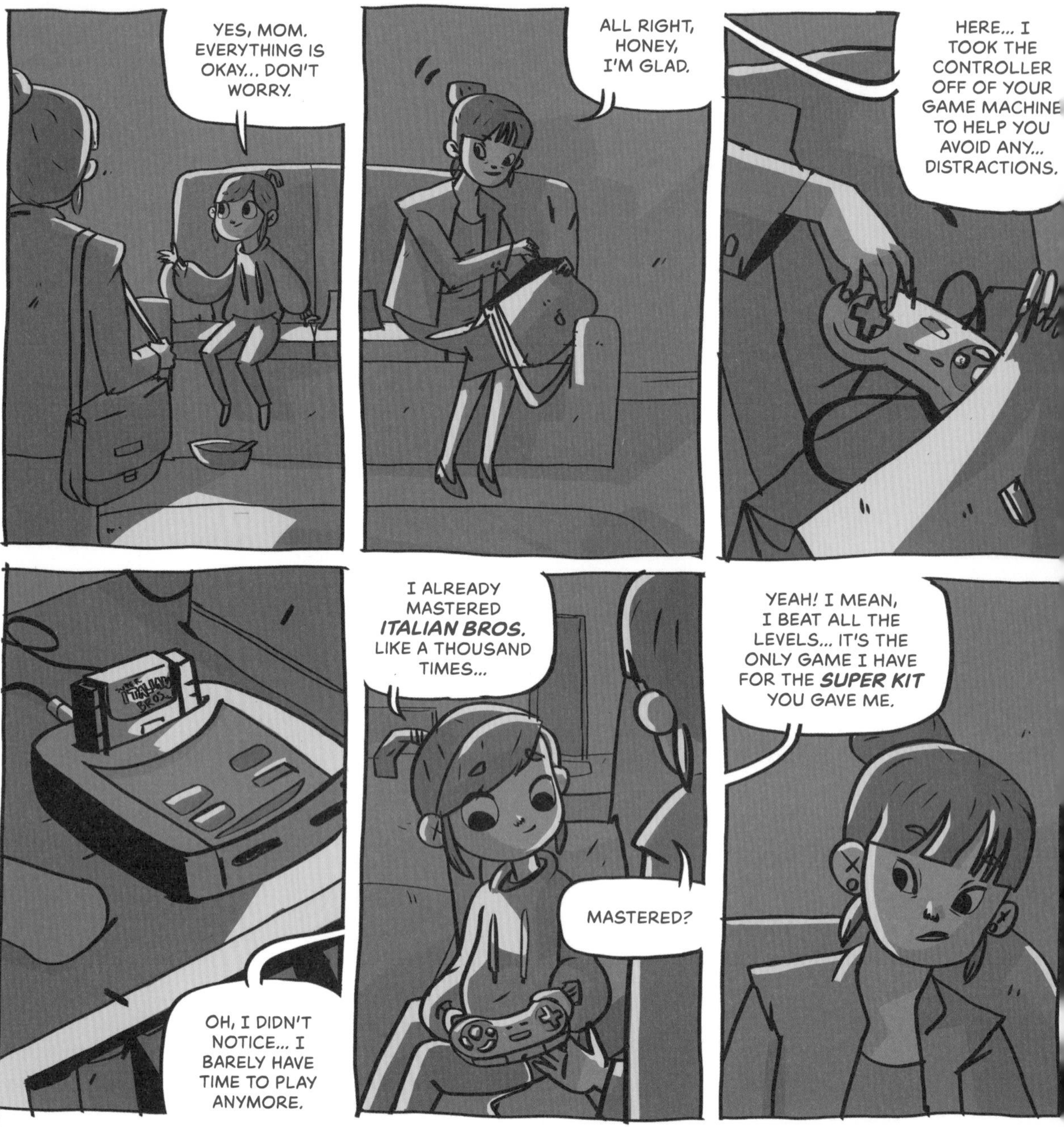
YES, MOM. EVERYTHING IS OKAY... DON'T WORRY.
ALL RIGHT, HONEY, I'M GLAD.
HERE... I TOOK THE CONTROLLER OFF OF YOUR GAME MACHINE TO HELP YOU AVOID ANY... DISTRACTIONS.
ITALIAN BROS.
OH, I DIDN'T NOTICE... I BARELY HAVE TIME TO PLAY ANYMORE.
I ALREADY MASTERED *ITALIAN BROS.* LIKE A THOUSAND TIMES...
MASTERED?
YEAH! I MEAN, I BEAT ALL THE LEVELS... IT'S THE ONLY GAME I HAVE FOR THE *SUPER KIT* YOU GAVE ME.

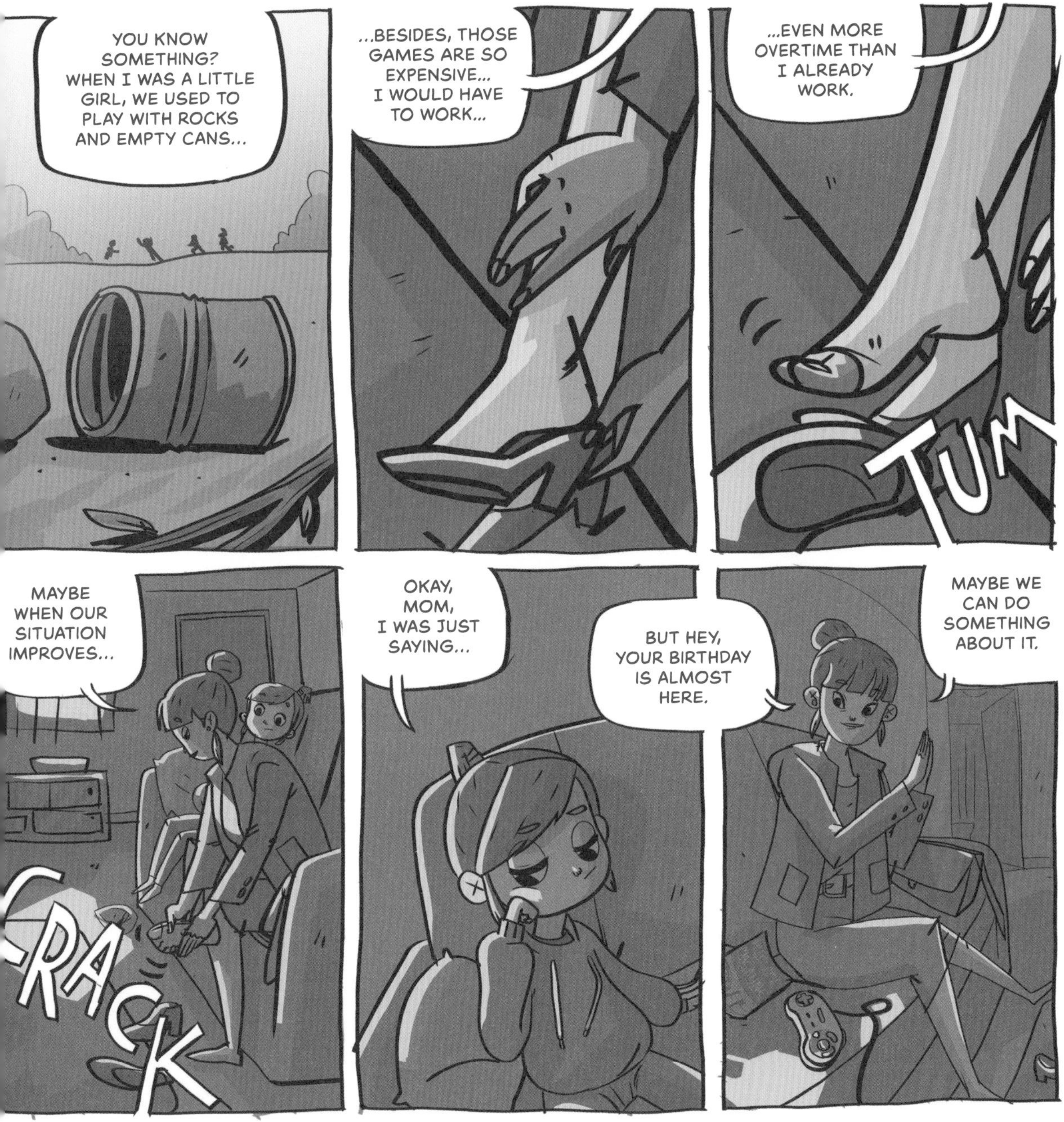
YOU KNOW SOMETHING? WHEN I WAS A LITTLE GIRL, WE USED TO PLAY WITH ROCKS AND EMPTY CANS...
...BESIDES, THOSE GAMES ARE SO EXPENSIVE... I WOULD HAVE TO WORK...
...EVEN MORE OVERTIME THAN I ALREADY WORK.
TUM
MAYBE WHEN OUR SITUATION IMPROVES...
CRACK
OKAY, MOM, I WAS JUST SAYING...
BUT HEY, YOUR BIRTHDAY IS ALMOST HERE.
MAYBE WE CAN DO SOMETHING ABOUT IT.

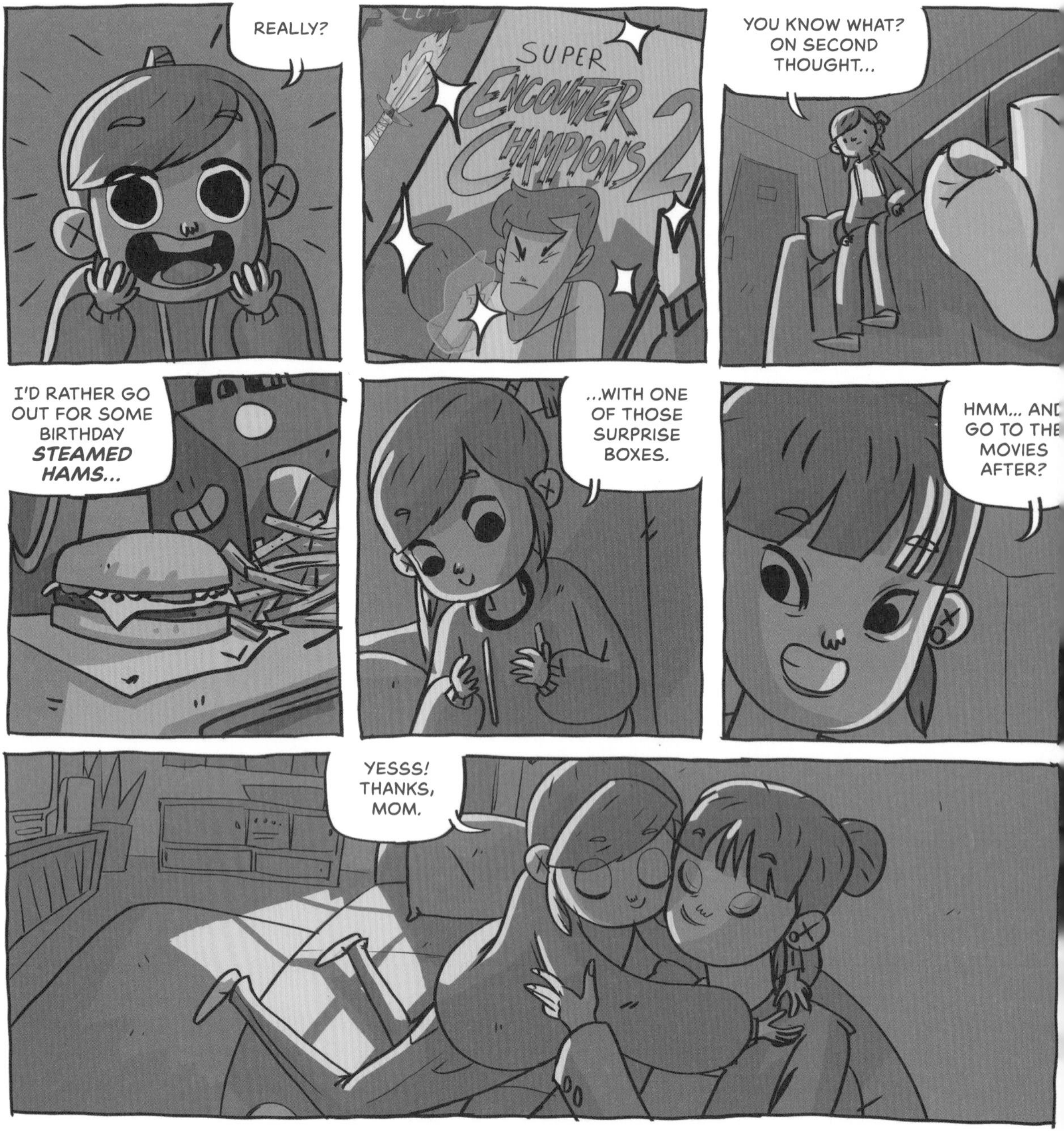
REALLY?
SUPER ENCOUNTER CHAMPIONS 2
YOU KNOW WHAT? ON SECOND THOUGHT...
I'D RATHER GO OUT FOR SOME BIRTHDAY **STEAMED HAMS...**
...WITH ONE OF THOSE SURPRISE BOXES.
HMM... AN GO TO TH MOVIES AFTER?
YESSS! THANKS, MOM.

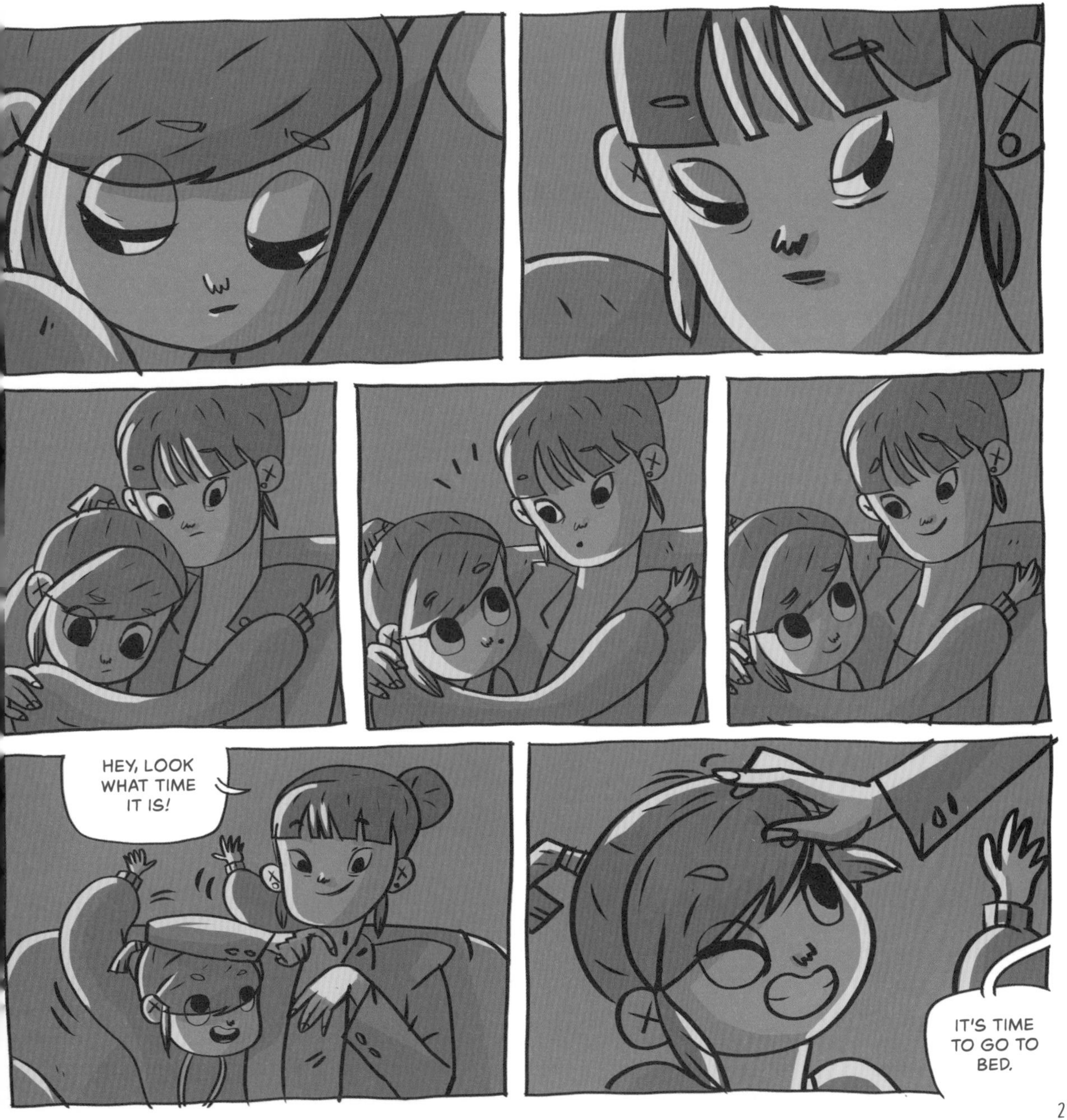
HEY, LOOK WHAT TIME IT IS!
IT'S TIME TO GO TO BED.

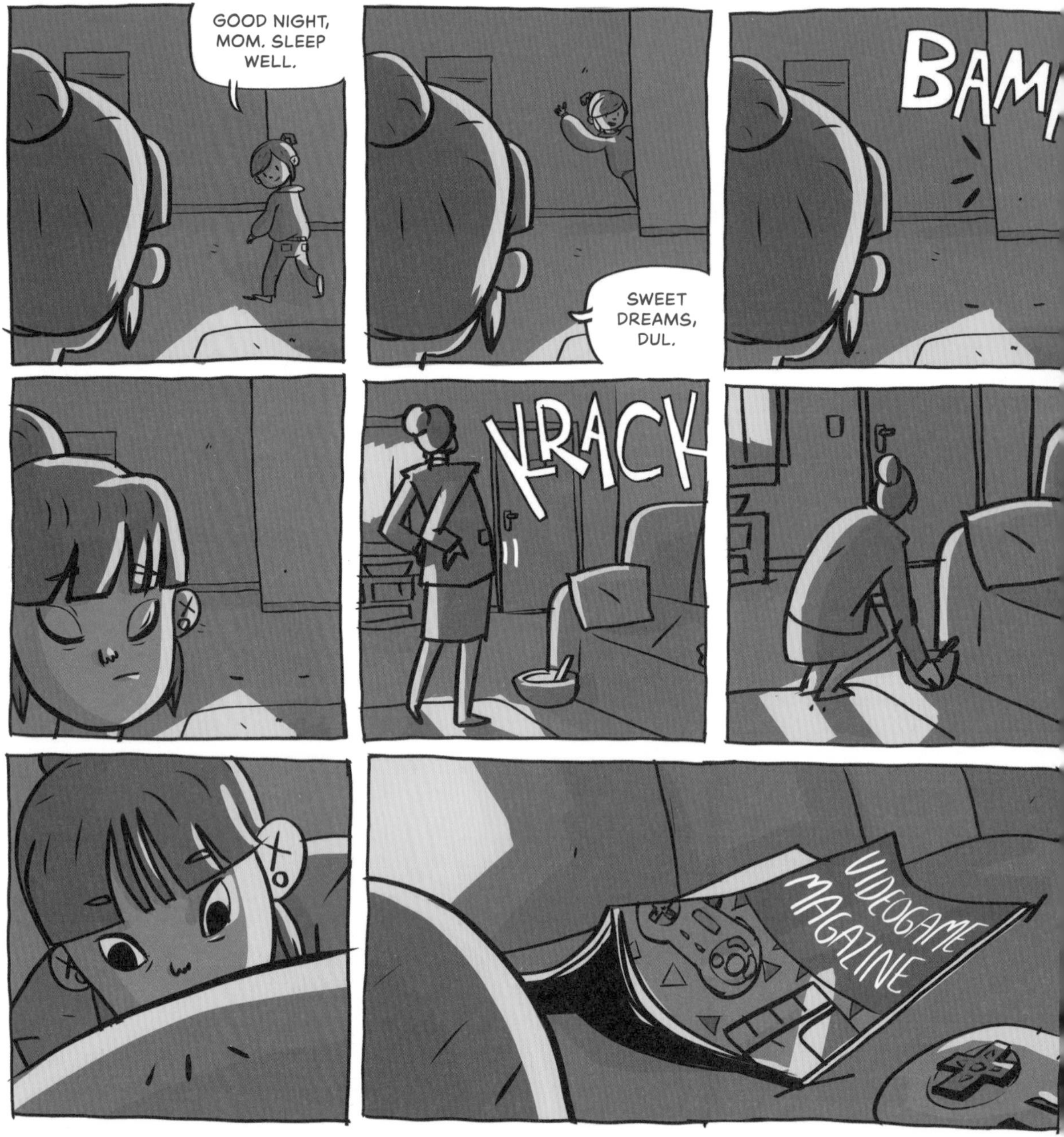
GOOD NIGHT, MOM. SLEEP WELL.
SWEET DREAMS, DUL.
BAM
KRACK
VIDEOGAME MAGAZINE

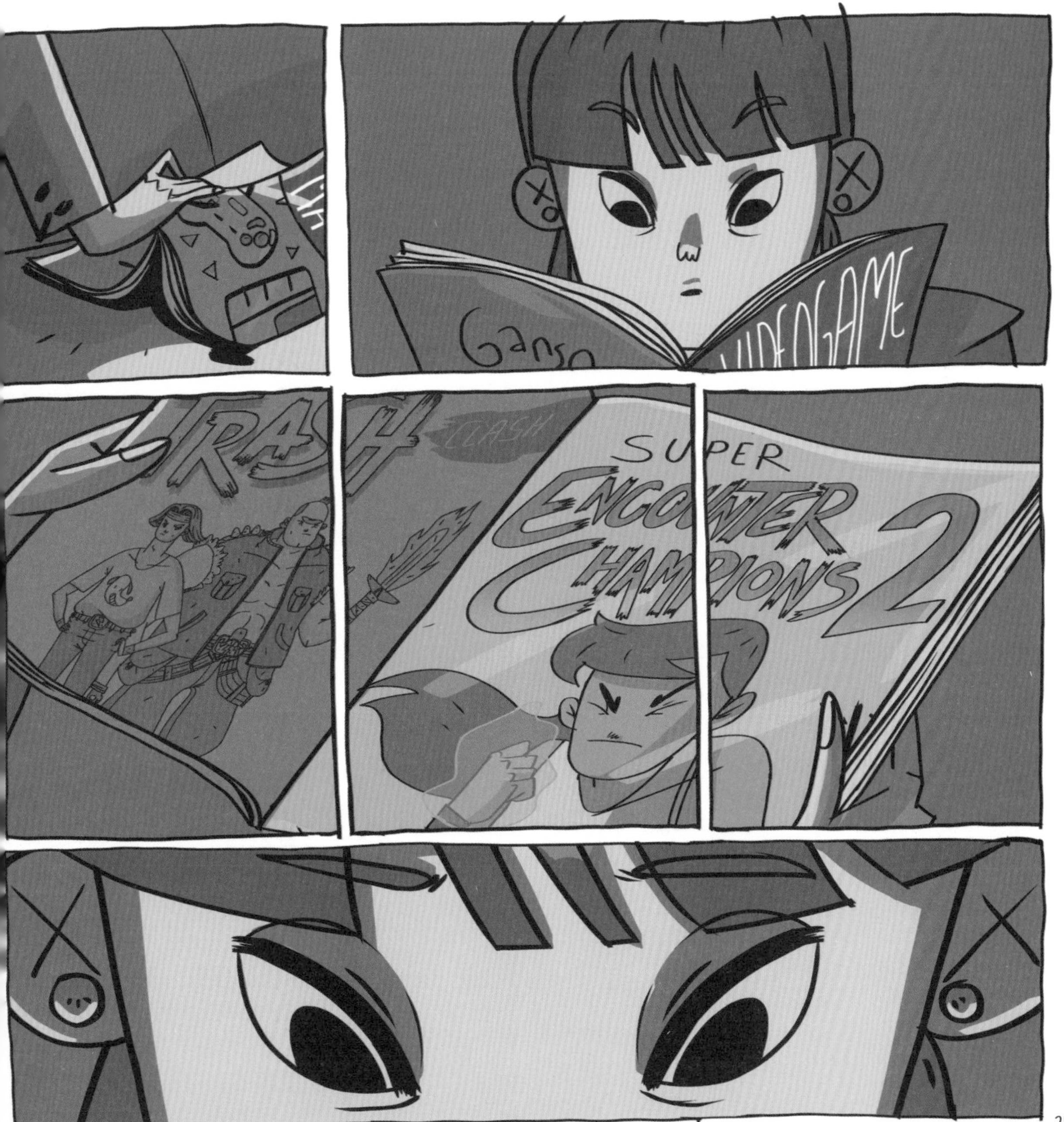
Ganso
VIDEOGAME
CLASH
SUPER
ENCOUNTER
CHAMPIONS 2

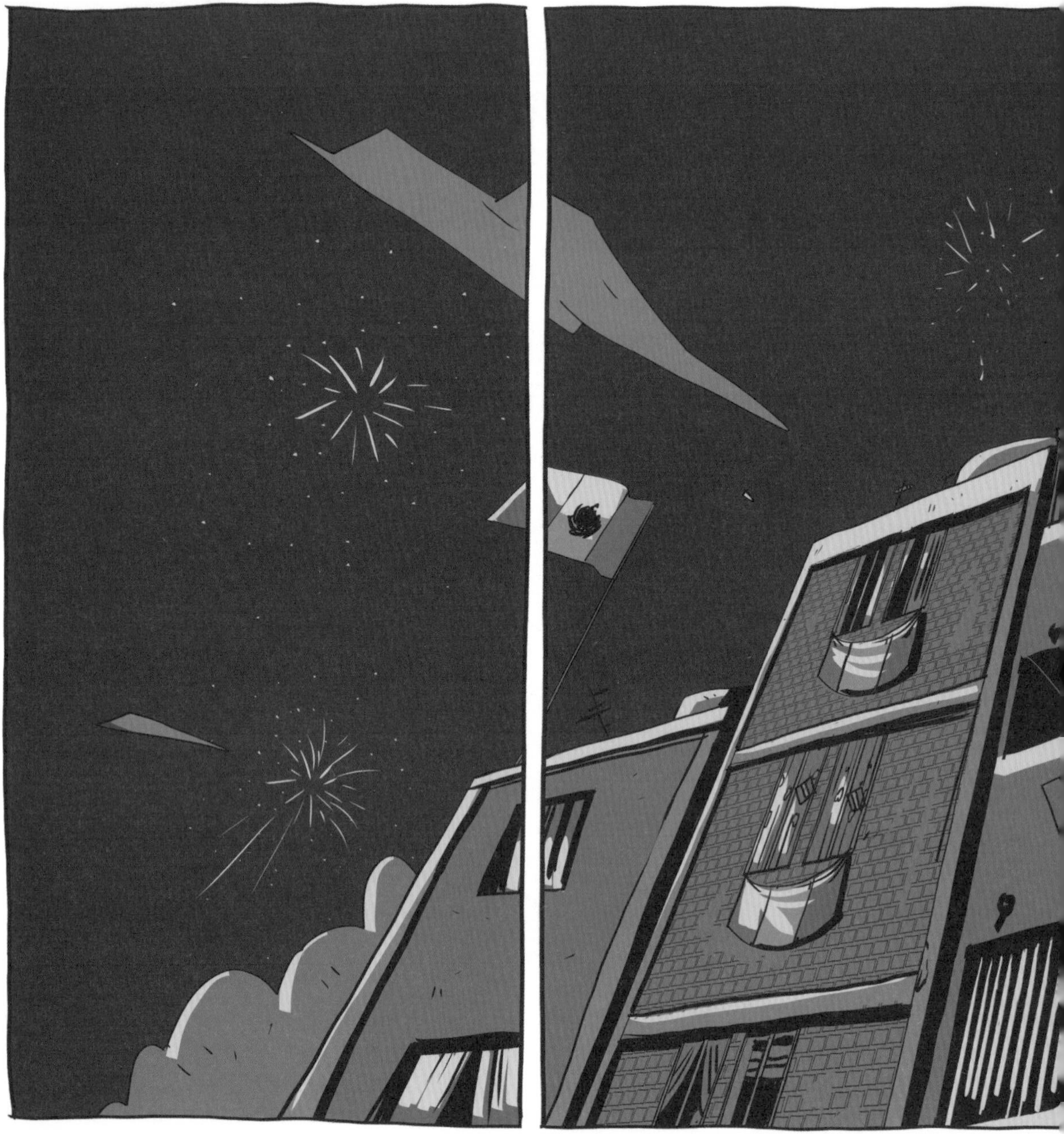

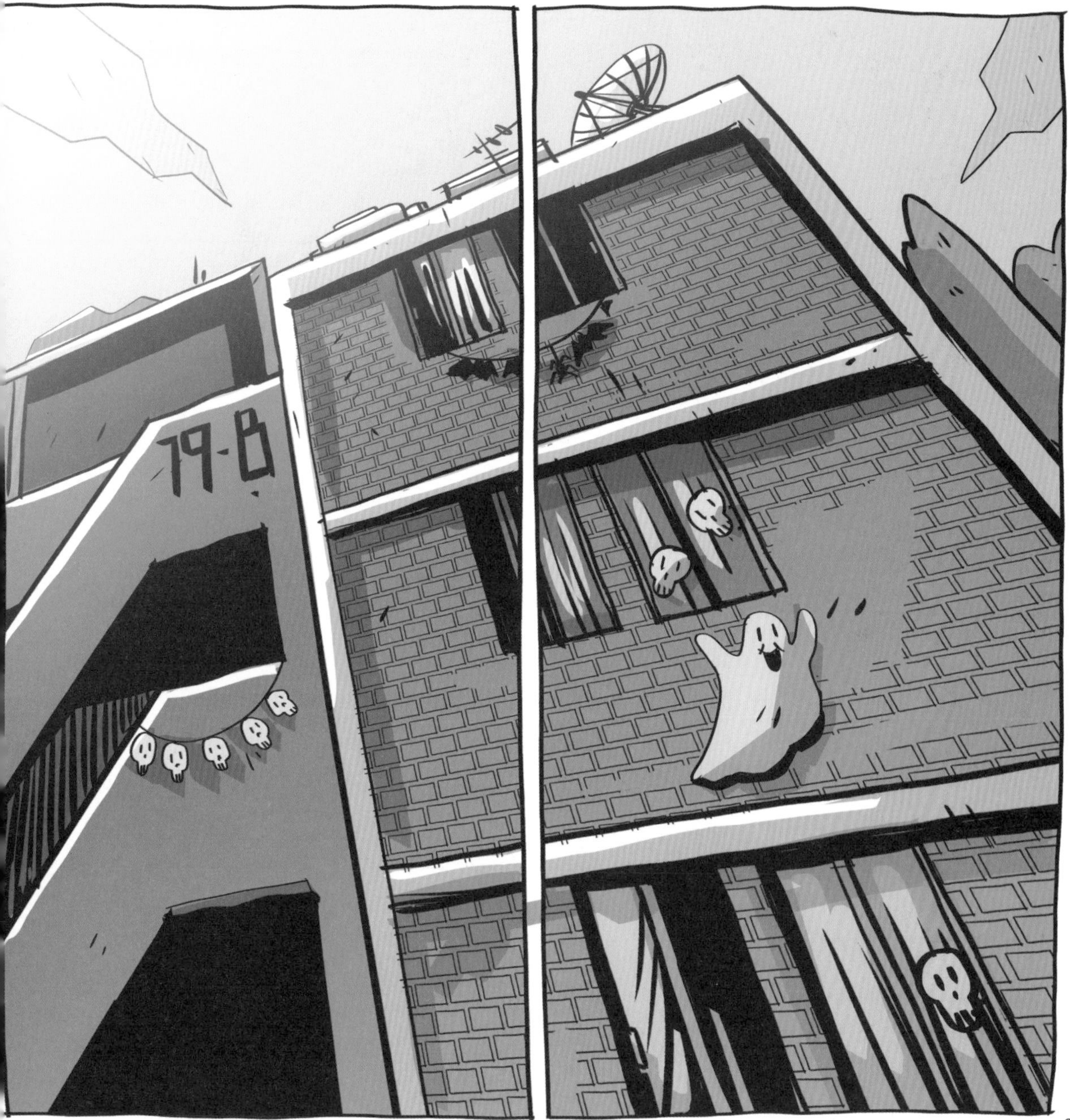
79-B

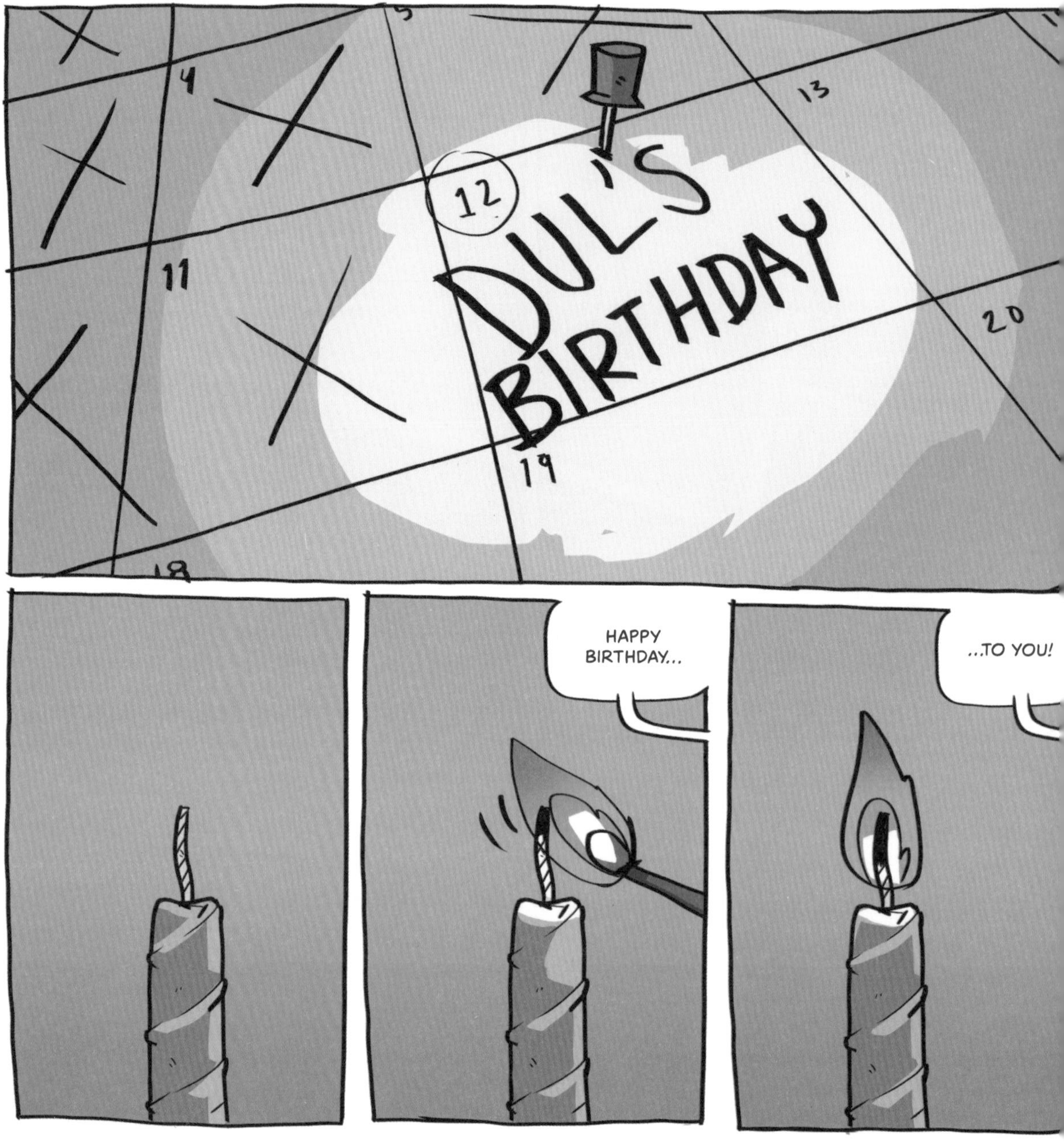
DUL'S BIRTHDAY
HAPPY BIRTHDAY...
...TO YOU!

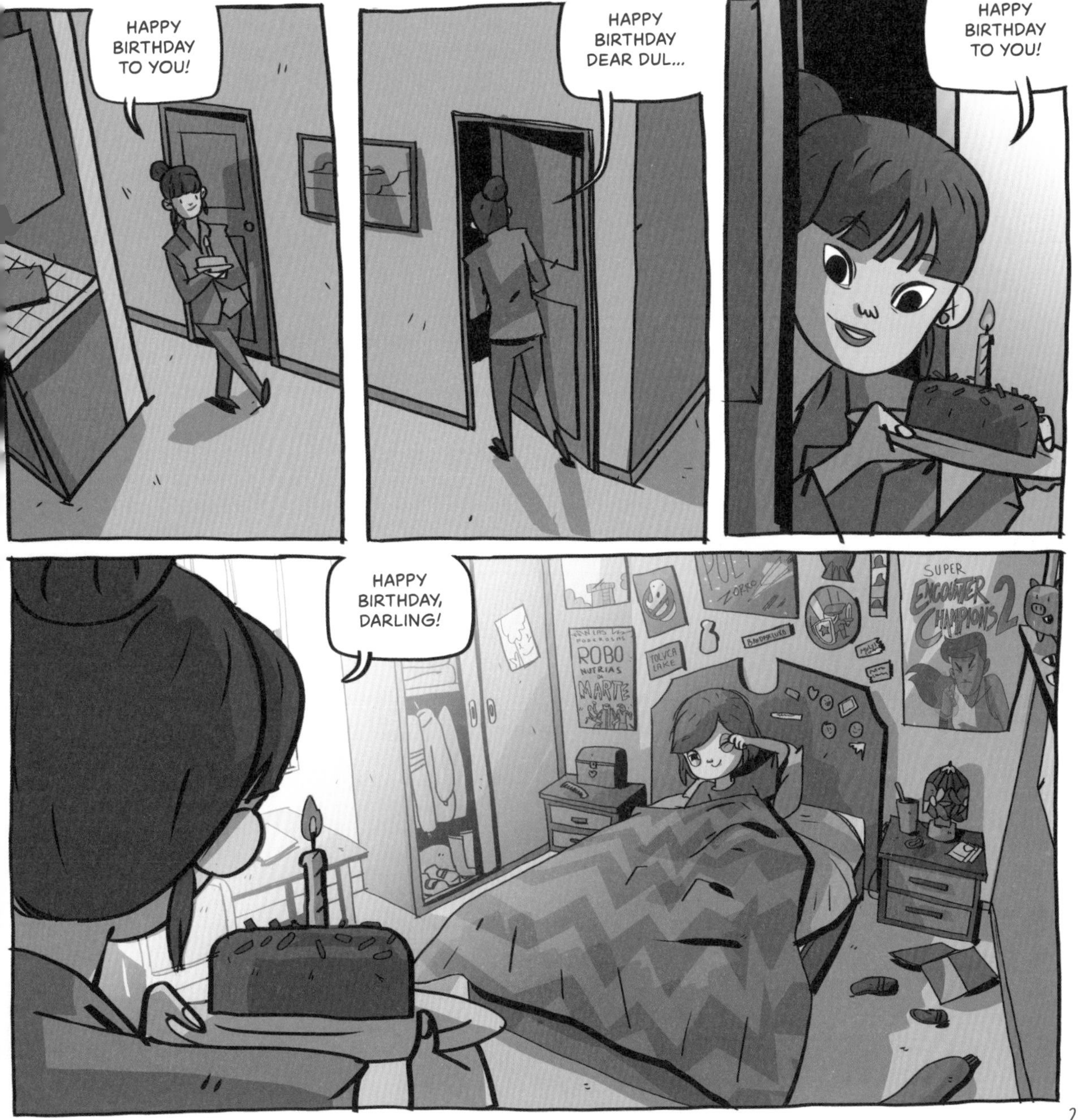
HAPPY BIRTHDAY TO YOU!
HAPPY BIRTHDAY DEAR DUL...
HAPPY BIRTHDAY TO YOU!
HAPPY BIRTHDAY, DARLING!
ROBO NUTRIAS MARTE
SUPER ENCOUNTER CHAMPIONS 2

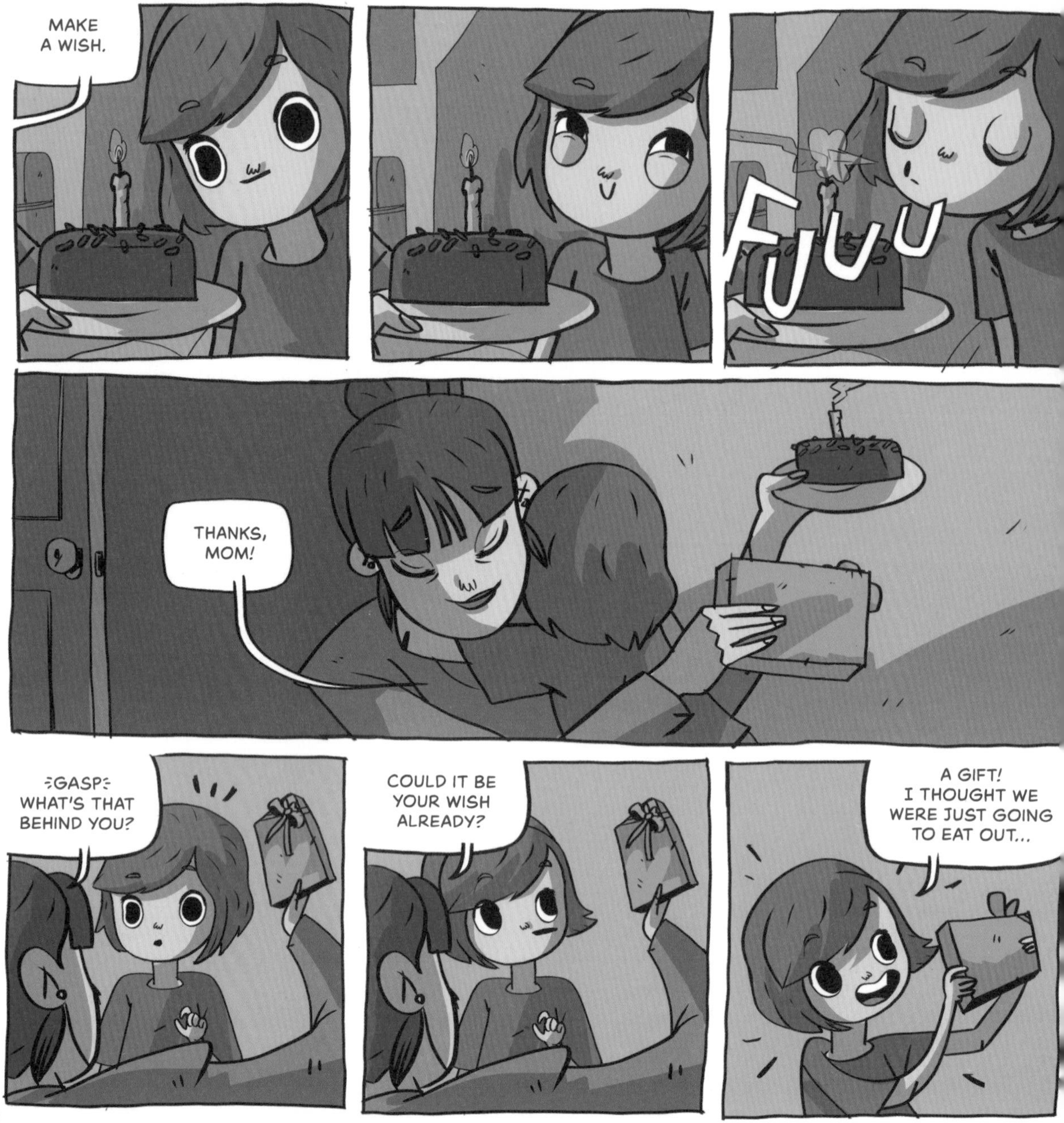

MAKE A WISH.
FUUUU
THANKS, MOM!
=GASP= WHAT'S THAT BEHIND YOU?
COULD IT BE YOUR WISH ALREADY?
A GIFT! I THOUGHT WE WERE JUST GOING TO EAT OUT...

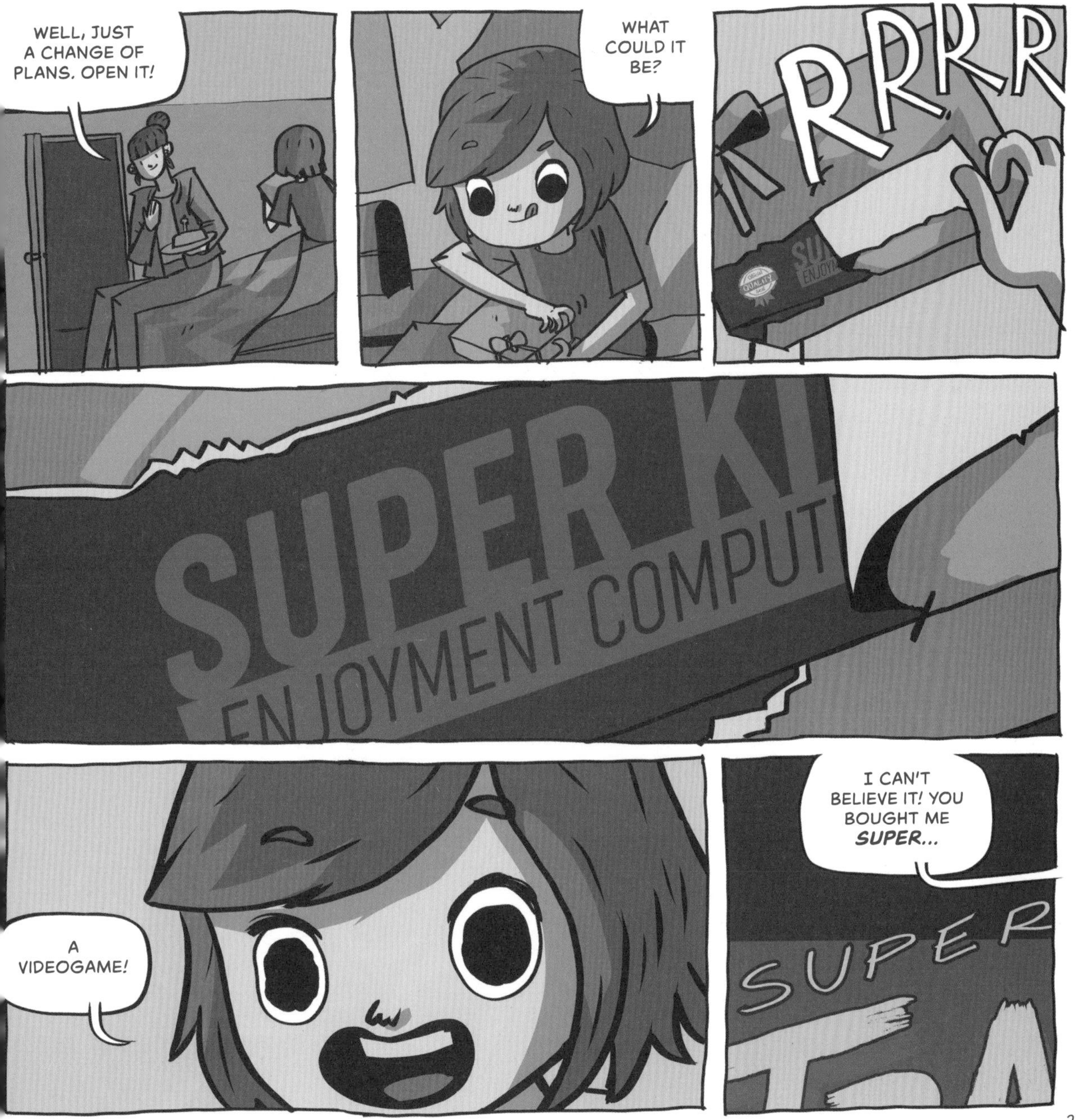
WELL, JUST A CHANGE OF PLANS. OPEN IT!
WHAT COULD IT BE?
RRRRR
SUPER KI
ENJOYMENT COMPUT
A VIDEOGAME!
I CAN'T BELIEVE IT! YOU BOUGHT ME *SUPER*...
SUPER

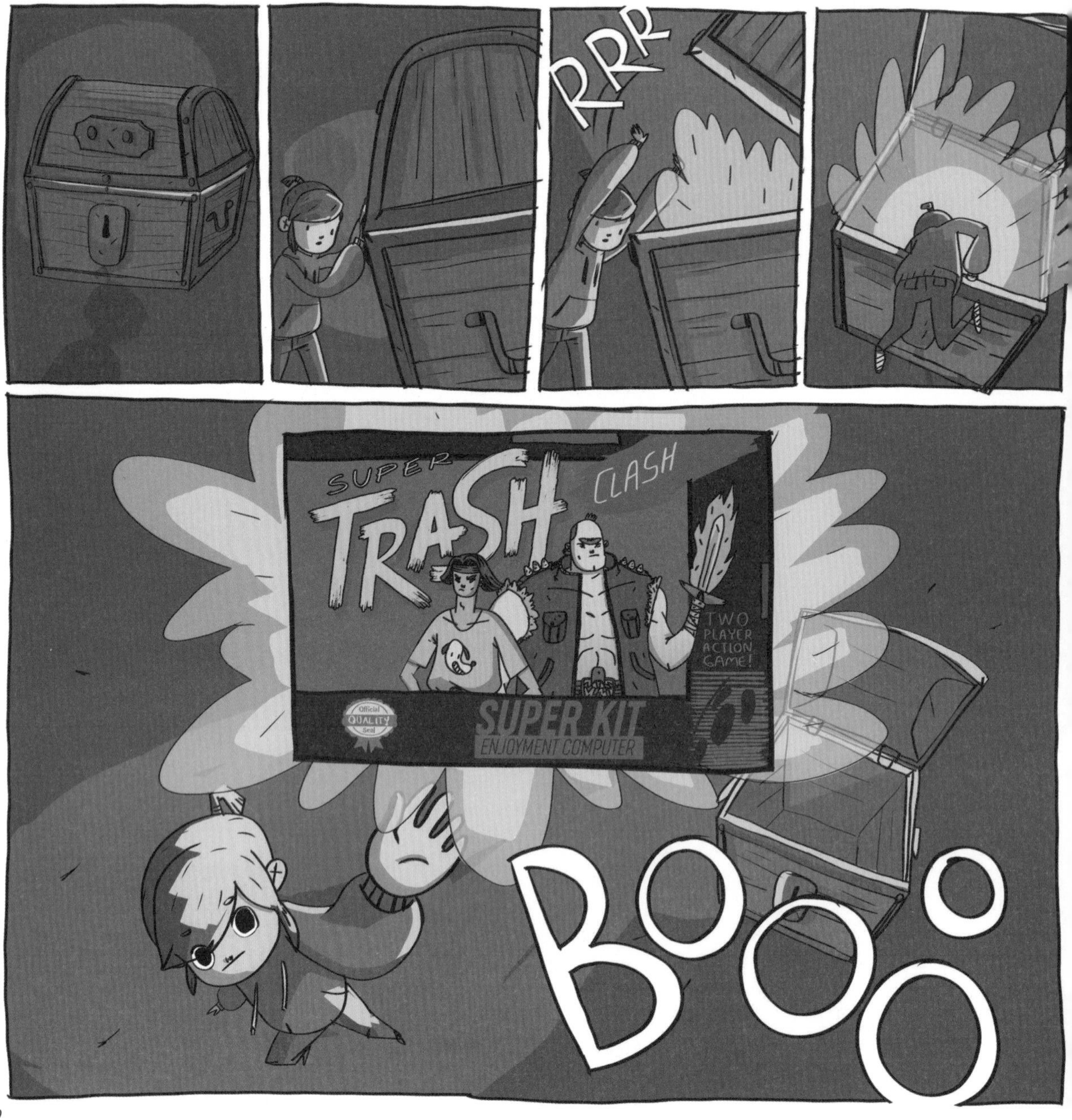
RRR
SUPER
TRASH
CLASH
TWO PLAYER ACTION GAME!
Official QUALITY Seal
SUPER KIT
ENJOYMENT COMPUTER
BOOOO

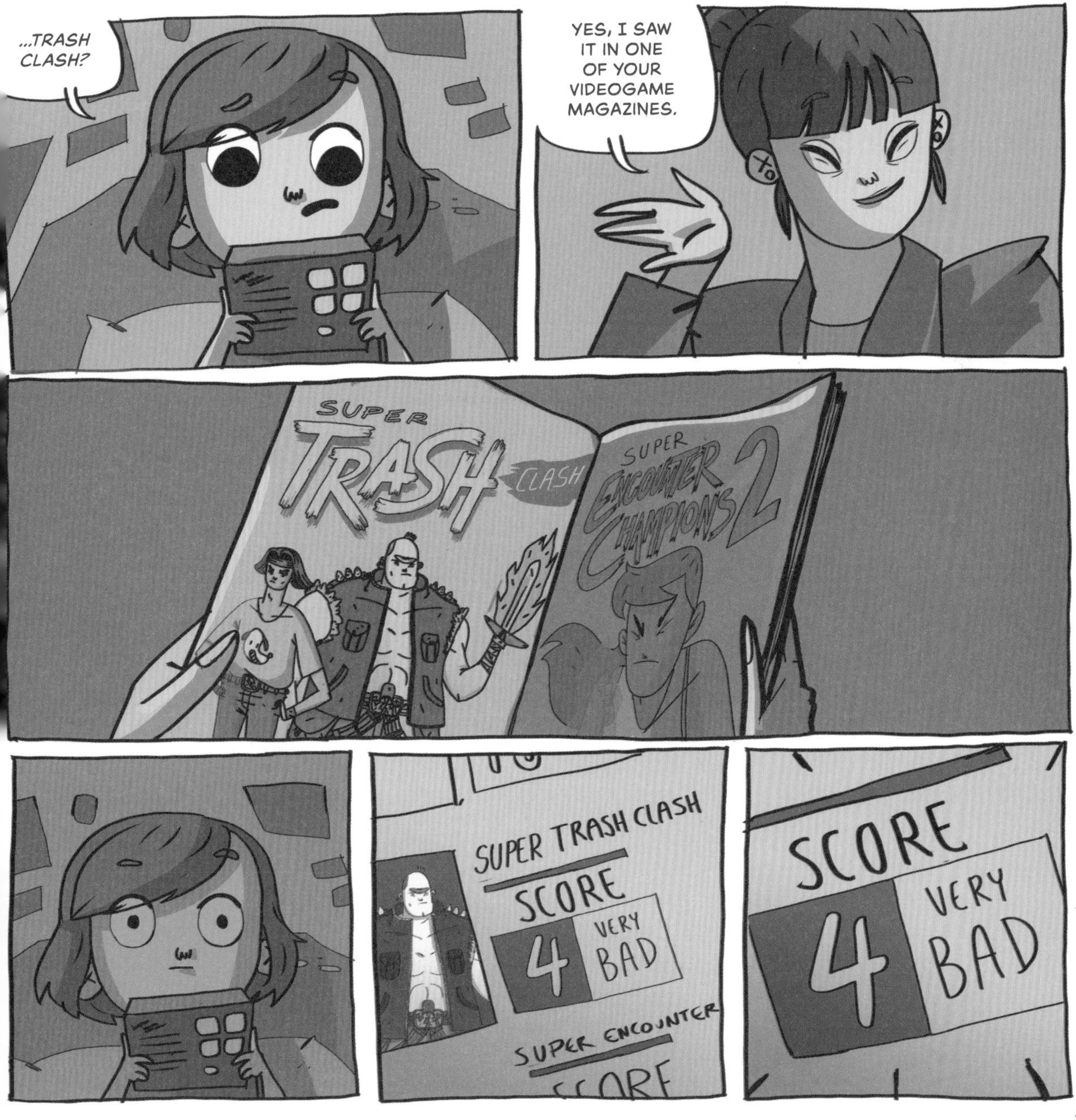

...TRASH CLASH?
YES, I SAW IT IN ONE OF YOUR VIDEOGAME MAGAZINES.
SUPER TRASH CLASH
SUPER ENCOUNTER CHAMPIONS 2
SUPER TRASH CLASH
SCORE
4
VERY BAD
SUPER ENCOUNTER
SCORE
4
VERY BAD

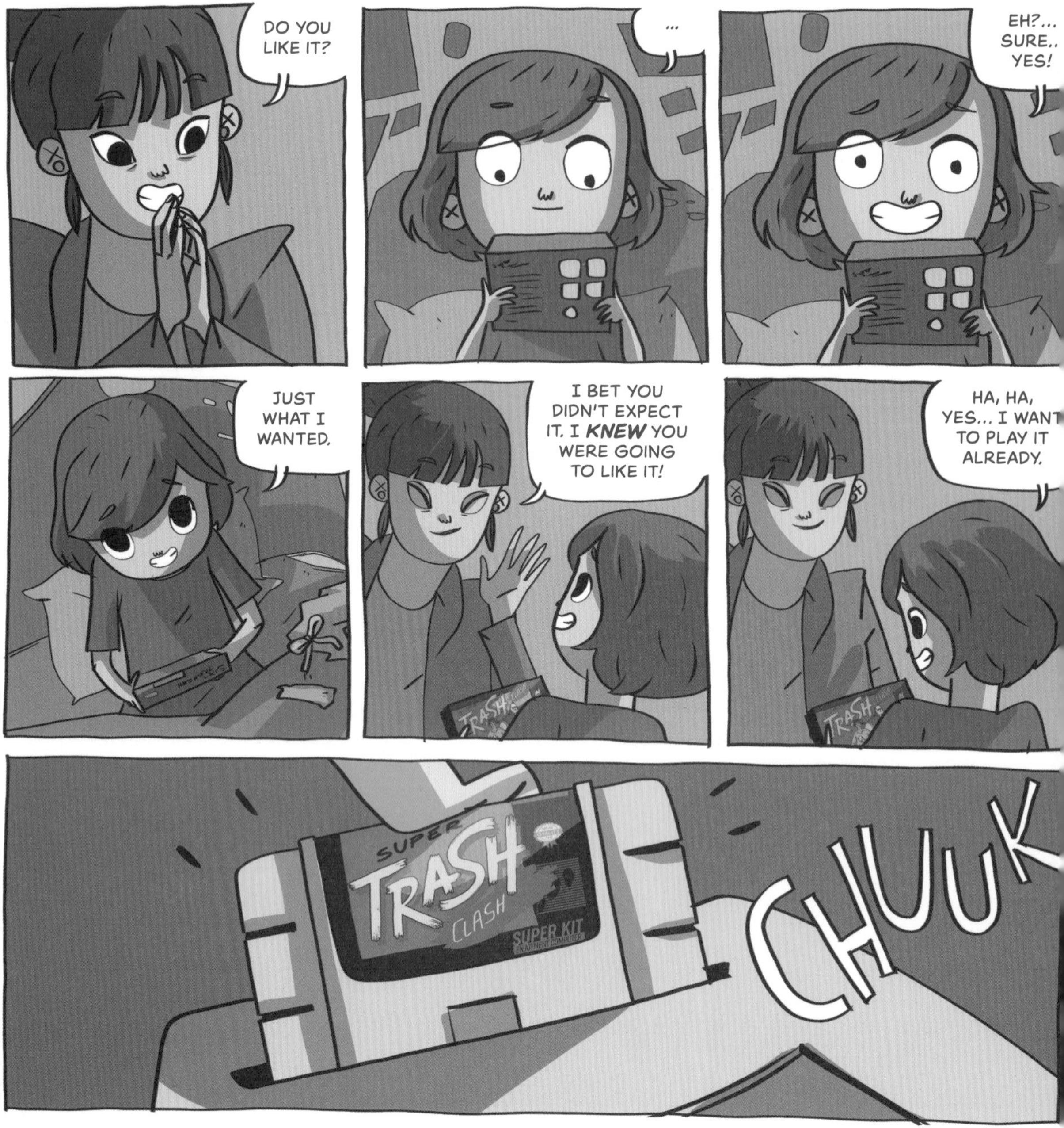
DO YOU LIKE IT?
...
EH?... SURE.. YES!
JUST WHAT I WANTED.
I BET YOU DIDN'T EXPECT IT. I KNEW YOU WERE GOING TO LIKE IT!
HA, HA, YES... I WANT TO PLAY IT ALREADY.
SUPER TRASH CLASH
SUPER KIT
CHUUK

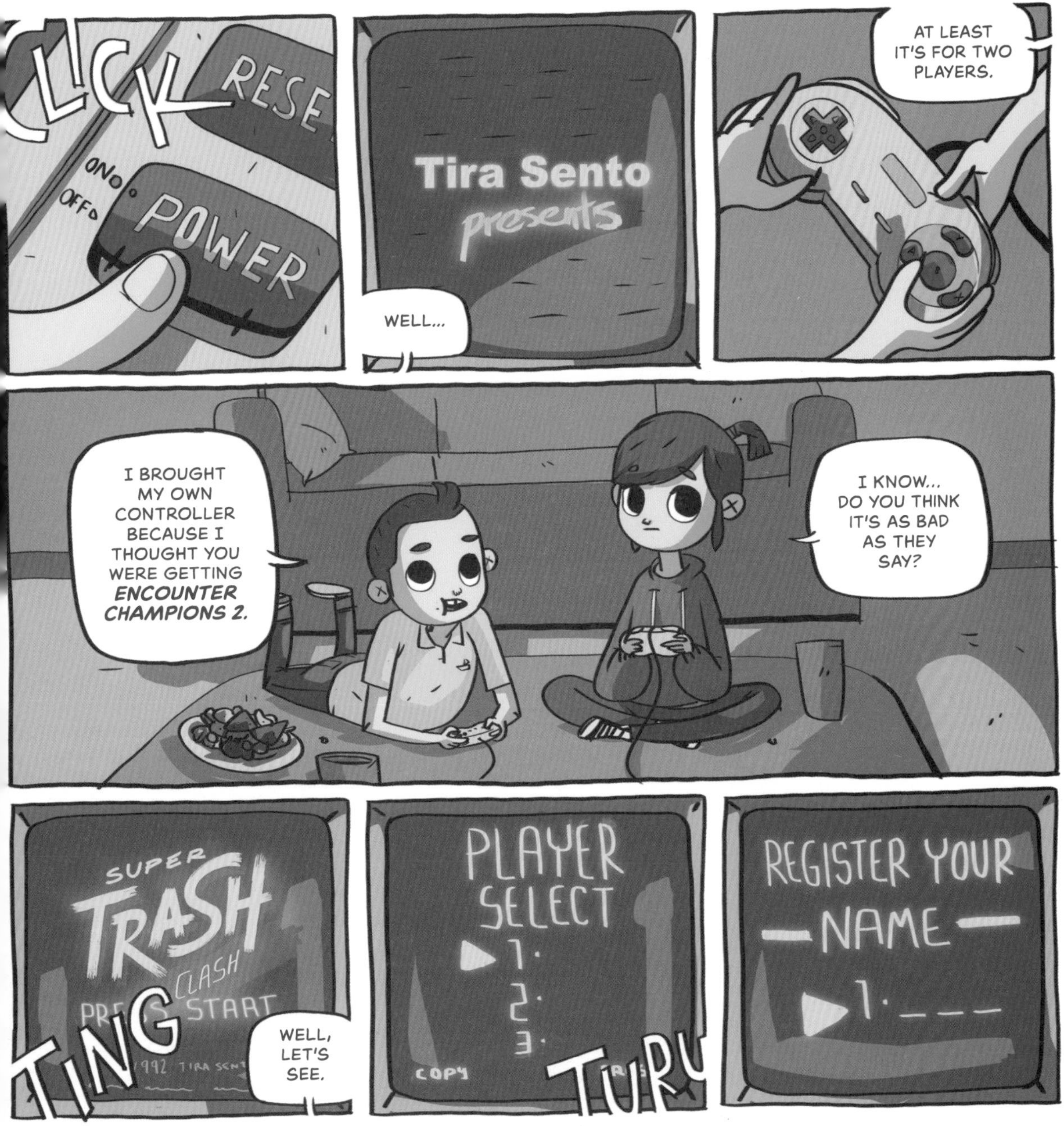
CLICK
RESET
ON
OFF
POWER
Tira Sento
presents
WELL...
AT LEAST IT'S FOR TWO PLAYERS.
I BROUGHT MY OWN CONTROLLER BECAUSE I THOUGHT YOU WERE GETTING ***ENCOUNTER CHAMPIONS 2.***
I KNOW... DO YOU THINK IT'S AS BAD AS THEY SAY?
SUPER TRASH CLASH
PRESS START
TING
WELL, LET'S SEE.
PLAYER SELECT
1.
2.
3.
COPY
TURU
REGISTER YOUR NAME
1. _ _ _

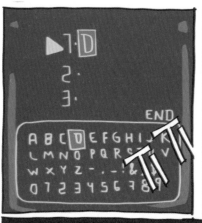

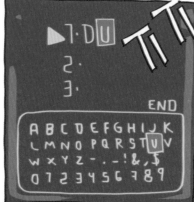

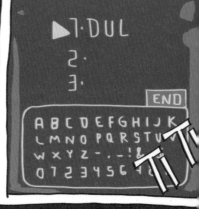

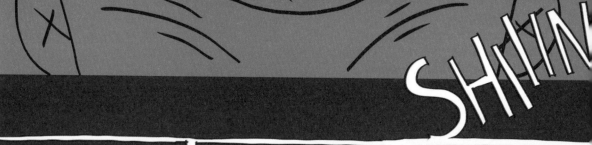

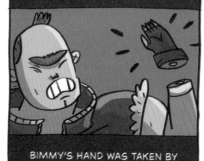

1·D
2·
3·
END
ABCDEFGHIJK
LMNOPQRSTUV
WXYZ-.-!&,$
0123456789
TI TI
1·DU
2·
3·
END
ABCDEFGHIJK
LMNOPQRSTUV
WXYZ-.-!&,$
0123456789
TI TI
1·DUL
2·
3·
END
TI TI
SHIIIN
BIMMY'S HAND WAS TAKEN BY THE EVIL DR. V. VELVET...
WHO STABBED A BURNING SWORD IN THE STUMP.
IF BIMMY DOESN'T GET BACK HIS HAND BY MIDNIGHT, THE BURNING SWORD WILL KILL HIM.

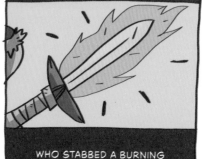

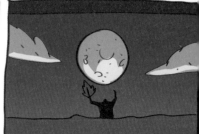

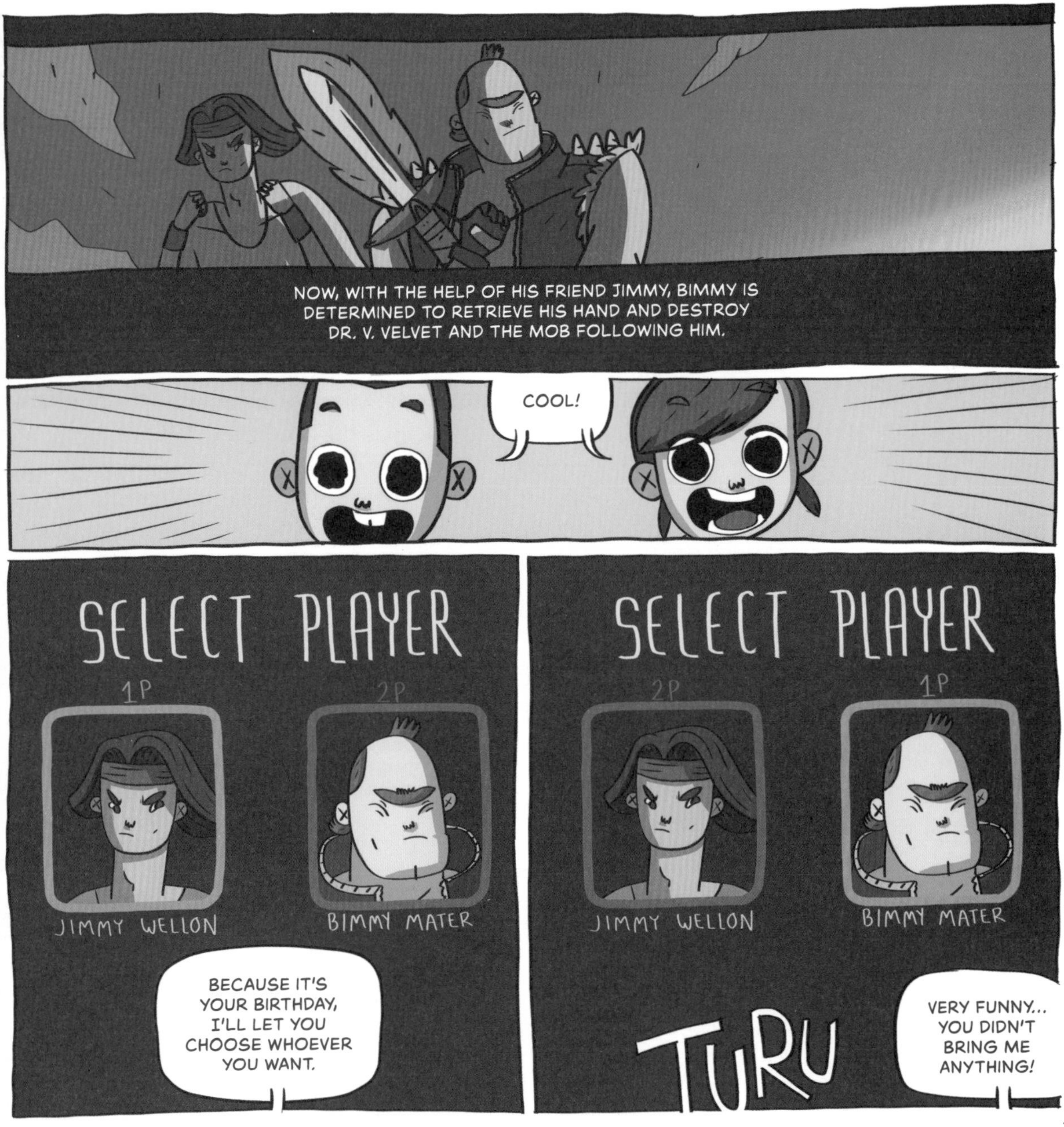

NOW, WITH THE HELP OF HIS FRIEND JIMMY, BIMMY IS DETERMINED TO RETRIEVE HIS HAND AND DESTROY DR. V. VELVET AND THE MOB FOLLOWING HIM.
COOL!
SELECT PLAYER
1P
2P
JIMMY WELLON
BIMMY MATER
BECAUSE IT'S YOUR BIRTHDAY, I'LL LET YOU CHOOSE WHOEVER YOU WANT.
SELECT PLAYER
2P
1P
JIMMY WELLON
BIMMY MATER
TURU
VERY FUNNY... YOU DIDN'T BRING ME ANYTHING!

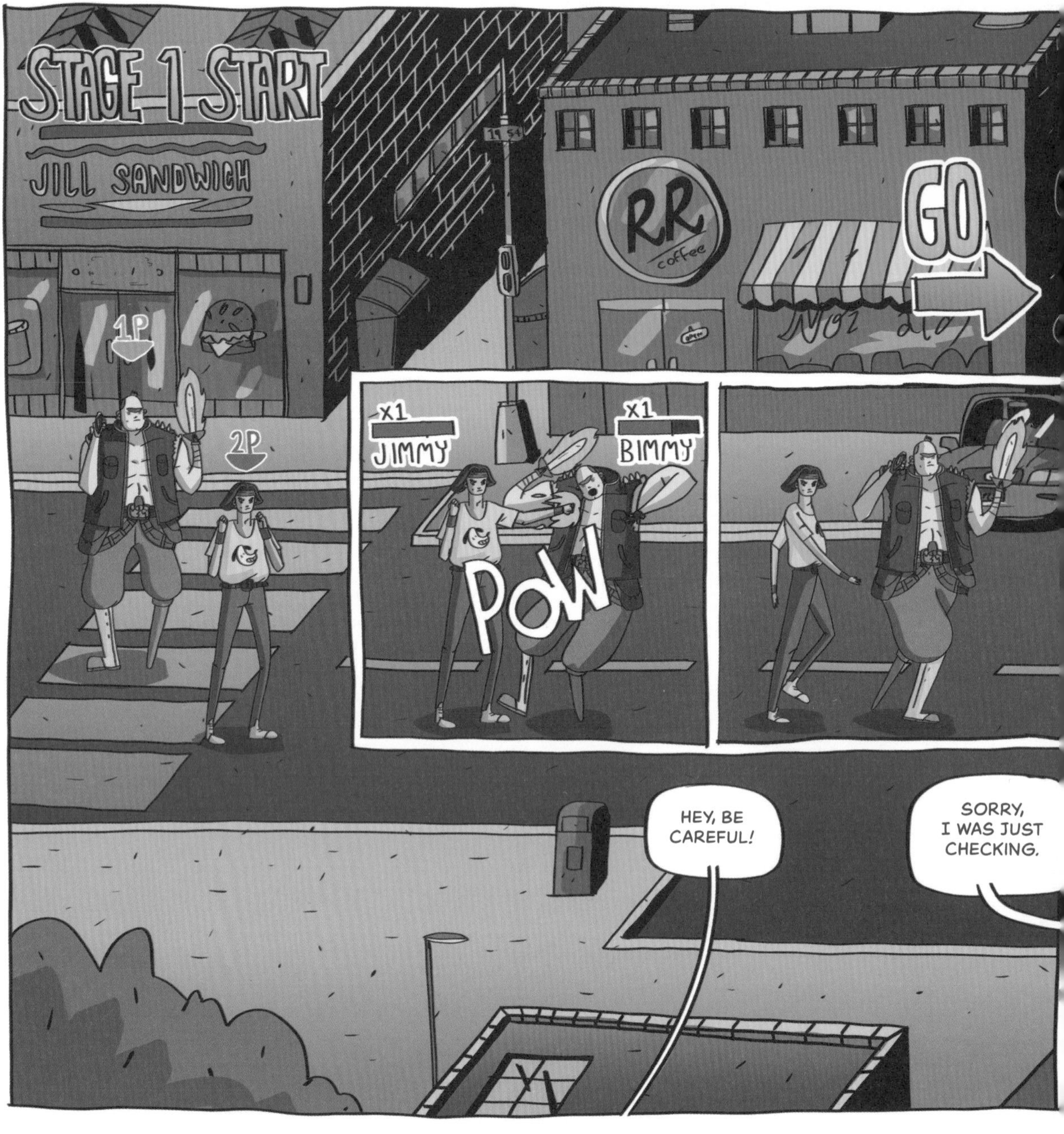
STAGE 1 START
JILL SANDWICH
1P
2P
RR coffee
GO
x1
JIMMY
x1
BIMMY
POW
HEY, BE CAREFUL!
SORRY, I WAS JUST CHECKING.

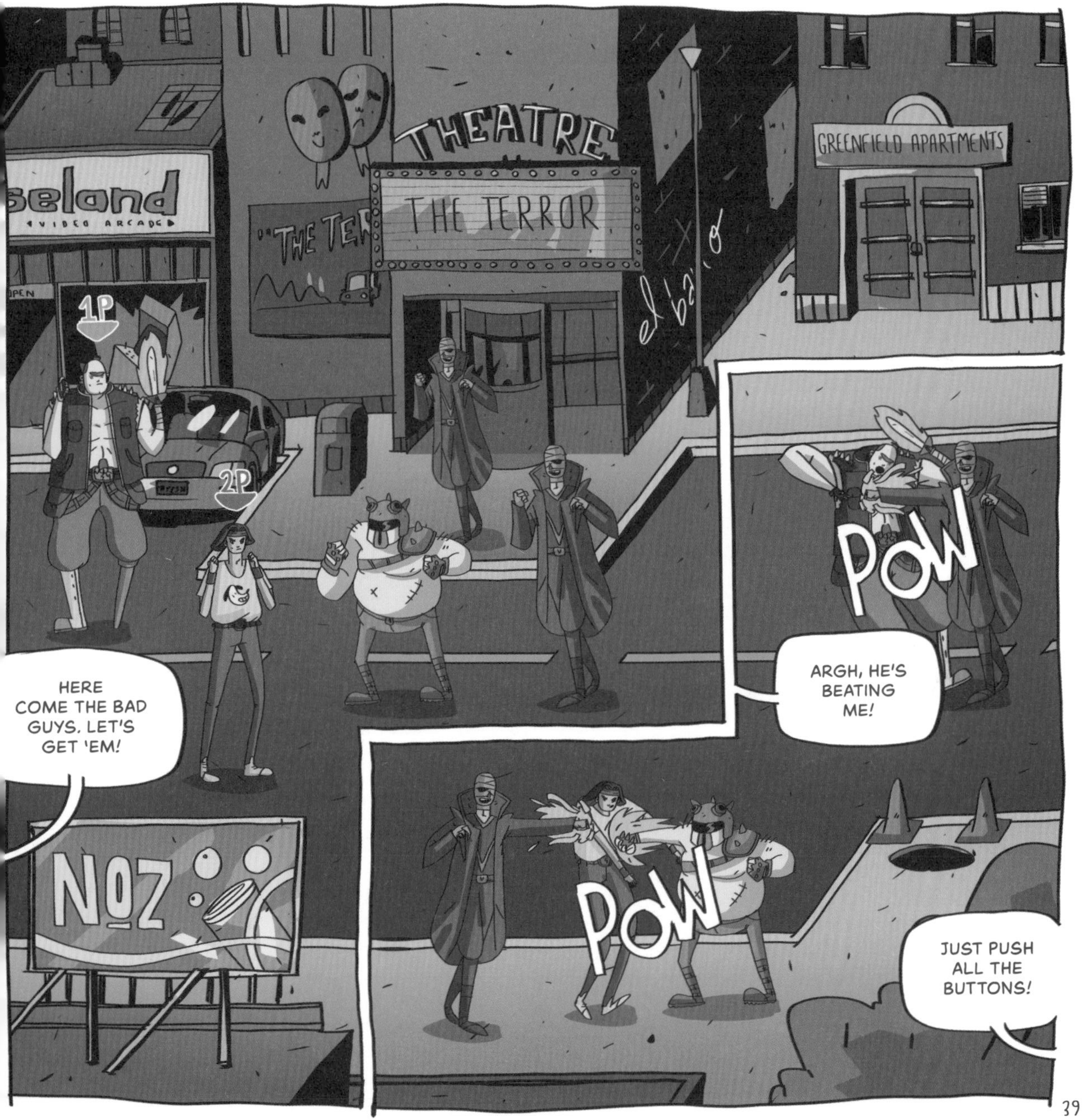

seland
VIDEO ARCADE
OPEN
THEATRE
"THE TER
THE TERROR
GREENFIELD APARTMENTS
1P
2P
HERE COME THE BAD GUYS. LET'S GET 'EM!
POW
ARGH, HE'S BEATING ME!
NO2
POW
JUST PUSH ALL THE BUTTONS!

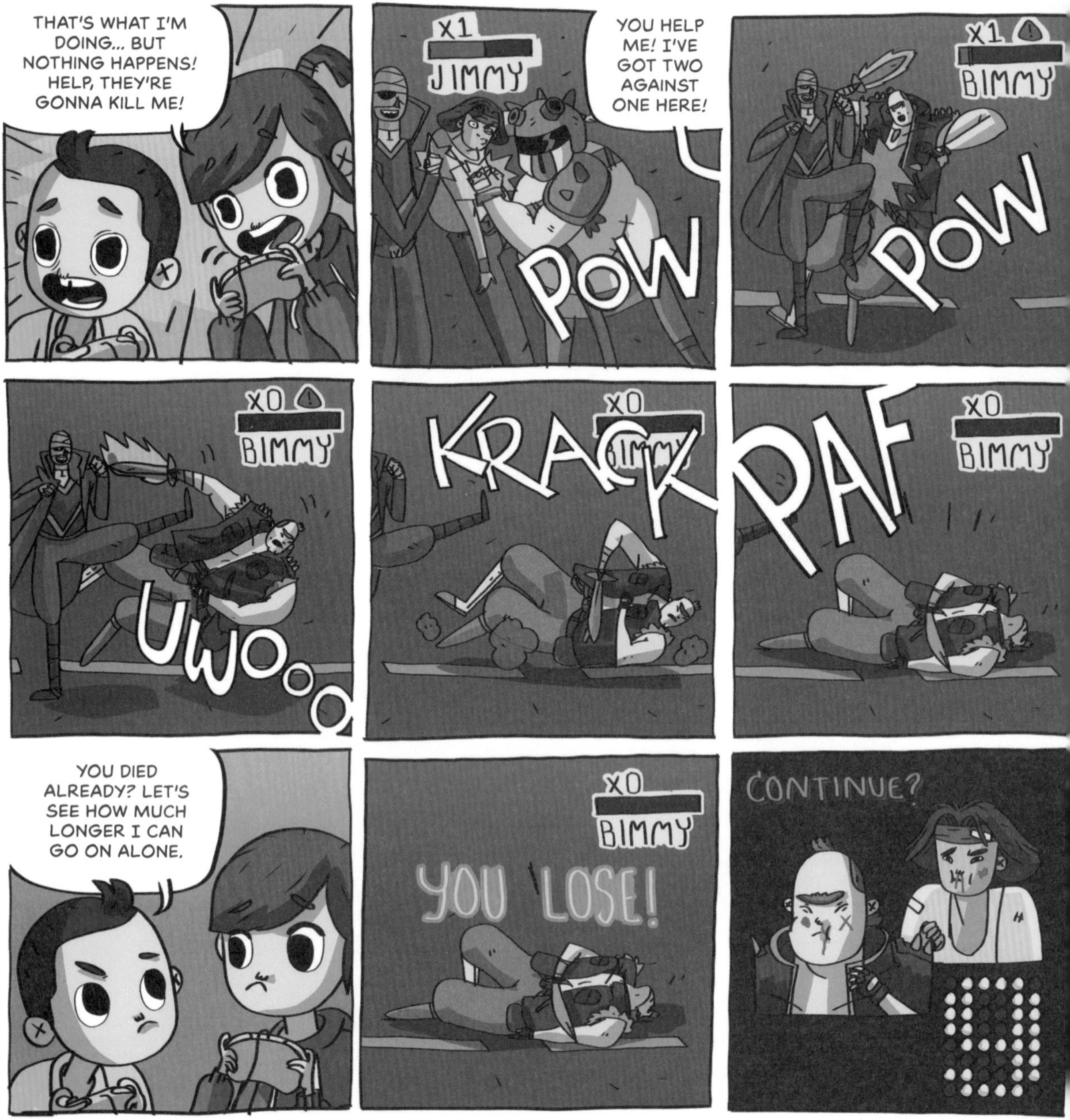
THAT'S WHAT I'M DOING... BUT NOTHING HAPPENS! HELP, THEY'RE GONNA KILL ME!
X1
JIMMY
YOU HELP ME! I'VE GOT TWO AGAINST ONE HERE!
POW
X1
BIMMY
POW
X0
BIMMY
UWOOOO
X0
KRACK
X0
BIMMY
PAF
YOU DIED ALREADY? LET'S SEE HOW MUCH LONGER I CAN GO ON ALONE.
X0
BIMMY
YOU LOSE!
CONTINUE?
9

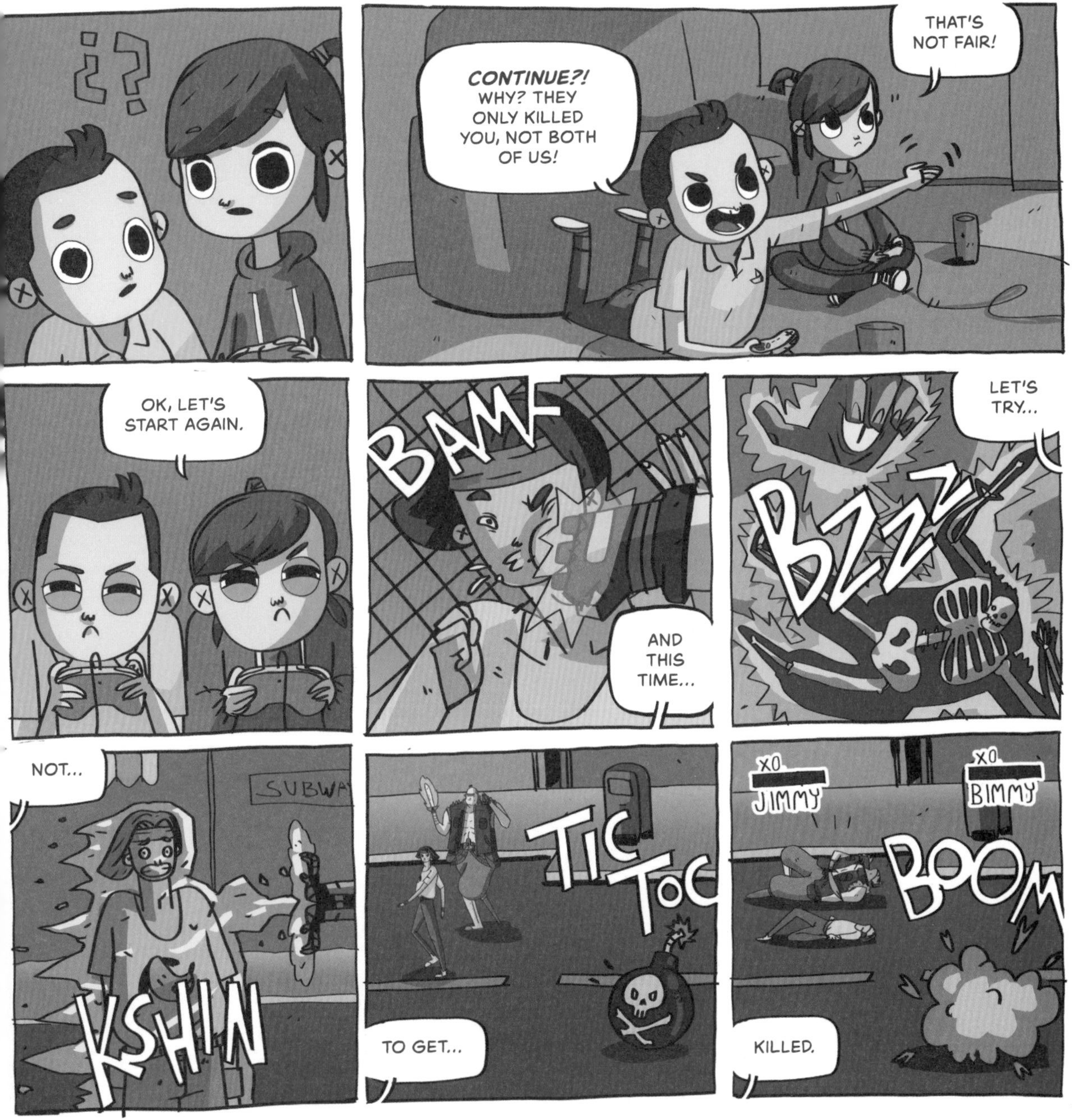
¿?
CONTINUE?! WHY? THEY ONLY KILLED YOU, NOT BOTH OF US!
THAT'S NOT FAIR!
OK, LET'S START AGAIN.
BAM
AND THIS TIME...
LET'S TRY...
BZZZ
NOT...
SUBWAY
KSHIN
TO GET...
TIC
TOC
XO
JIMMY
XO
BIMMY
BOOM
KILLED.

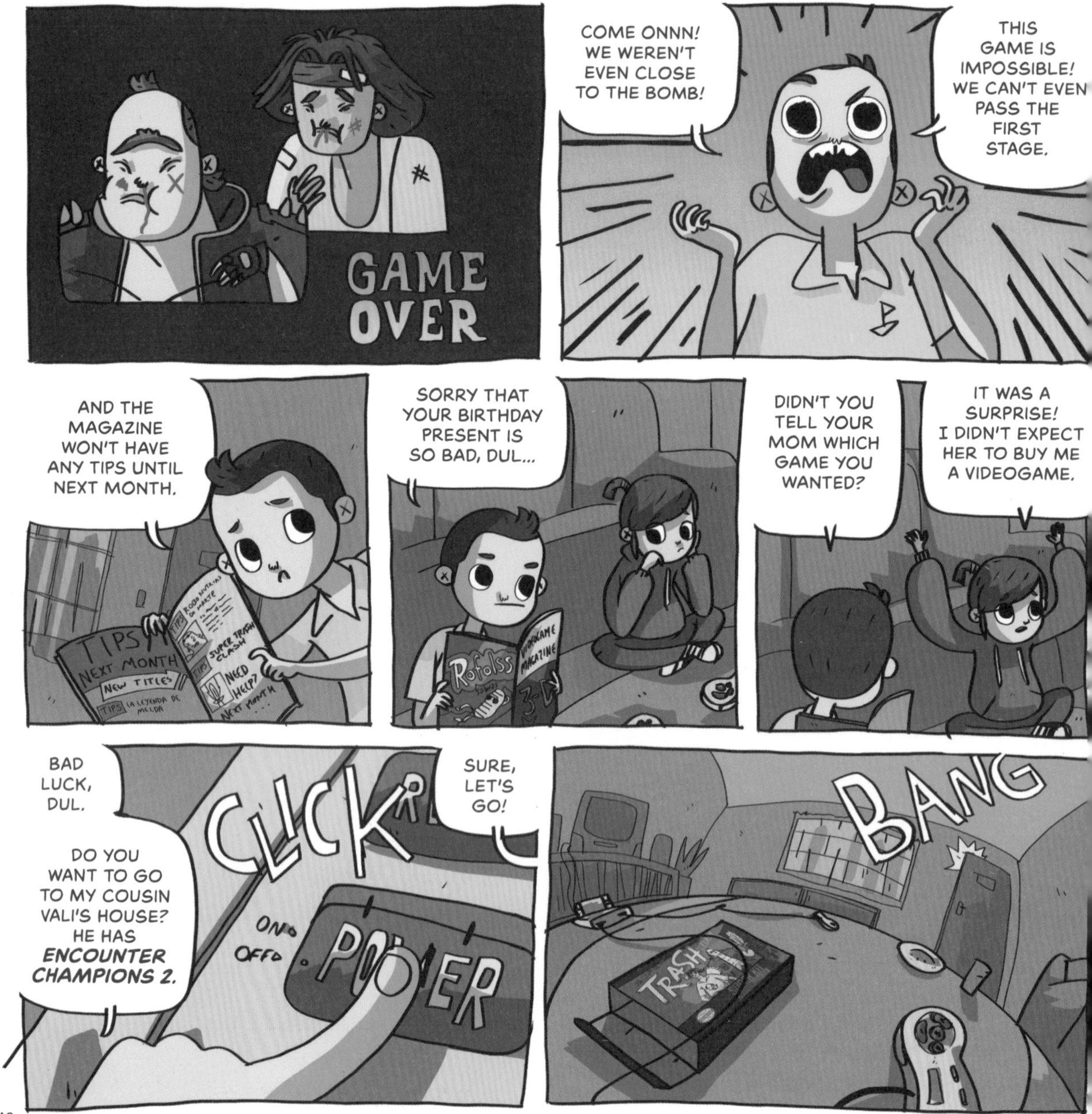
GAME OVER
COME ONNN! WE WEREN'T EVEN CLOSE TO THE BOMB!
THIS GAME IS IMPOSSIBLE! WE CAN'T EVEN PASS THE FIRST STAGE.
AND THE MAGAZINE WON'T HAVE ANY TIPS UNTIL NEXT MONTH.
TIPS NEXT MONTH
NEW TITLES
SUPER TRASH CLASH
NEED HELP?
SORRY THAT YOUR BIRTHDAY PRESENT IS SO BAD, DUL...
VIDEOGAME MAGAZINE
DIDN'T YOU TELL YOUR MOM WHICH GAME YOU WANTED?
IT WAS A SURPRISE! I DIDN'T EXPECT HER TO BUY ME A VIDEOGAME.
BAD LUCK, DUL.
DO YOU WANT TO GO TO MY COUSIN VALI'S HOUSE? HE HAS ***ENCOUNTER CHAMPIONS 2.***
CLICK
SURE, LET'S GO!
ON
OFF
POWER
BANG
TRASH

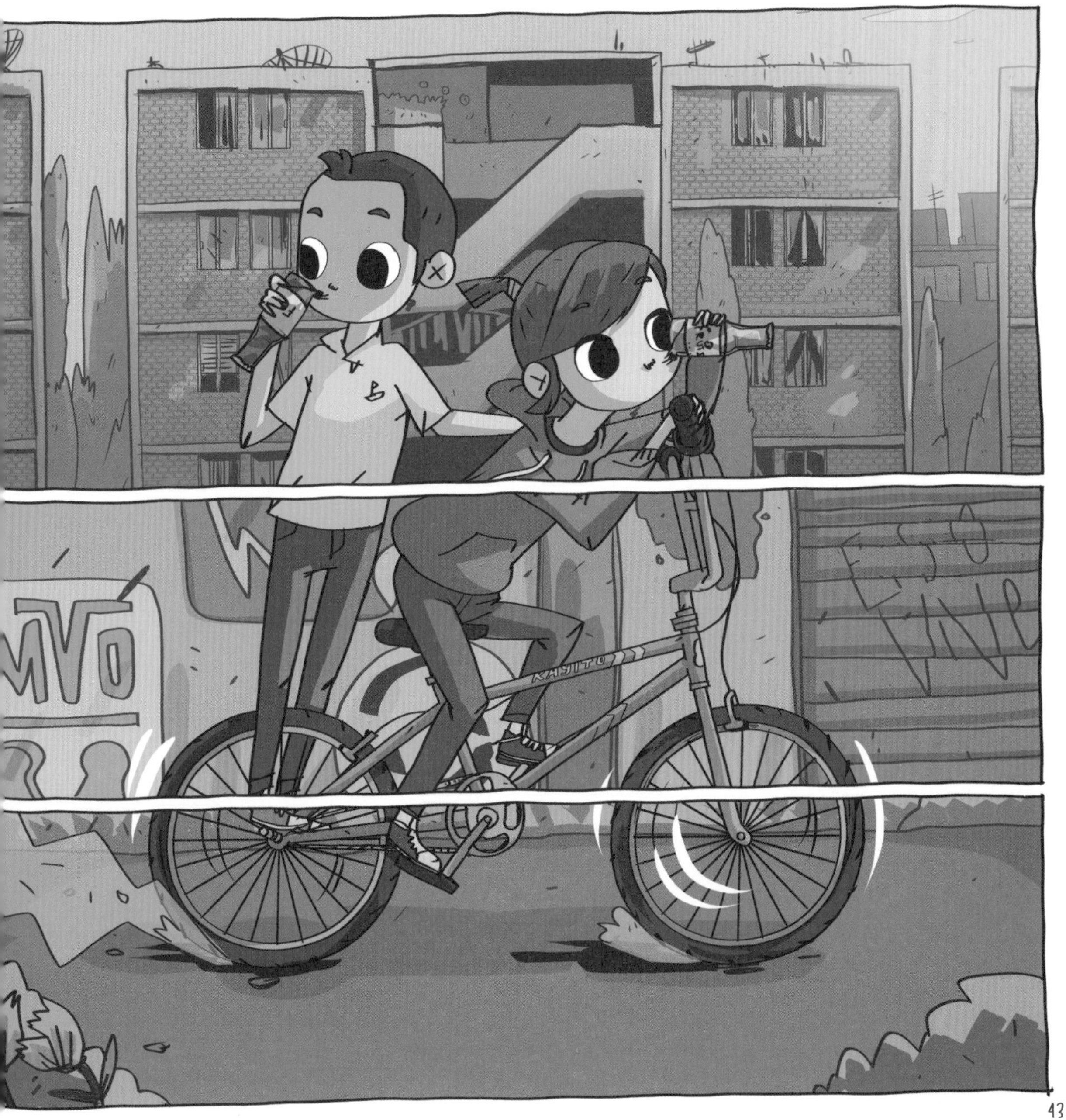

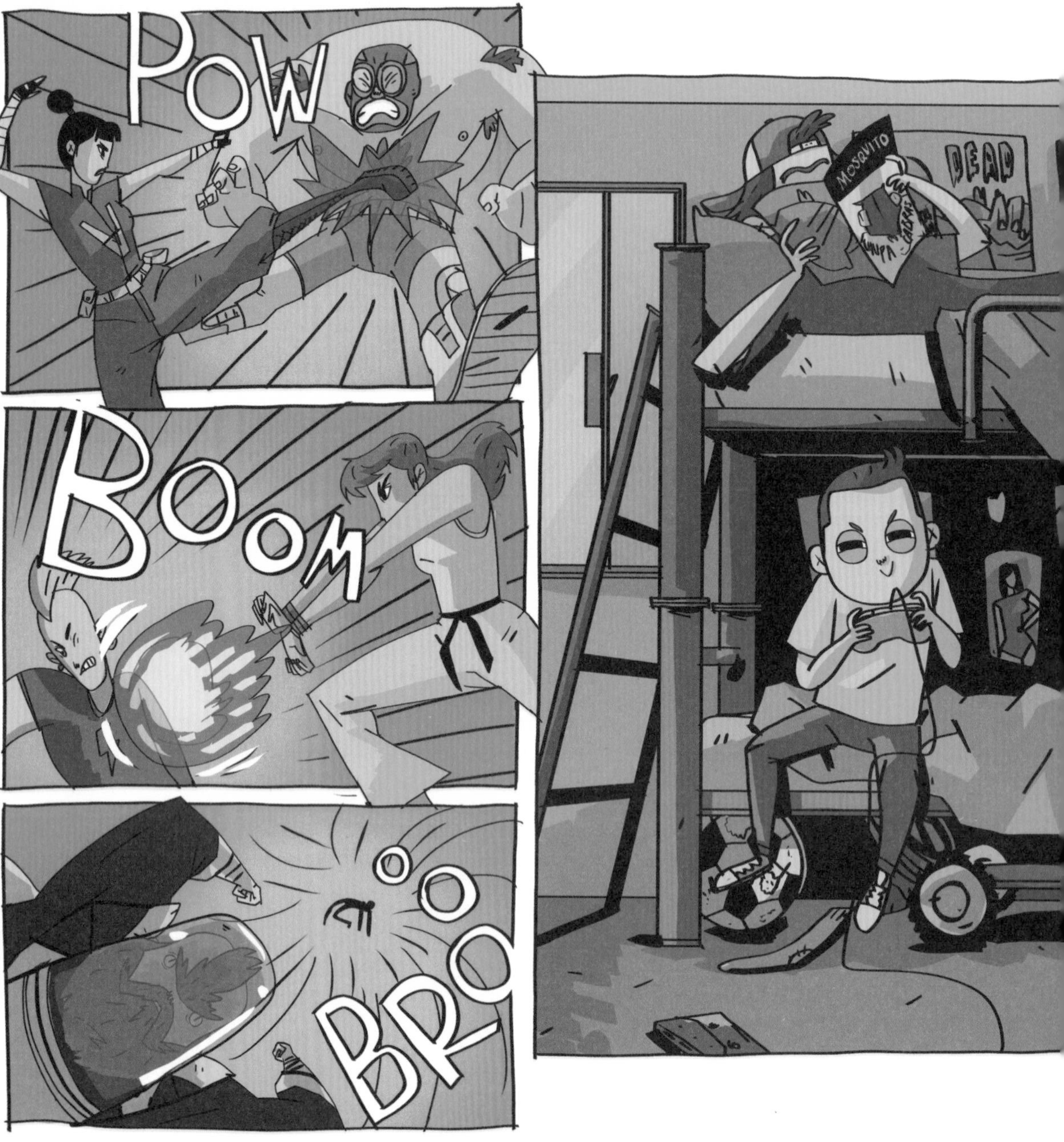
POW
BOOM
BROOOO
MOSQUITO
DEAD

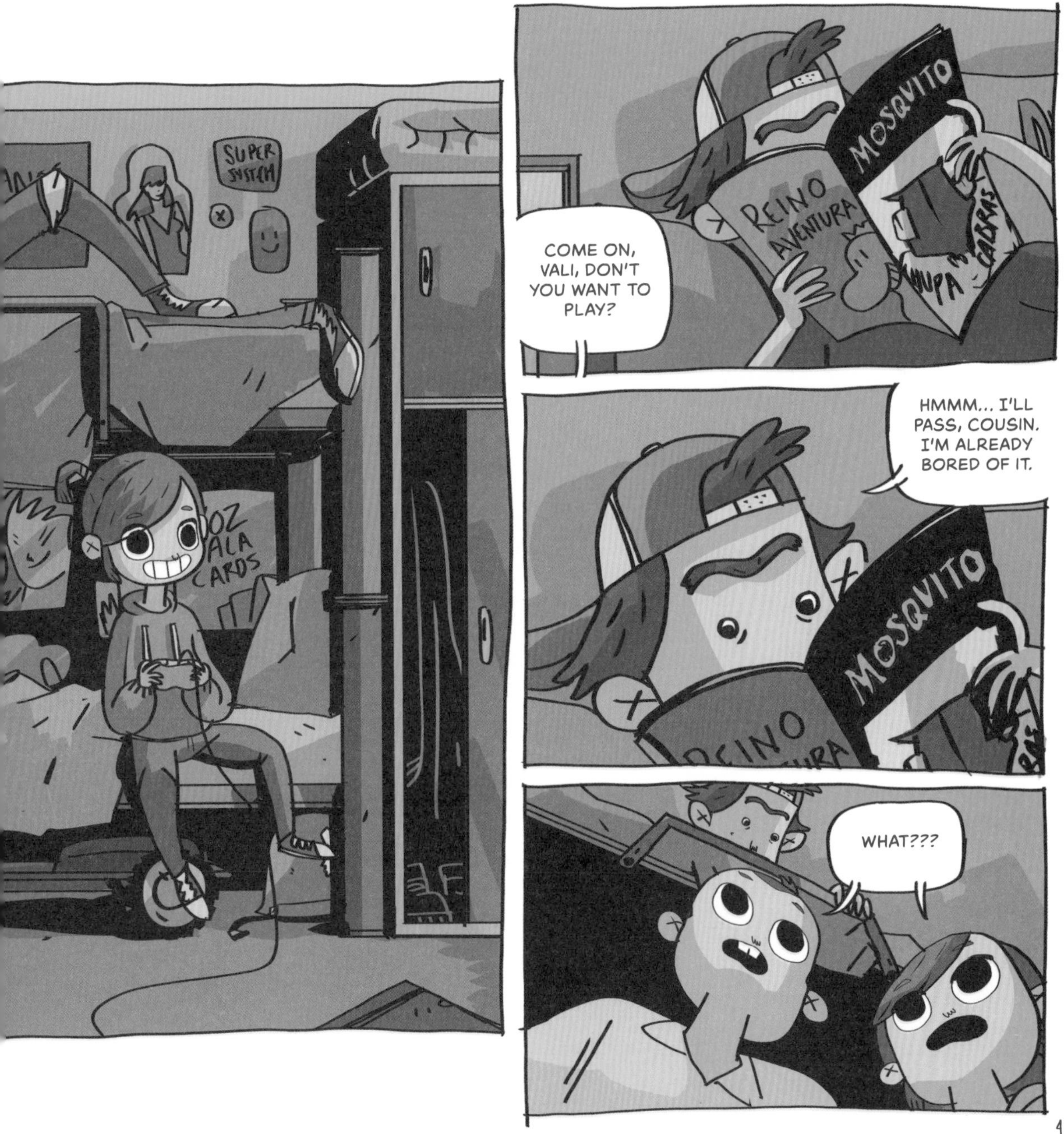
SUPER SYSTEM
REINO AVENTURA
MOSQUITO
COME ON, VALI, DON'T YOU WANT TO PLAY?
HMMM... I'LL PASS, COUSIN. I'M ALREADY BORED OF IT.
MOSQUITO
WHAT???

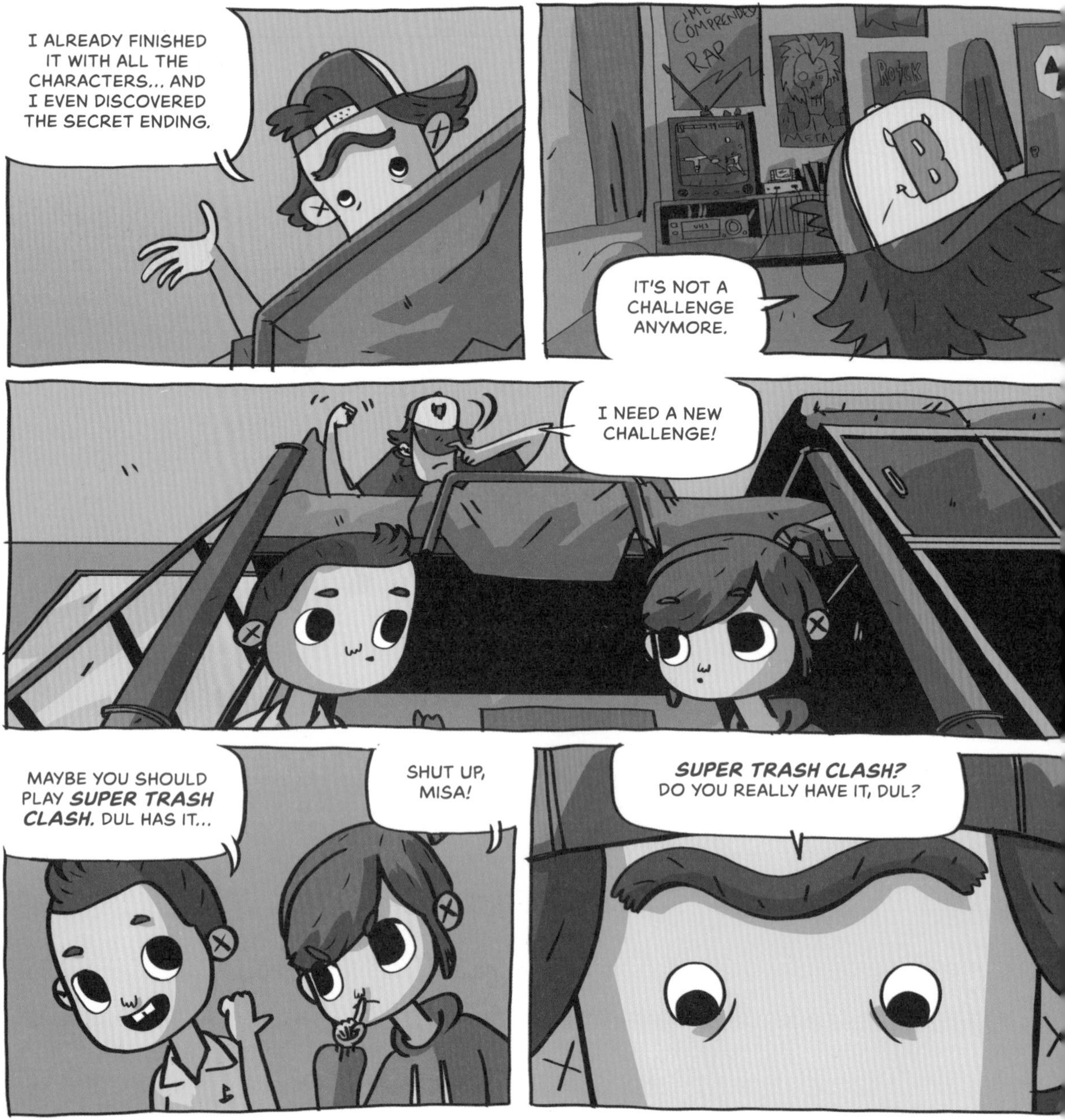

I ALREADY FINISHED IT WITH ALL THE CHARACTERS... AND I EVEN DISCOVERED THE SECRET ENDING.
¡ME COMPRENDES RAP
ROCK
METAL
VHS
IT'S NOT A CHALLENGE ANYMORE.
I NEED A NEW CHALLENGE!
MAYBE YOU SHOULD PLAY *SUPER TRASH CLASH.* DUL HAS IT...
SHUT UP, MISA!
SUPER TRASH CLASH? DO YOU REALLY HAVE IT, DUL?

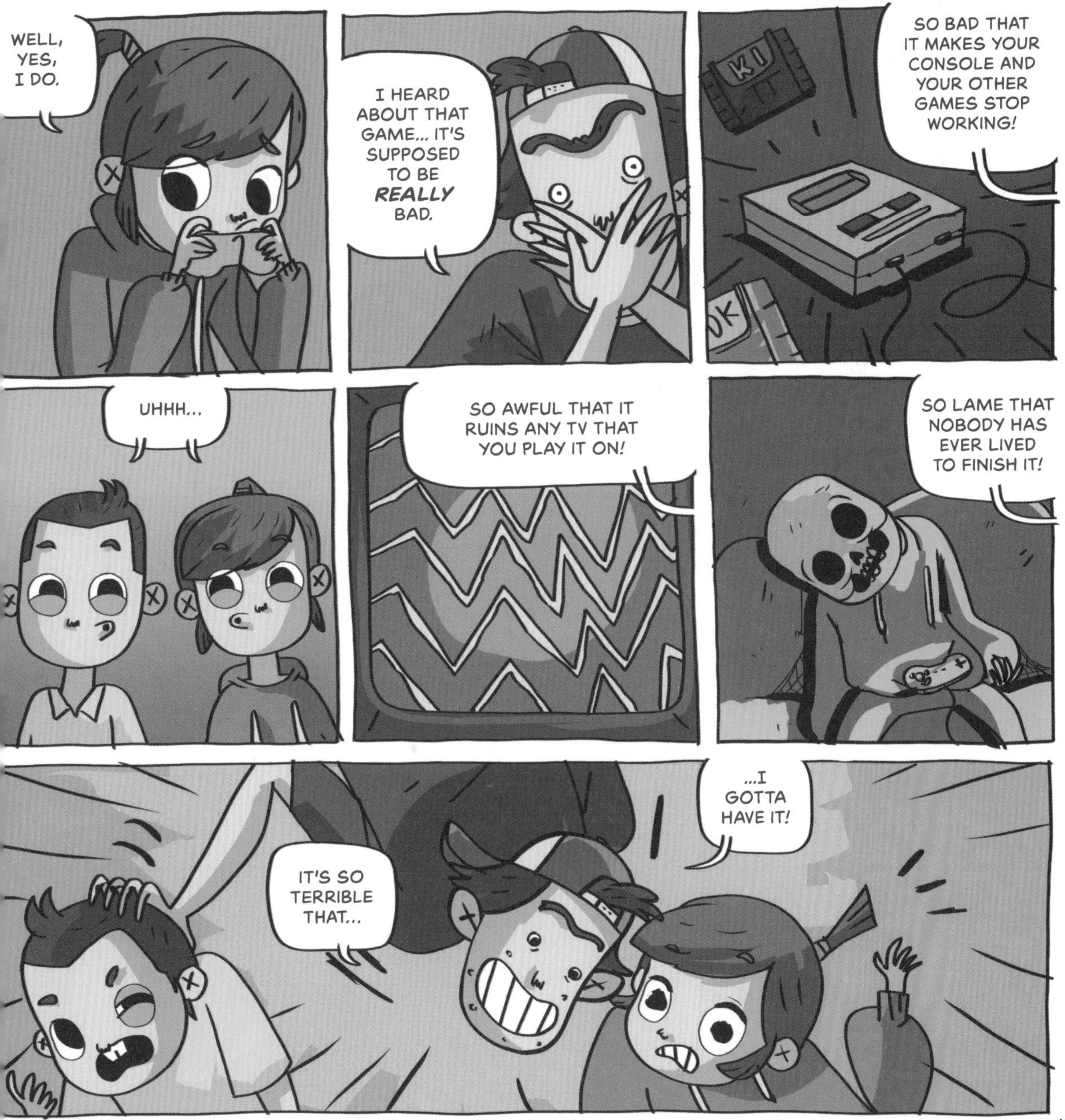
WELL, YES, I DO.
I HEARD ABOUT THAT GAME... IT'S SUPPOSED TO BE *REALLY* BAD.
SO BAD THAT IT MAKES YOUR CONSOLE AND YOUR OTHER GAMES STOP WORKING!
KI
DK
UHHH...
SO AWFUL THAT IT RUINS ANY TV THAT YOU PLAY IT ON!
SO LAME THAT NOBODY HAS EVER LIVED TO FINISH IT!
IT'S SO TERRIBLE THAT...
...I GOTTA HAVE IT!

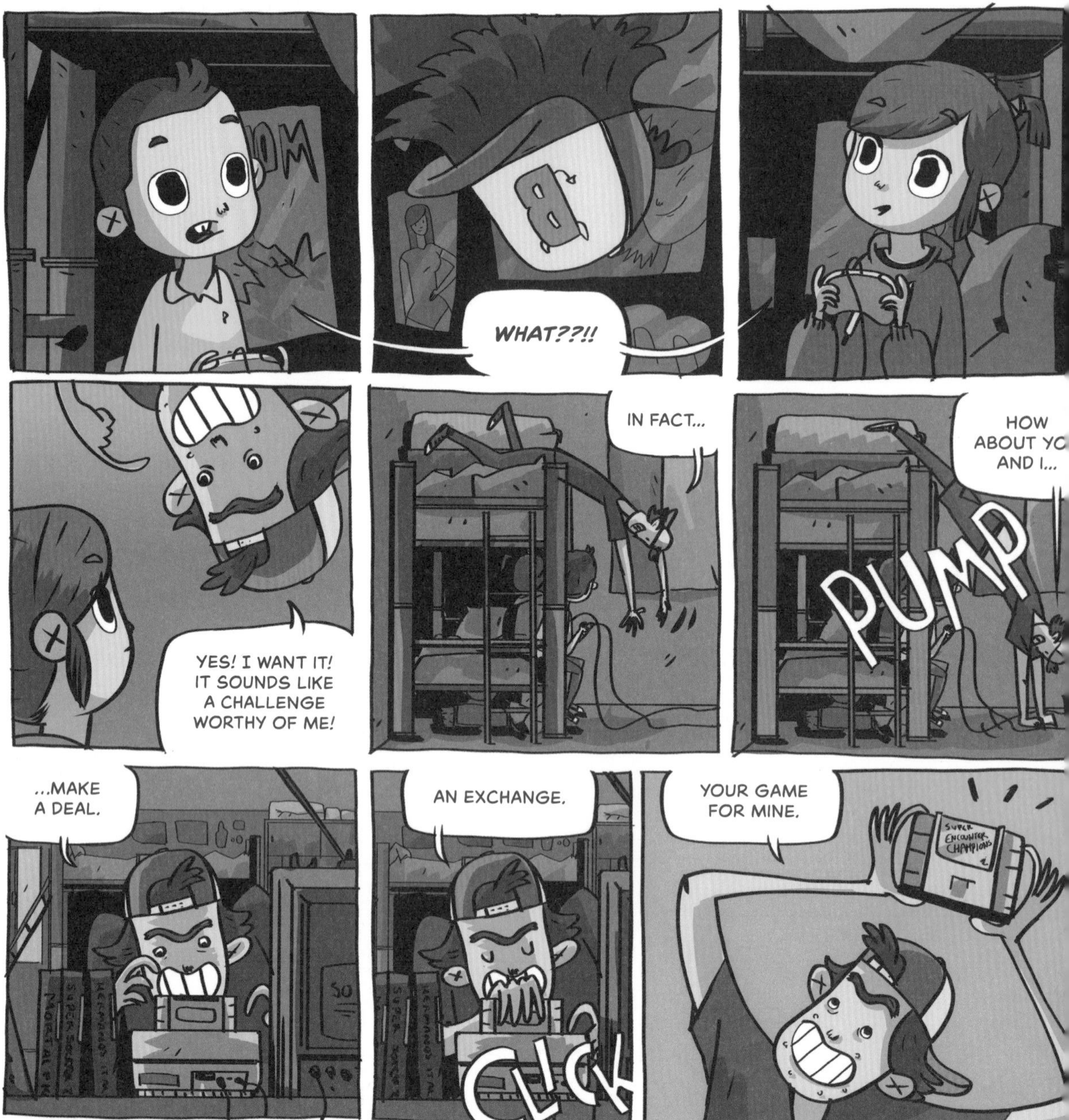
WHAT??!!
YES! I WANT IT! IT SOUNDS LIKE A CHALLENGE WORTHY OF ME!
IN FACT...
HOW ABOUT YO AND I...
PUMP
...MAKE A DEAL.
AN EXCHANGE.
CLICK
YOUR GAME FOR MINE.
SUPER ENCOUNTER CHAMPIONS 2

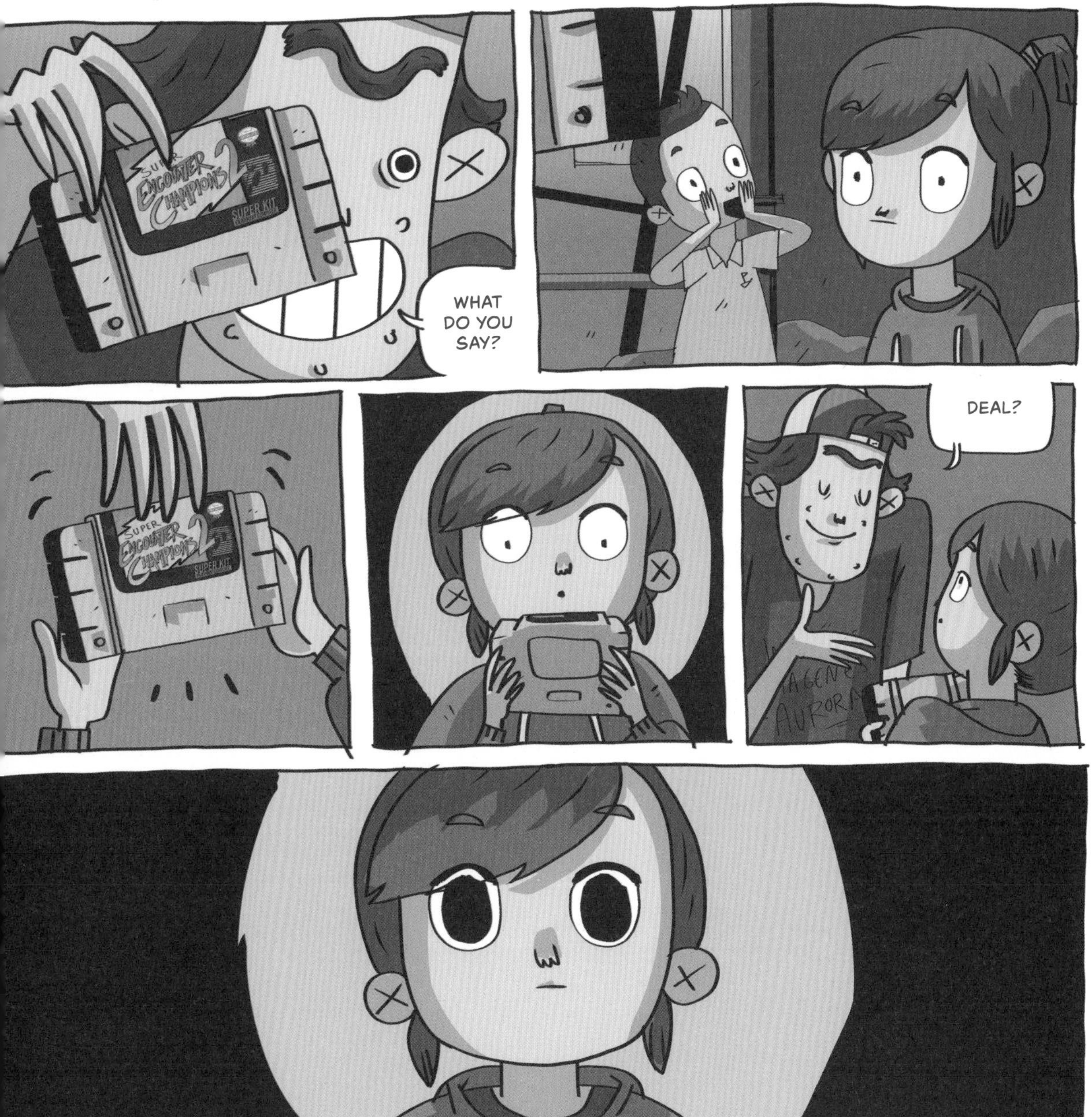
SUPER ENCOUNTER CHAMPIONS 2
SUPER KIT
WHAT DO YOU SAY?
SUPER ENCOUNTER CHAMPIONS 2
SUPER KIT
DEAL?

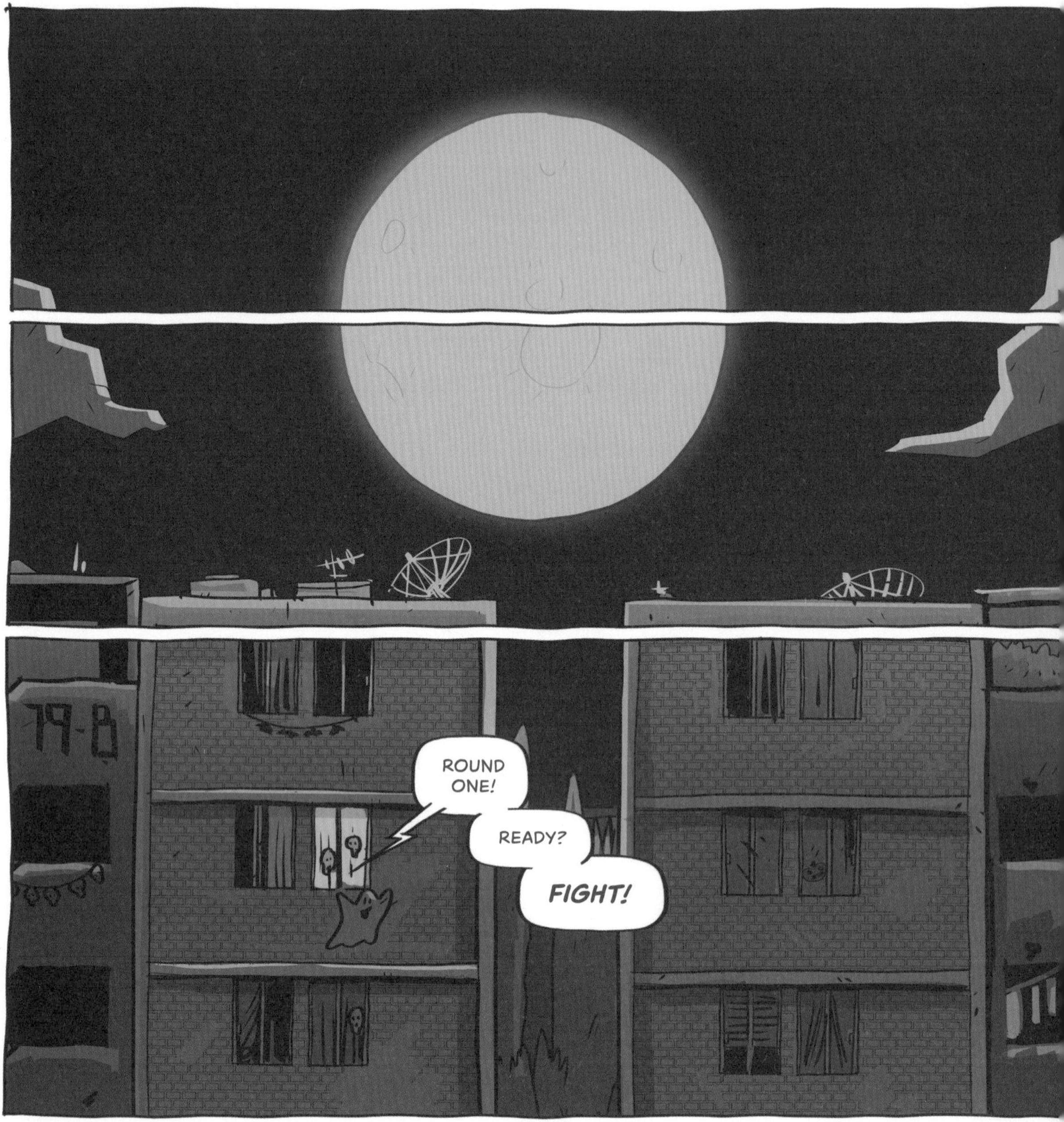
79-B
ROUND ONE!
READY?
FIGHT!

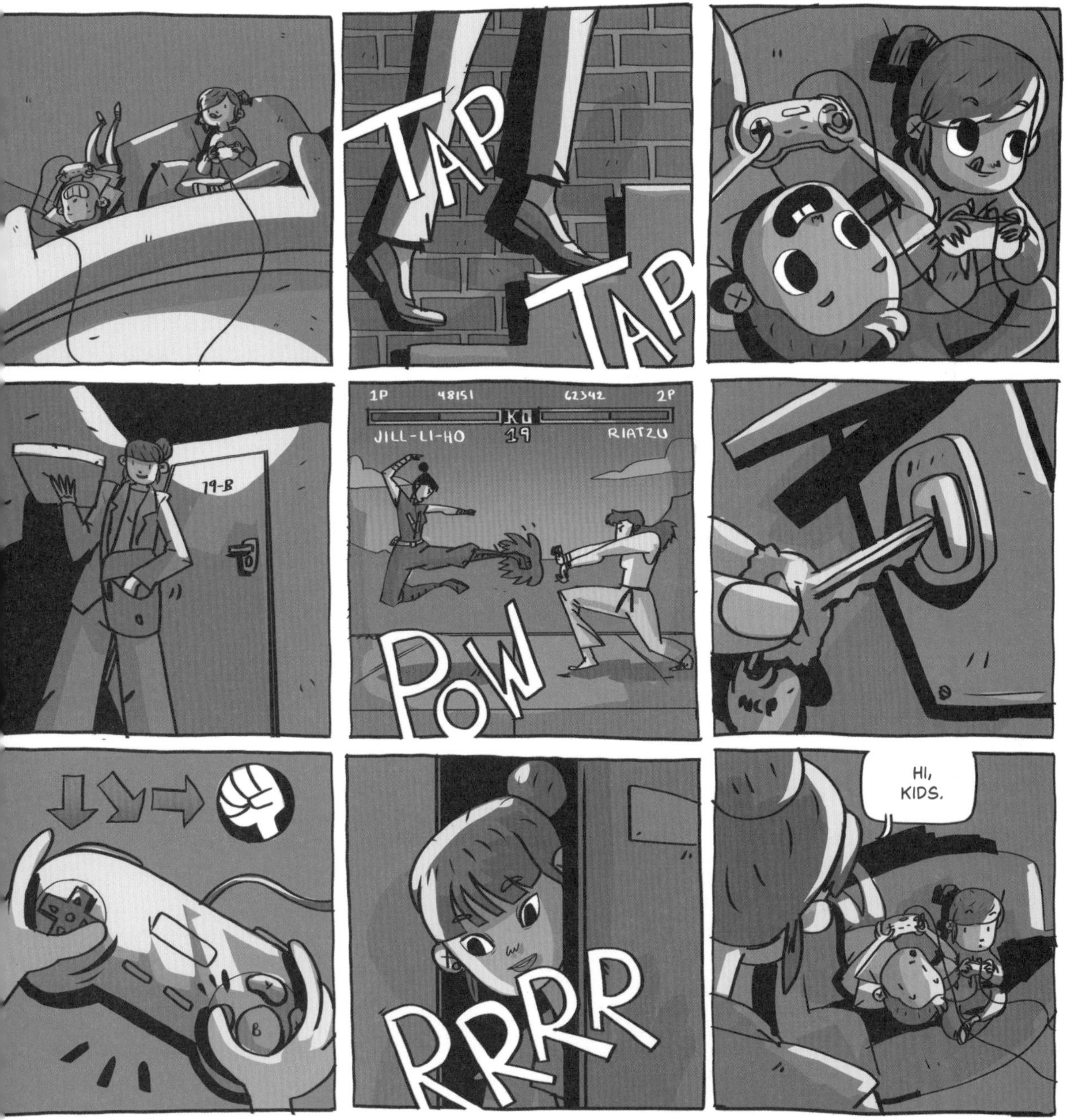
TAP
TAP
19-B
1P 48151
62342 2P
KO
JILL-LI-HO
19
RIATZU
POW
RRRR
HI, KIDS.

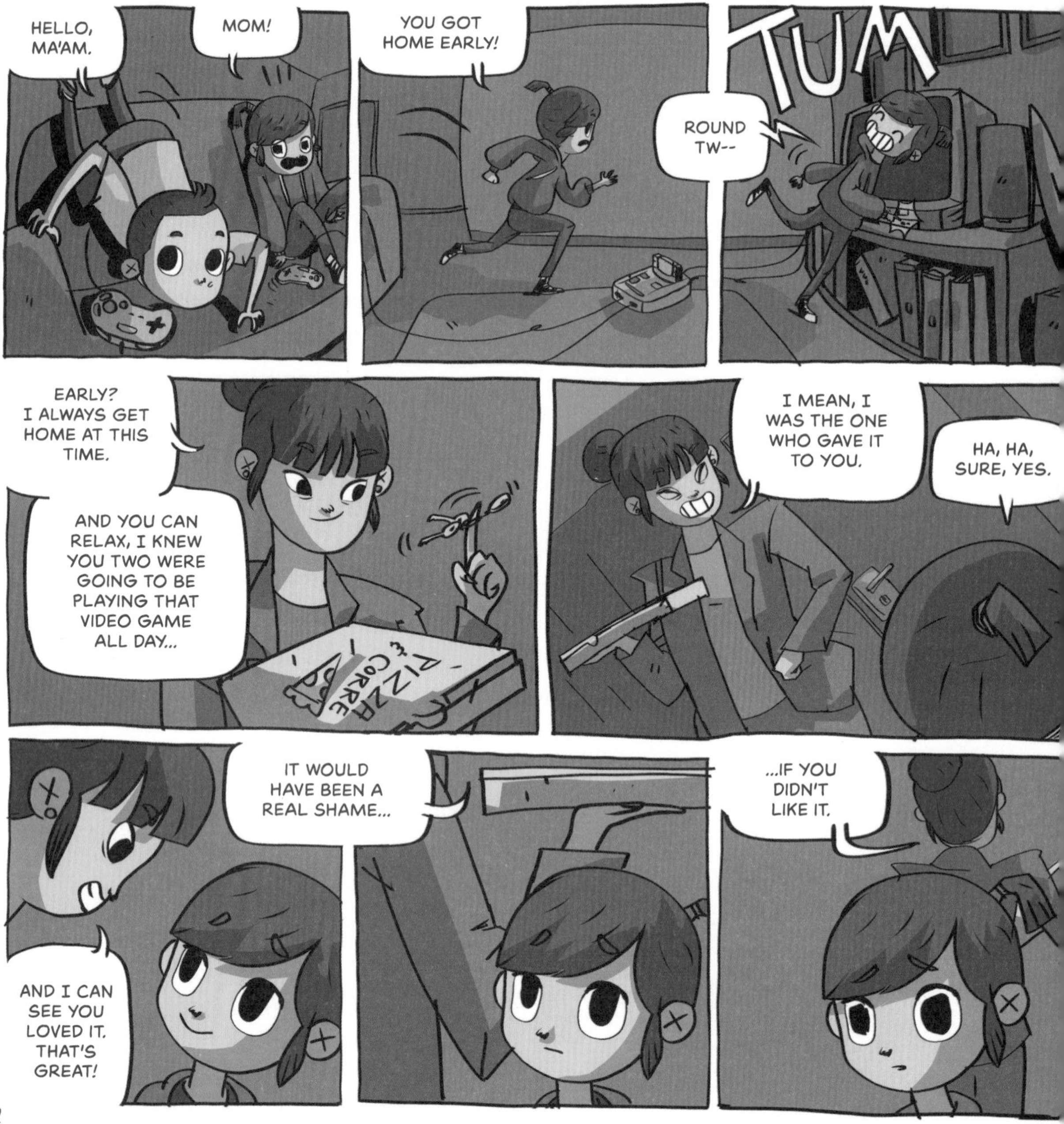
HELLO, MA'AM.
MOM!
YOU GOT HOME EARLY!
TUM
ROUND TW--
EARLY? I ALWAYS GET HOME AT THIS TIME.
AND YOU CAN RELAX, I KNEW YOU TWO WERE GOING TO BE PLAYING THAT VIDEO GAME ALL DAY...
PIZZA CORRE
I MEAN, I WAS THE ONE WHO GAVE IT TO YOU.
HA, HA, SURE, YES.
AND I CAN SEE YOU LOVED IT. THAT'S GREAT!
IT WOULD HAVE BEEN A REAL SHAME...
...IF YOU DIDN'T LIKE IT.

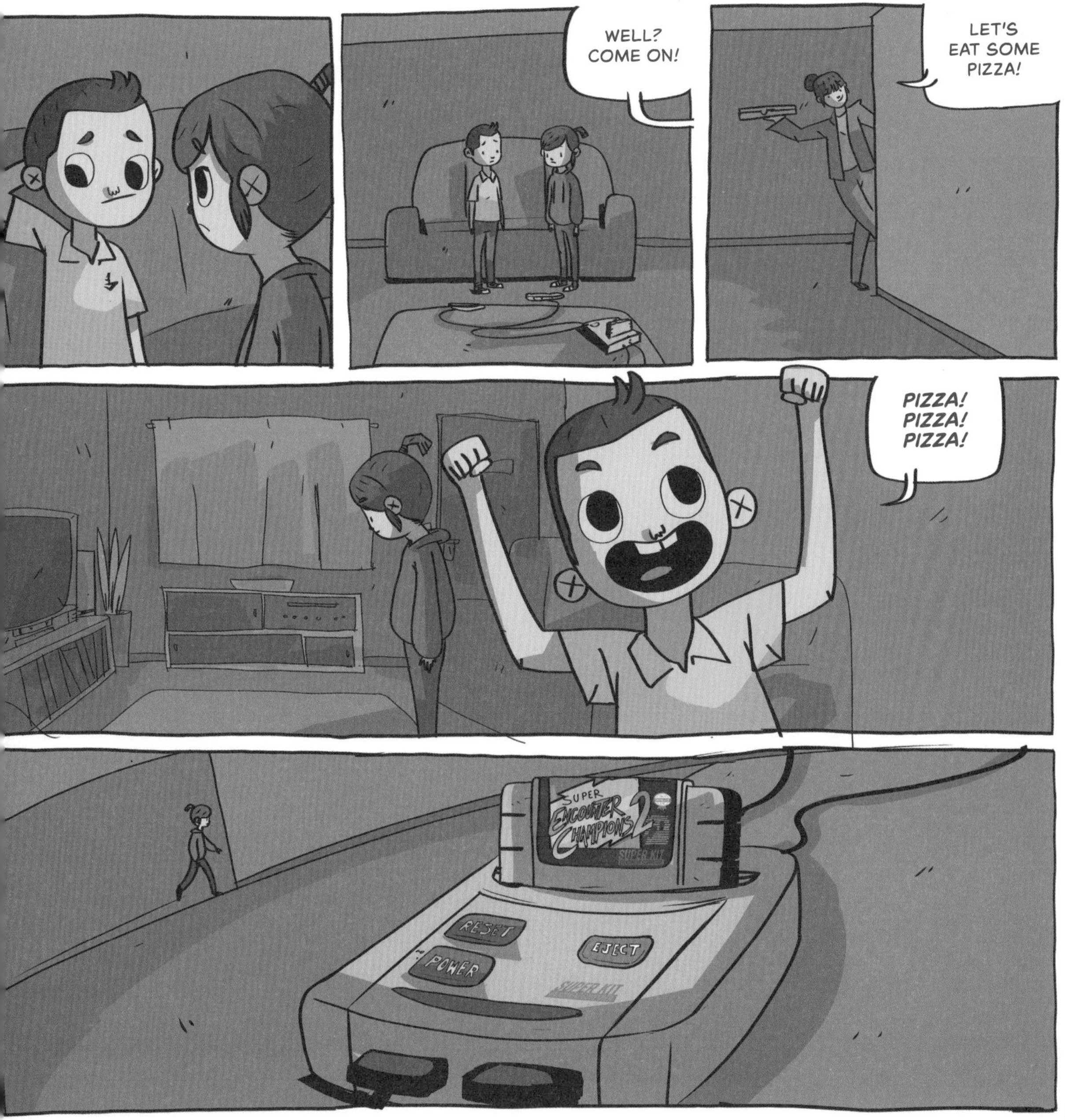
WELL? COME ON!
LET'S EAT SOME PIZZA!
PIZZA! PIZZA! PIZZA!
SUPER ENCOUNTER CHAMPIONS 2
SUPER KIT
RESET
POWER
EJECT
SUPER KIT

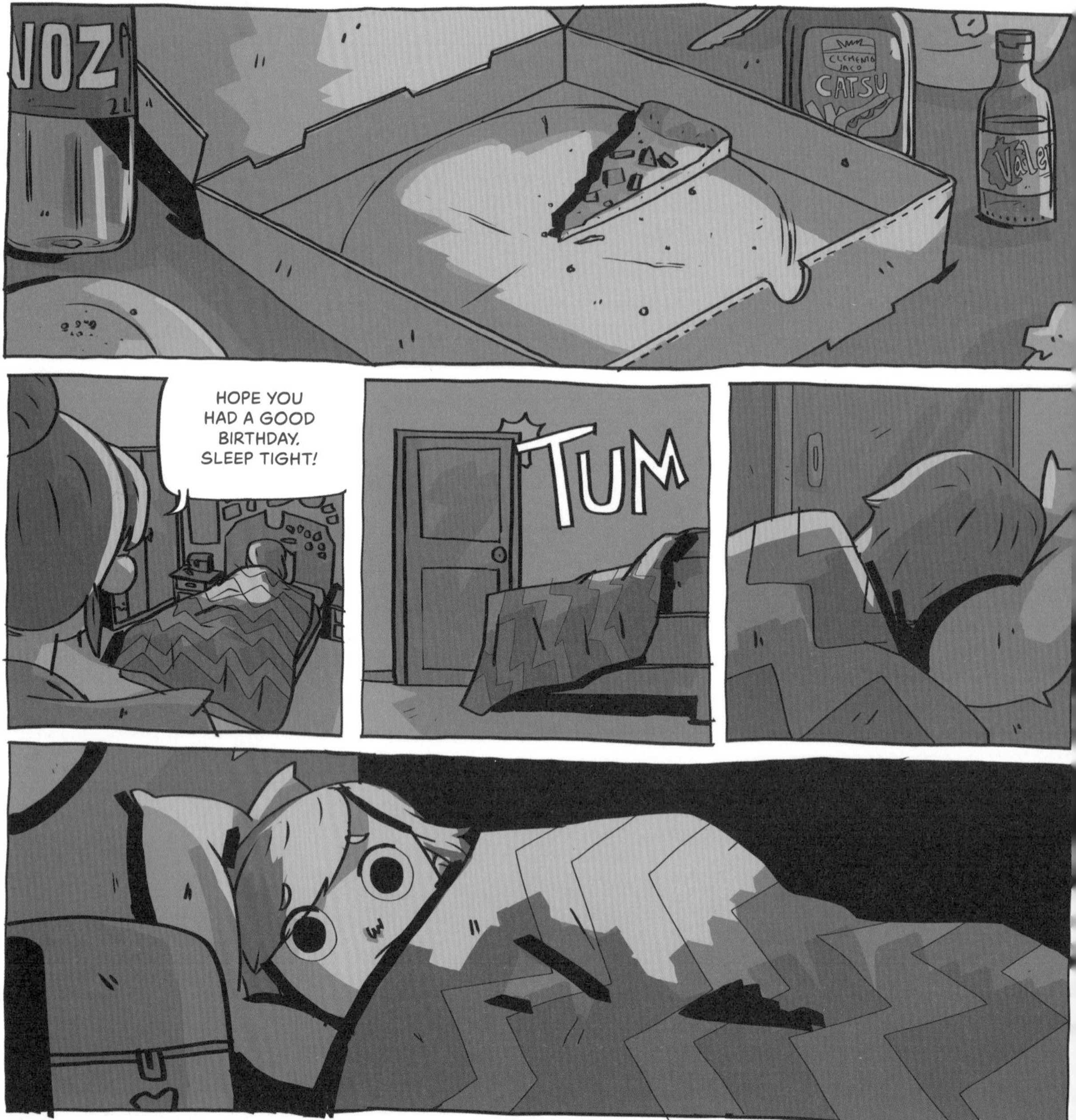
CATSU
HOPE YOU HAD A GOOD BIRTHDAY. SLEEP TIGHT!
TUM

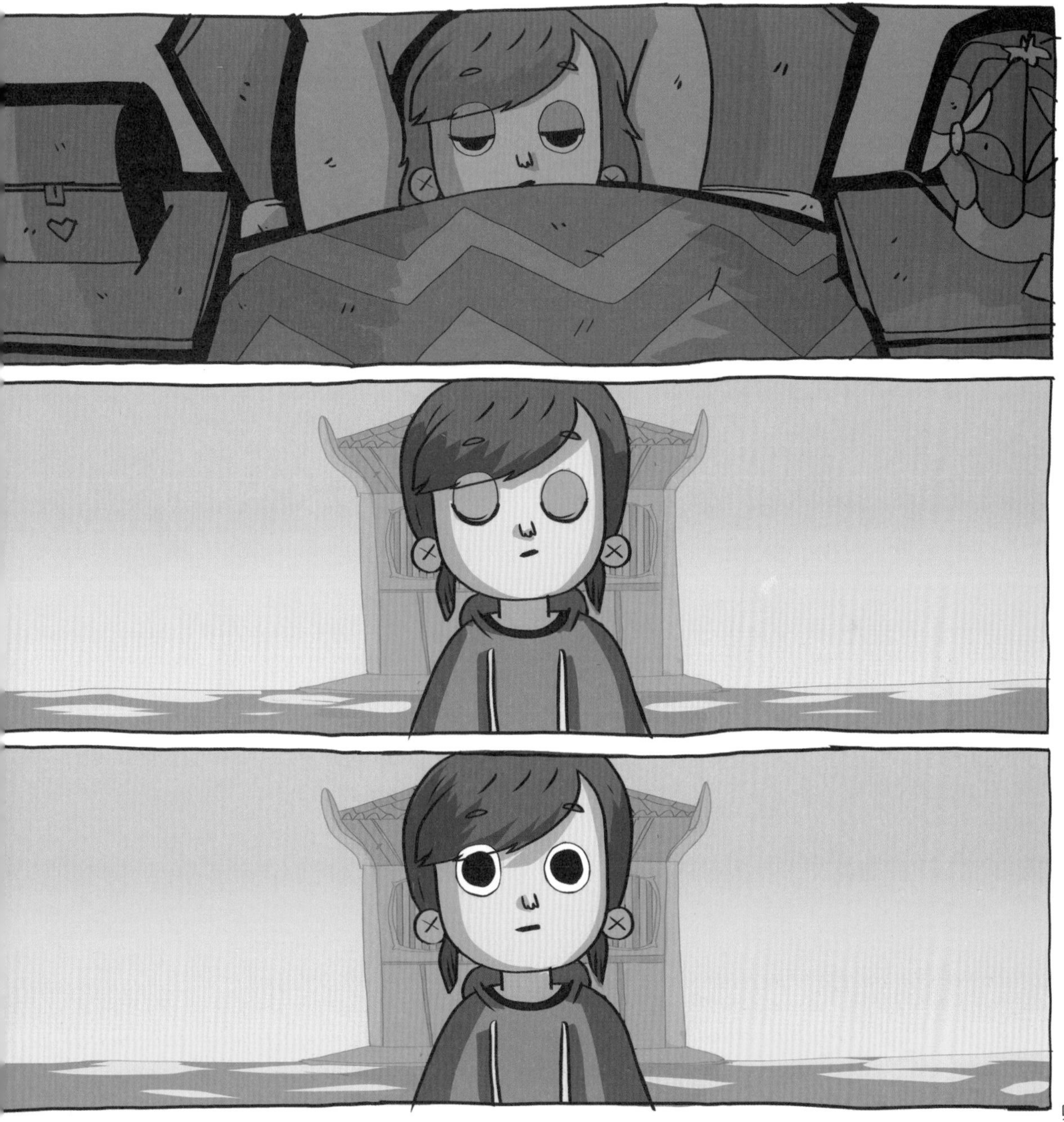

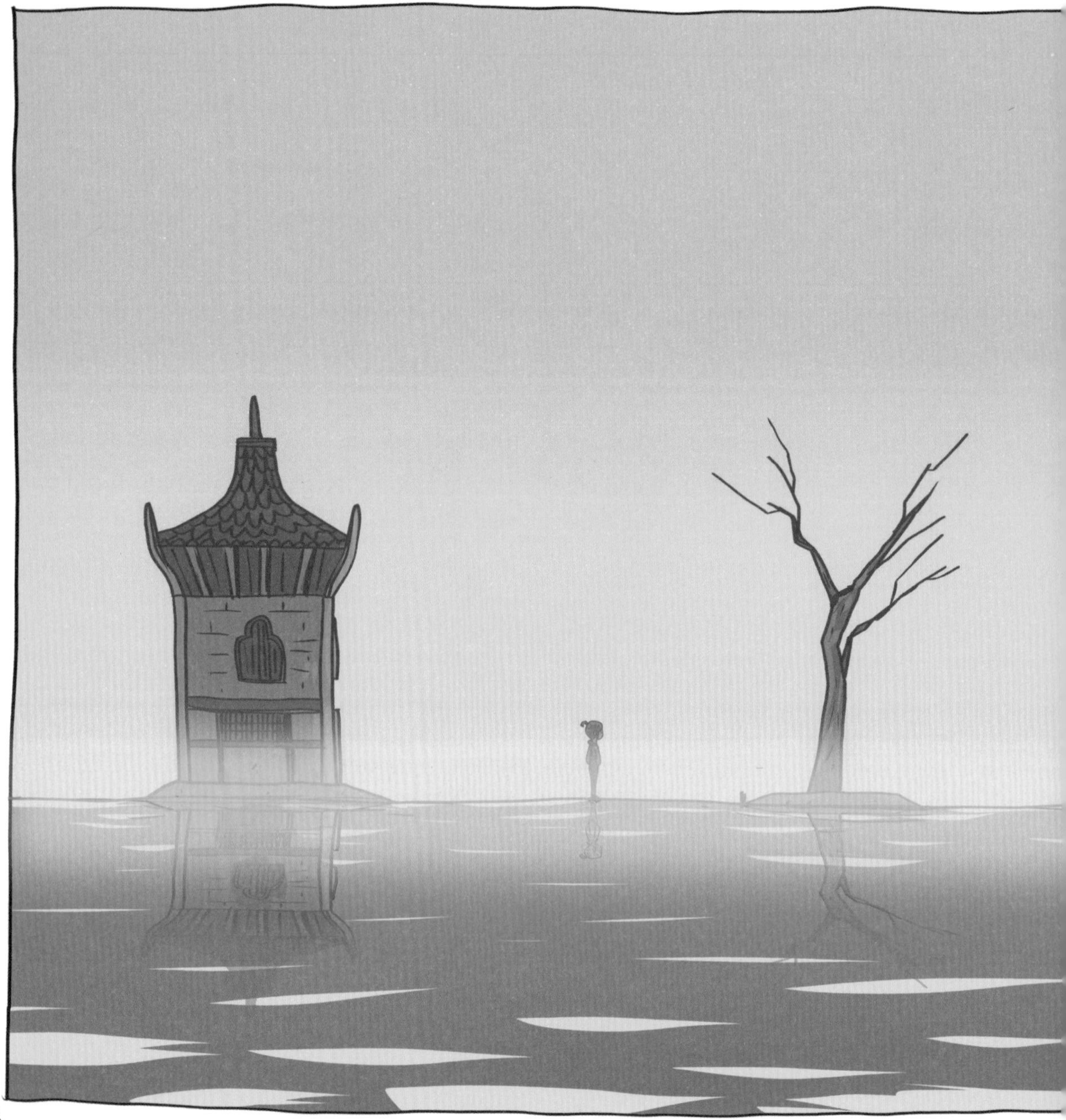

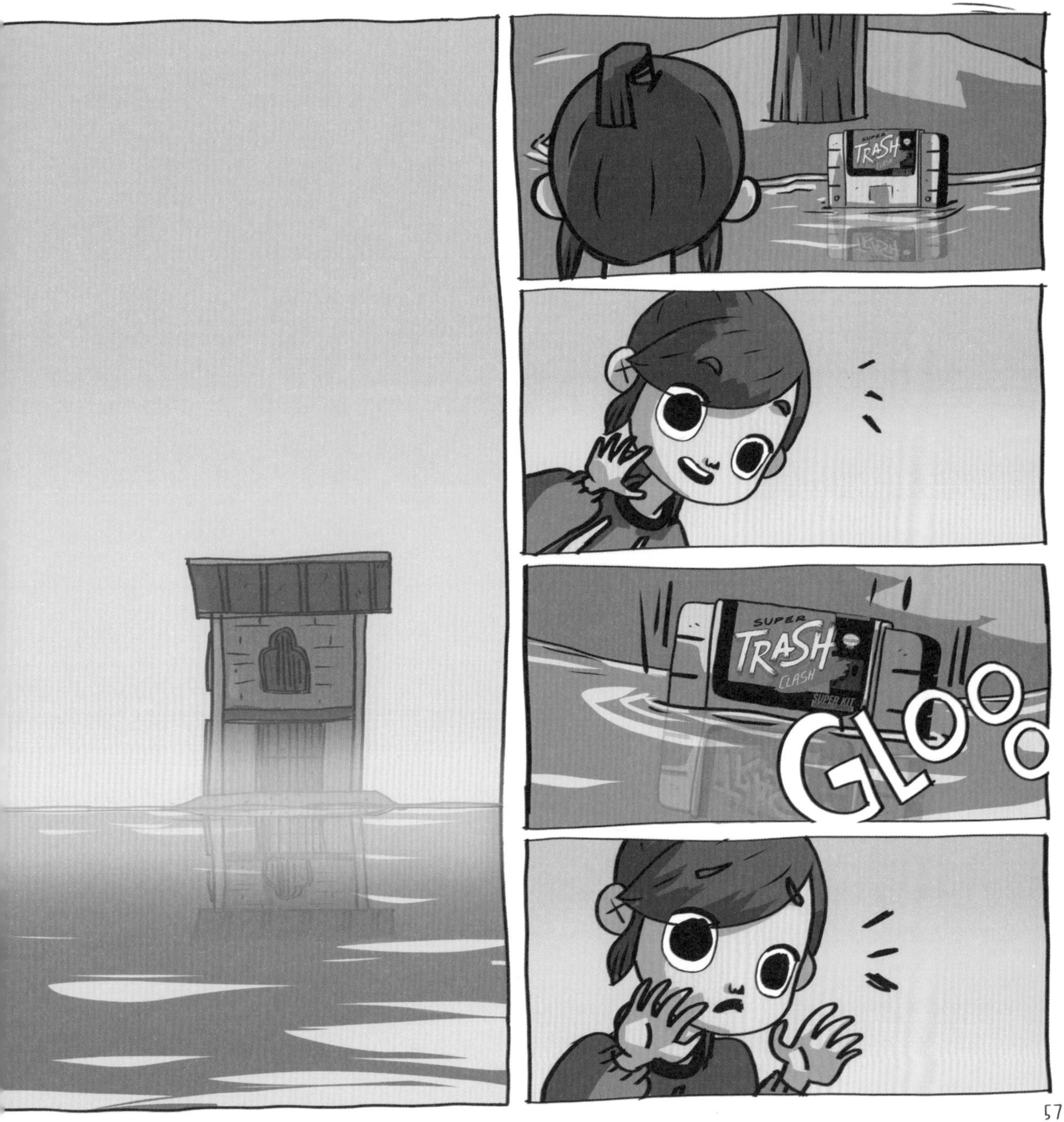
SUPER TRASH CLASH
SUPER TRASH CLASH
SUPER KIT
GLOOO

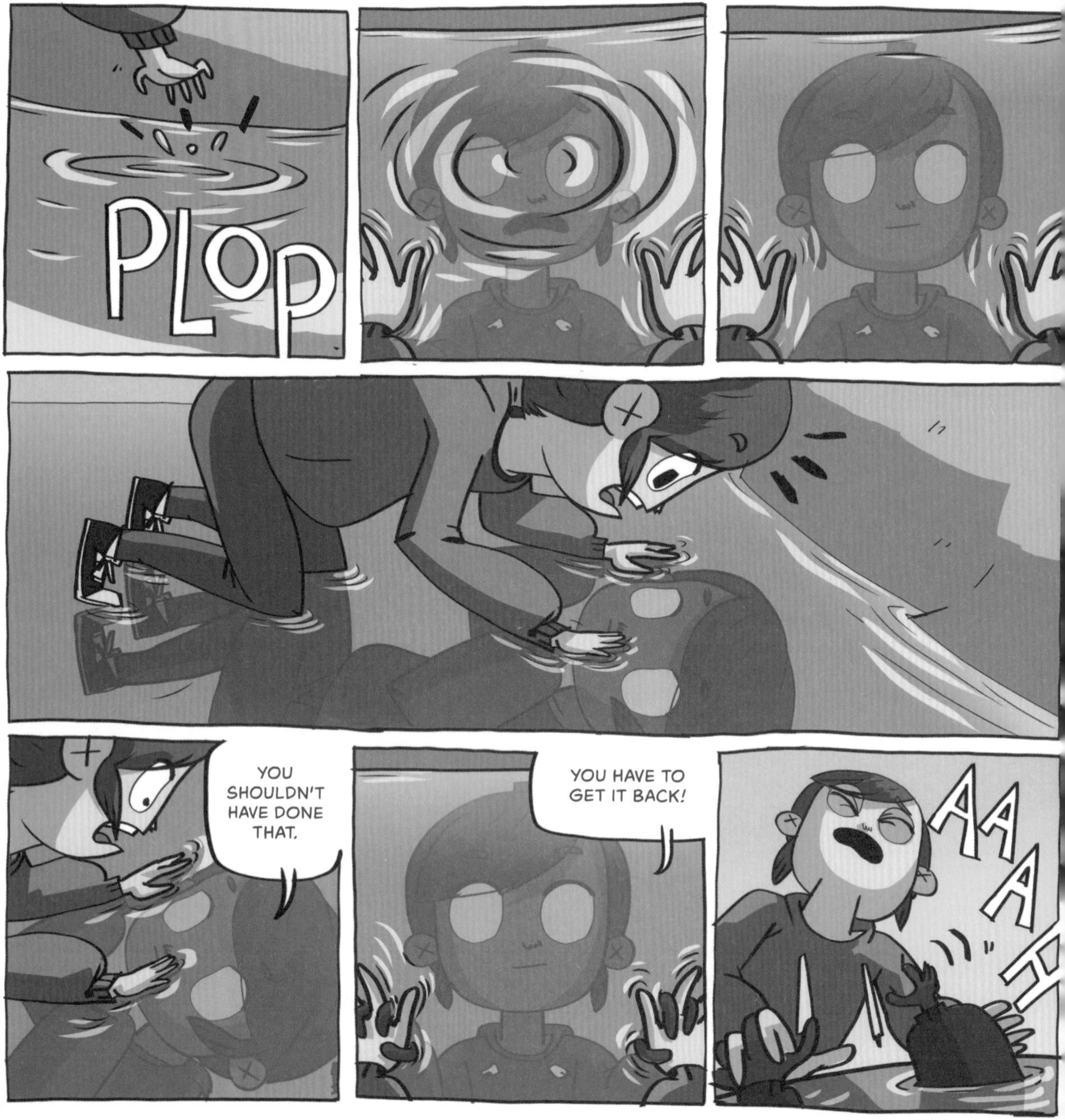
PLOP
YOU SHOULDN'T HAVE DONE THAT.
YOU HAVE TO GET IT BACK!
AAAH

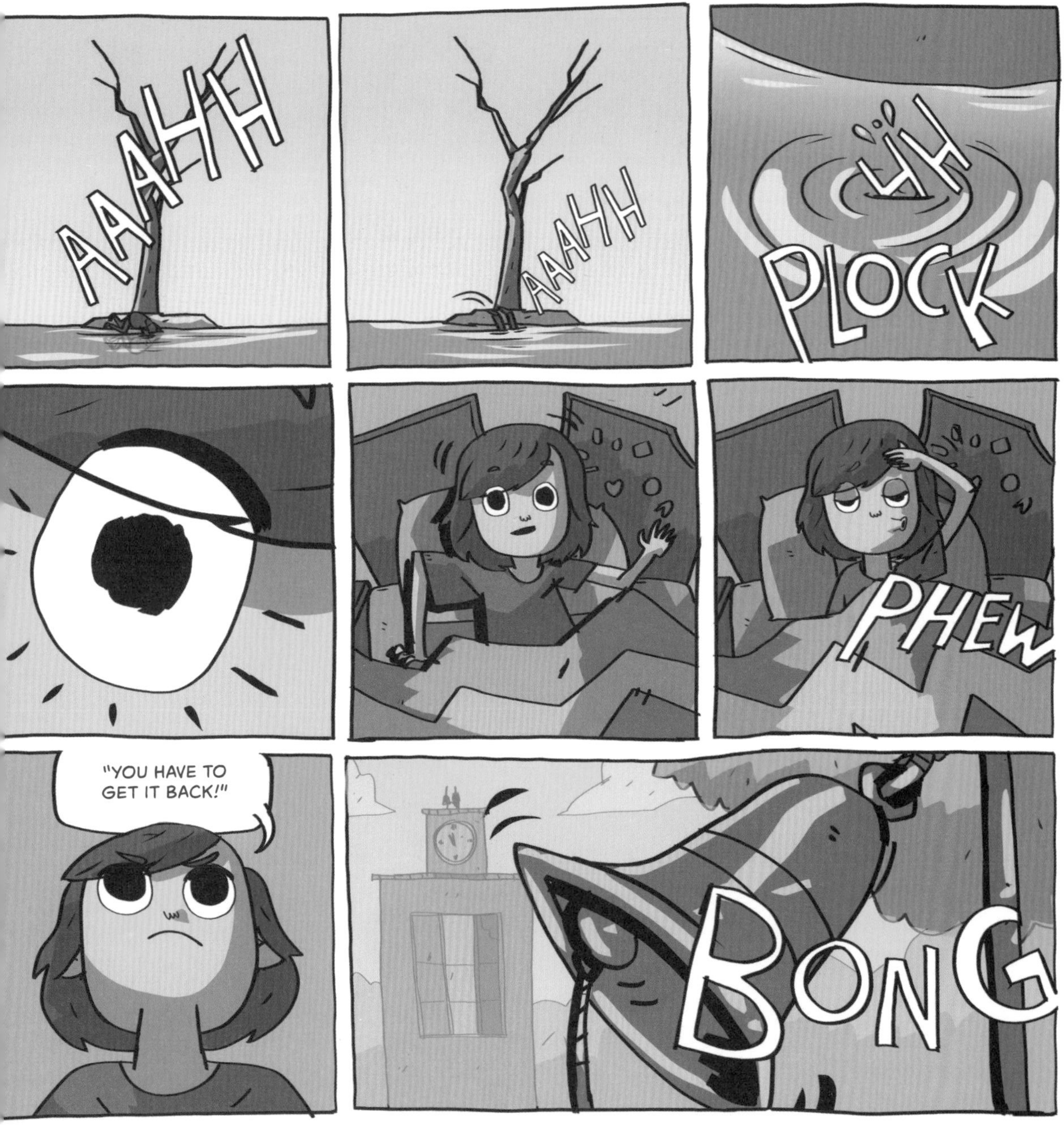
AAAHHH
AAAHH
UHH
PLOCK
PHEW
"YOU HAVE TO GET IT BACK!"
BONG

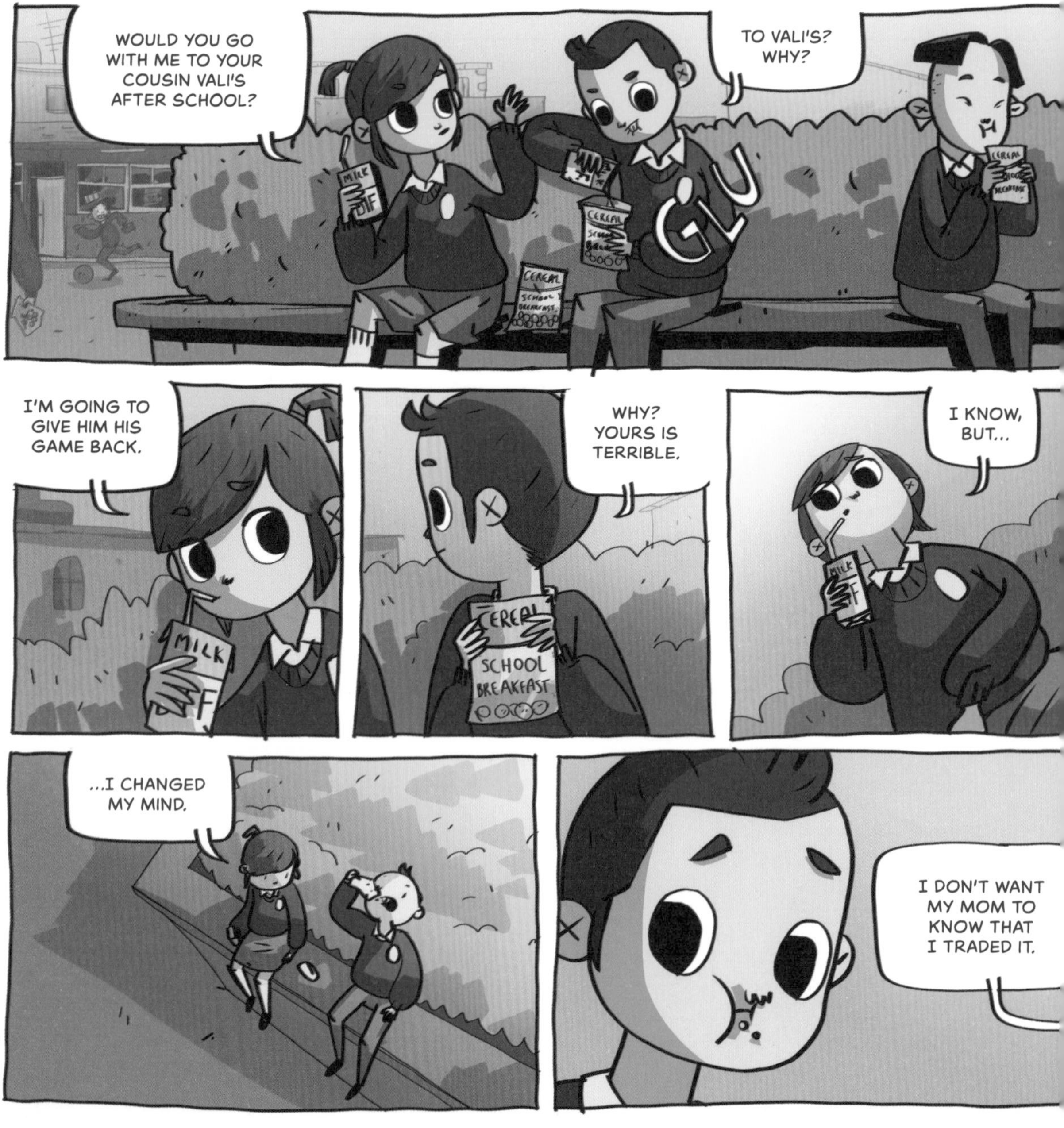
WOULD YOU GO WITH ME TO YOUR COUSIN VALI'S AFTER SCHOOL?
TO VALI'S? WHY?
MILK
CEREAL
GLU
I'M GOING TO GIVE HIM HIS GAME BACK.
WHY? YOURS IS TERRIBLE.
CEREAL SCHOOL BREAKFAST
I KNOW, BUT...
...I CHANGED MY MIND.
I DON'T WANT MY MOM TO KNOW THAT I TRADED IT.

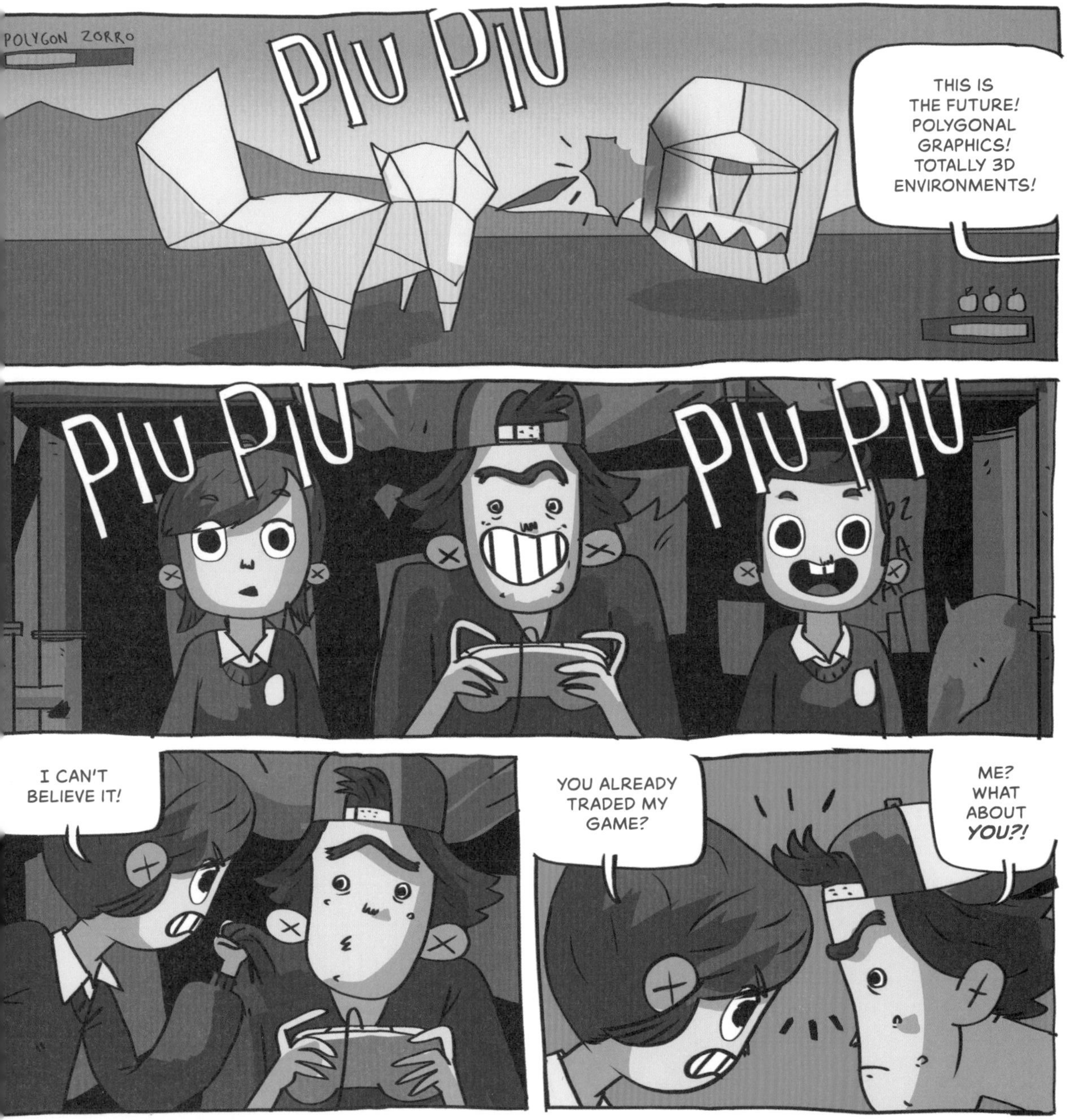
POLYGON ZORRO
PIU PIU
THIS IS THE FUTURE! POLYGONAL GRAPHICS! TOTALLY 3D ENVIRONMENTS!
PIU PIU
PIU PIU
I CAN'T BELIEVE IT!
YOU ALREADY TRADED MY GAME?
ME? WHAT ABOUT *YOU?!*

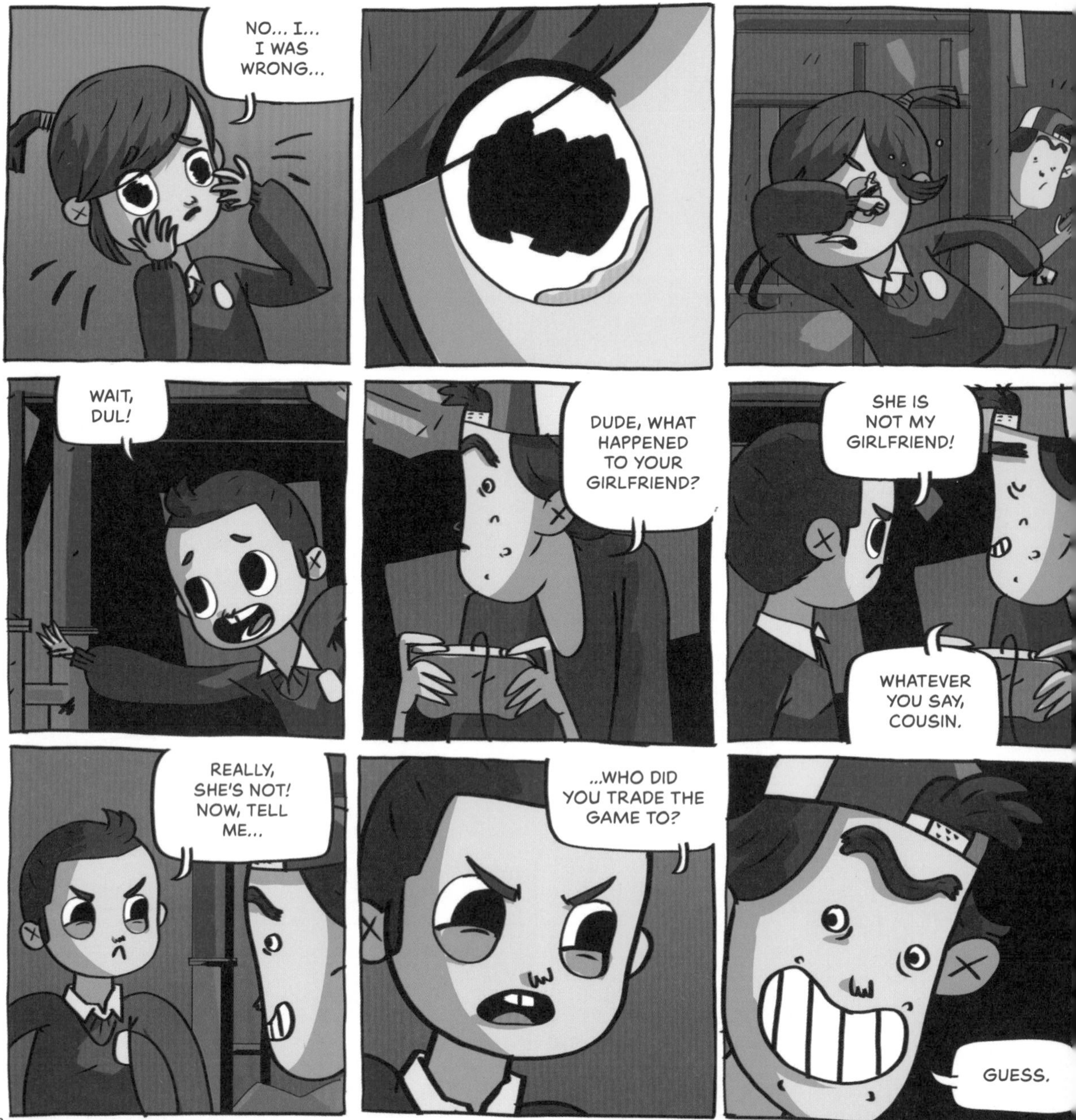
NO... I...
I WAS
WRONG...
WAIT,
DUL!
DUDE, WHAT
HAPPENED
TO YOUR
GIRLFRIEND?
SHE IS
NOT MY
GIRLFRIEND!
WHATEVER
YOU SAY,
COUSIN.
REALLY,
SHE'S NOT!
NOW, TELL
ME...
...WHO DID
YOU TRADE THE
GAME TO?
GUESS.

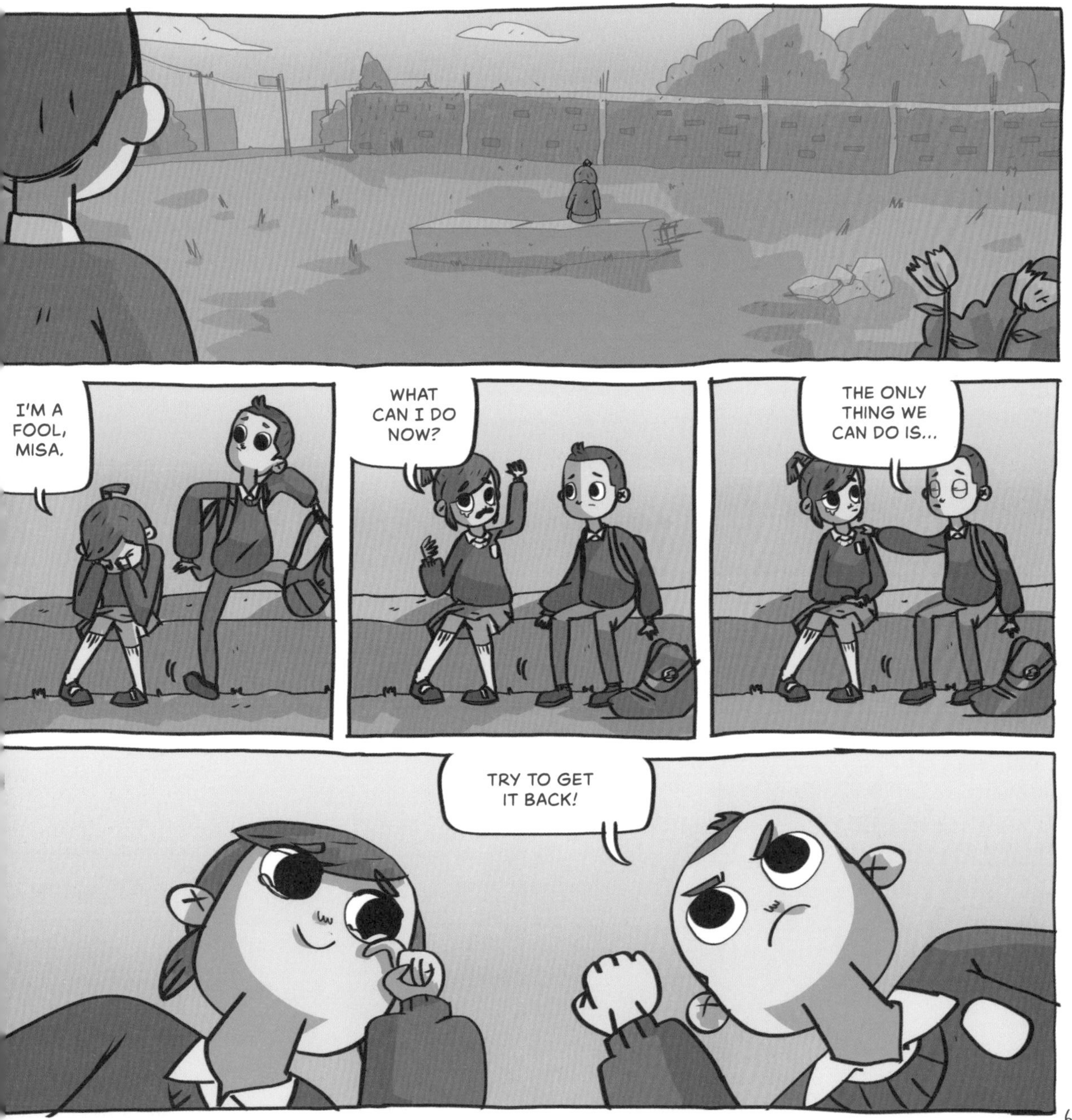

I'M A FOOL, MISA.
WHAT CAN I DO NOW?
THE ONLY THING WE CAN DO IS...
TRY TO GET IT BACK!

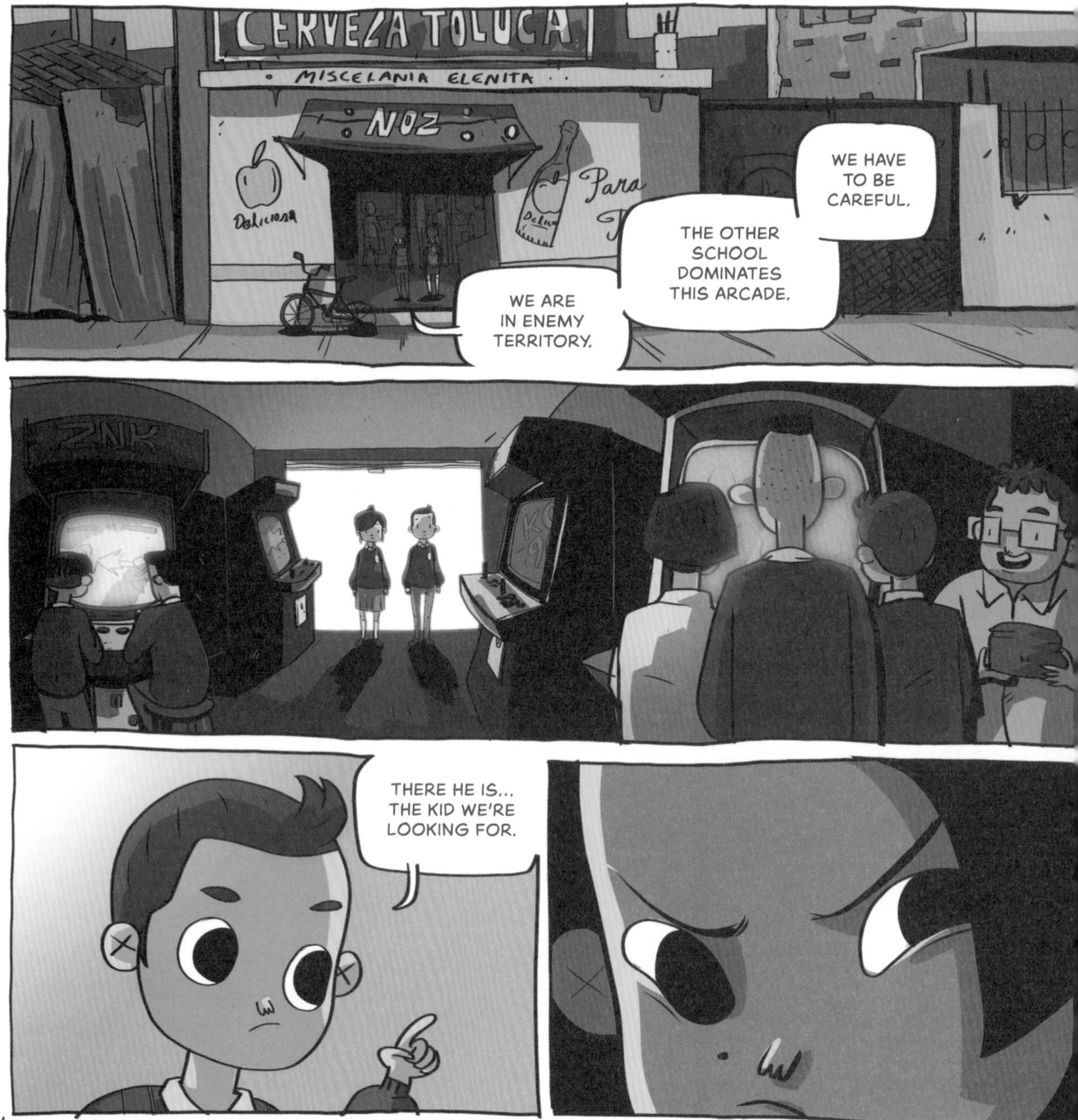
CERVEZA TOLUCA
MISCELANIA ELENITA
NOZ
Deliciosa
WE ARE IN ENEMY TERRITORY.
THE OTHER SCHOOL DOMINATES THIS ARCADE.
WE HAVE TO BE CAREFUL.
ZNK
THERE HE IS... THE KID WE'RE LOOKING FOR.

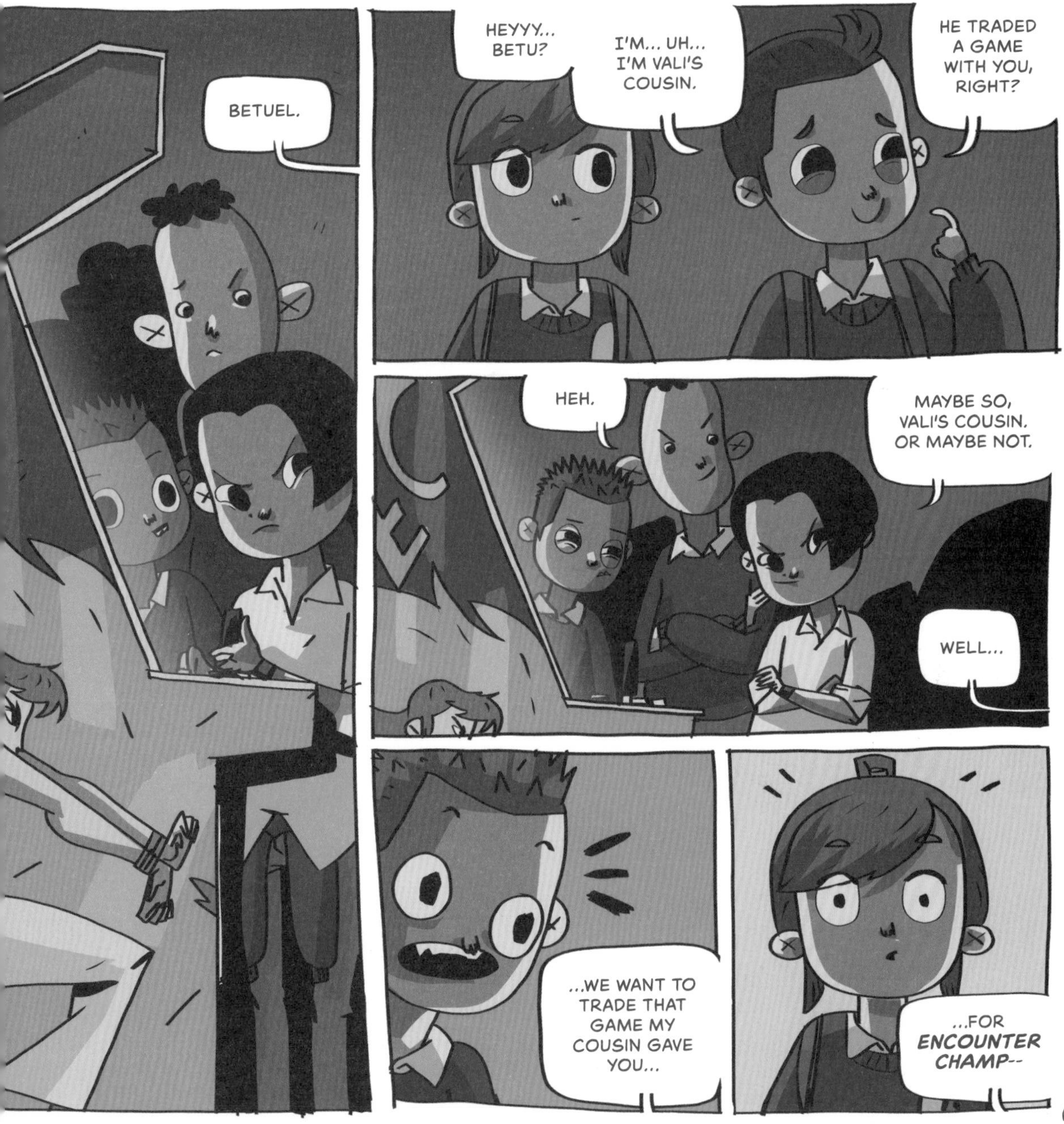
BETUEL.
HEYYY... BETU?
I'M... UH... I'M VALI'S COUSIN.
HE TRADED A GAME WITH YOU, RIGHT?
HEH.
MAYBE SO, VALI'S COUSIN. OR MAYBE NOT.
WELL...
...WE WANT TO TRADE THAT GAME MY COUSIN GAVE YOU...
...FOR *ENCOUNTER CHAMP*--

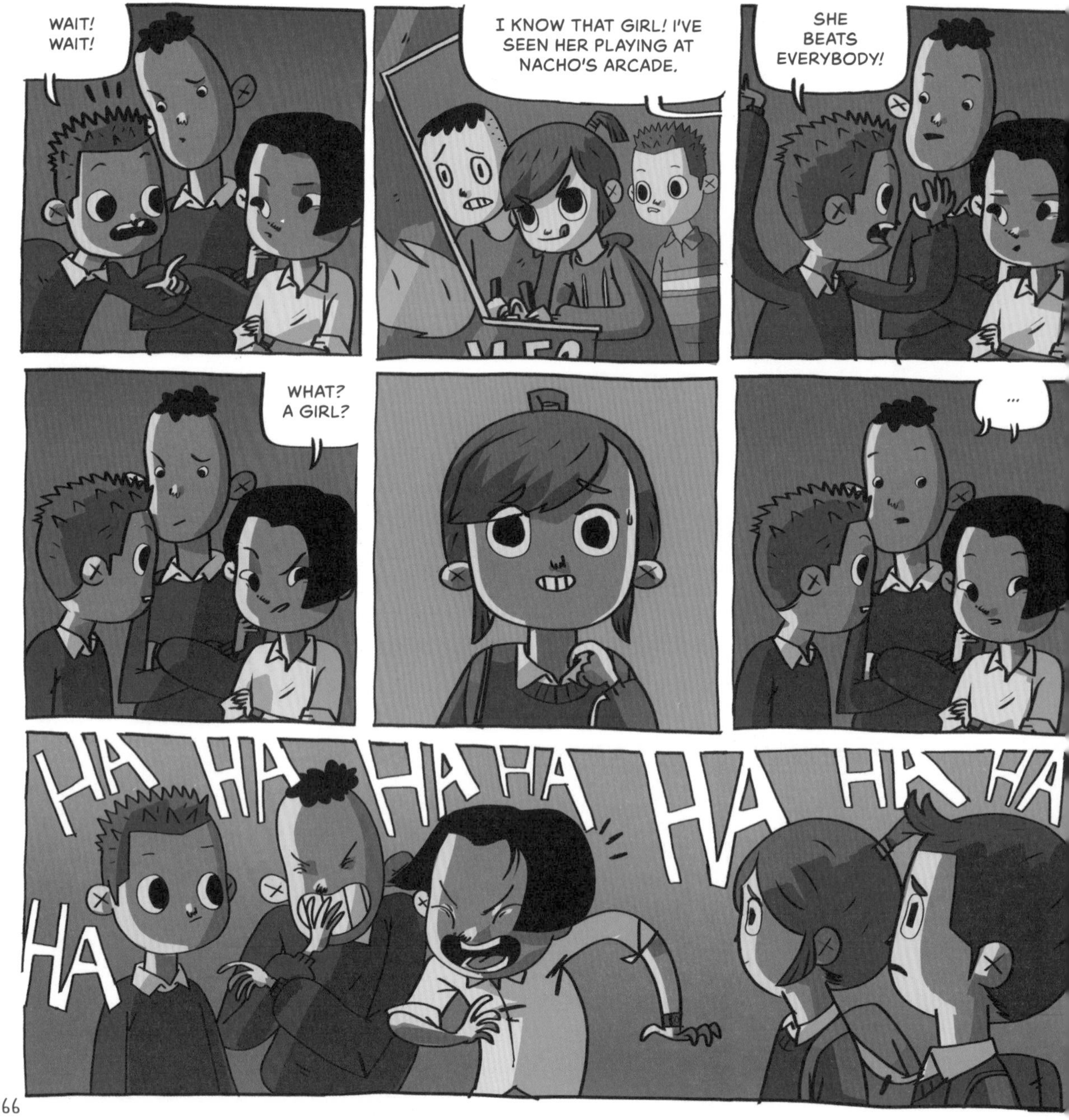
WAIT! WAIT!
I KNOW THAT GIRL! I'VE SEEN HER PLAYING AT NACHO'S ARCADE.
SHE BEATS EVERYBODY!
WHAT? A GIRL?
...
HA HA HA HA HA HA HA HA HA HA

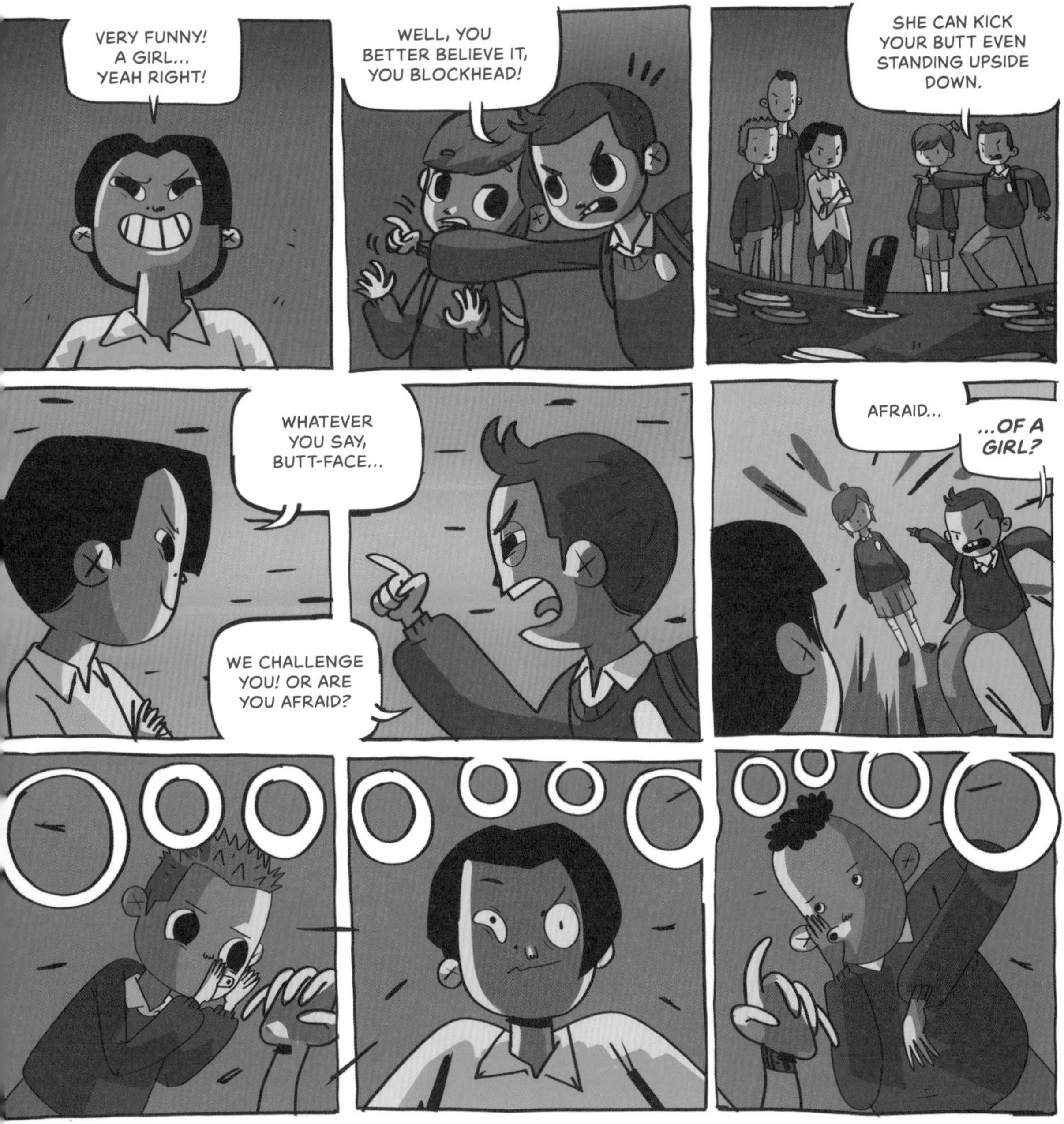
VERY FUNNY! A GIRL... YEAH RIGHT!
WELL, YOU BETTER BELIEVE IT, YOU BLOCKHEAD!
SHE CAN KICK YOUR BUTT EVEN STANDING UPSIDE DOWN.
WHATEVER YOU SAY, BUTT-FACE...
WE CHALLENGE YOU! OR ARE YOU AFRAID?
AFRAID...
...OF A GIRL?

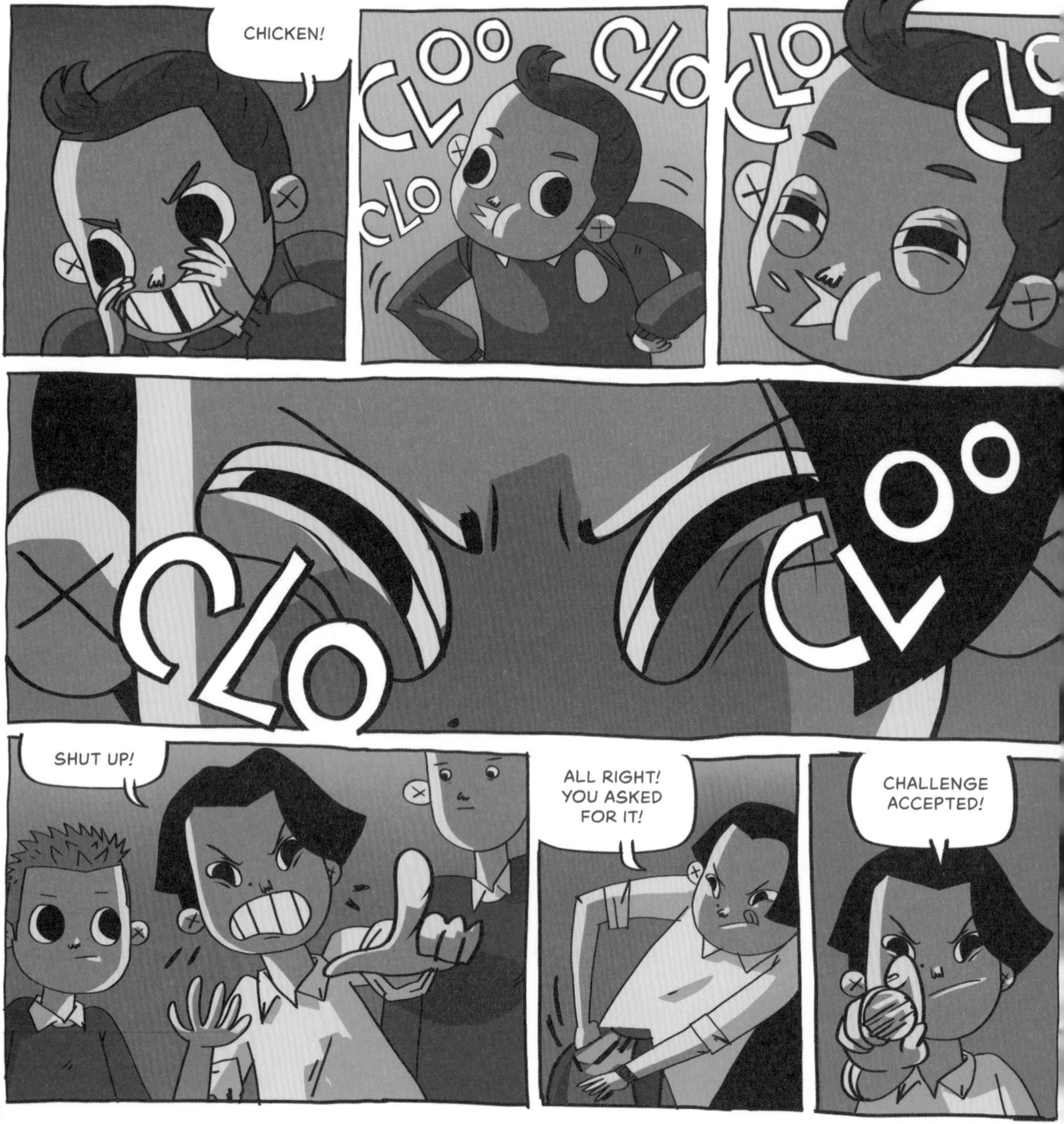
CHICKEN!
CLOO
CLO
CLO
CLO
CLO
CLO
CLOO
SHUT UP!
ALL RIGHT! YOU ASKED FOR IT!
CHALLENGE ACCEPTED!

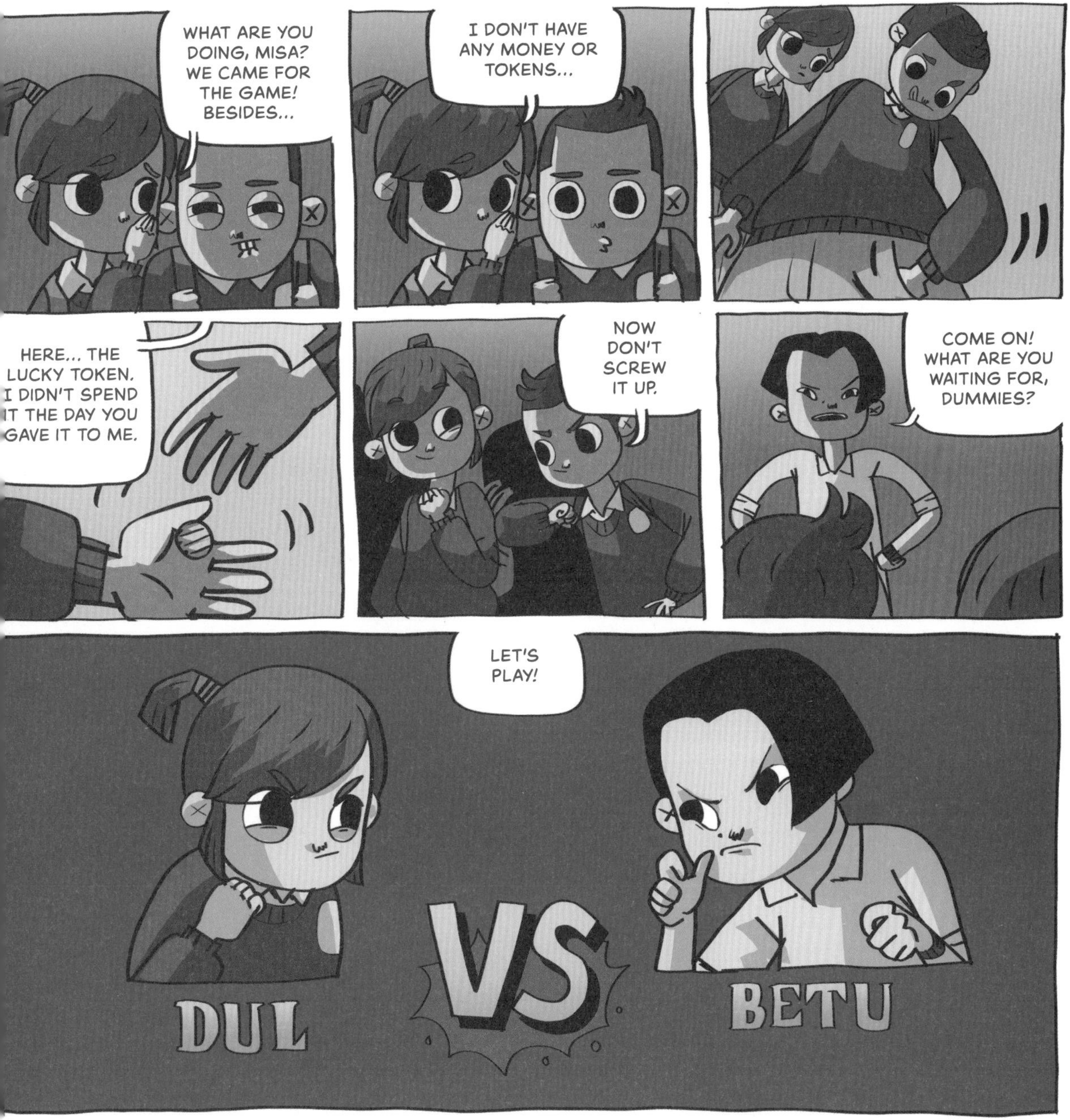
WHAT ARE YOU DOING, MISA? WE CAME FOR THE GAME! BESIDES...
I DON'T HAVE ANY MONEY OR TOKENS...
HERE... THE LUCKY TOKEN. I DIDN'T SPEND IT THE DAY YOU GAVE IT TO ME.
NOW DON'T SCREW IT UP.
COME ON! WHAT ARE YOU WAITING FOR, DUMMIES?
LET'S PLAY!
DUL
VS
BETU

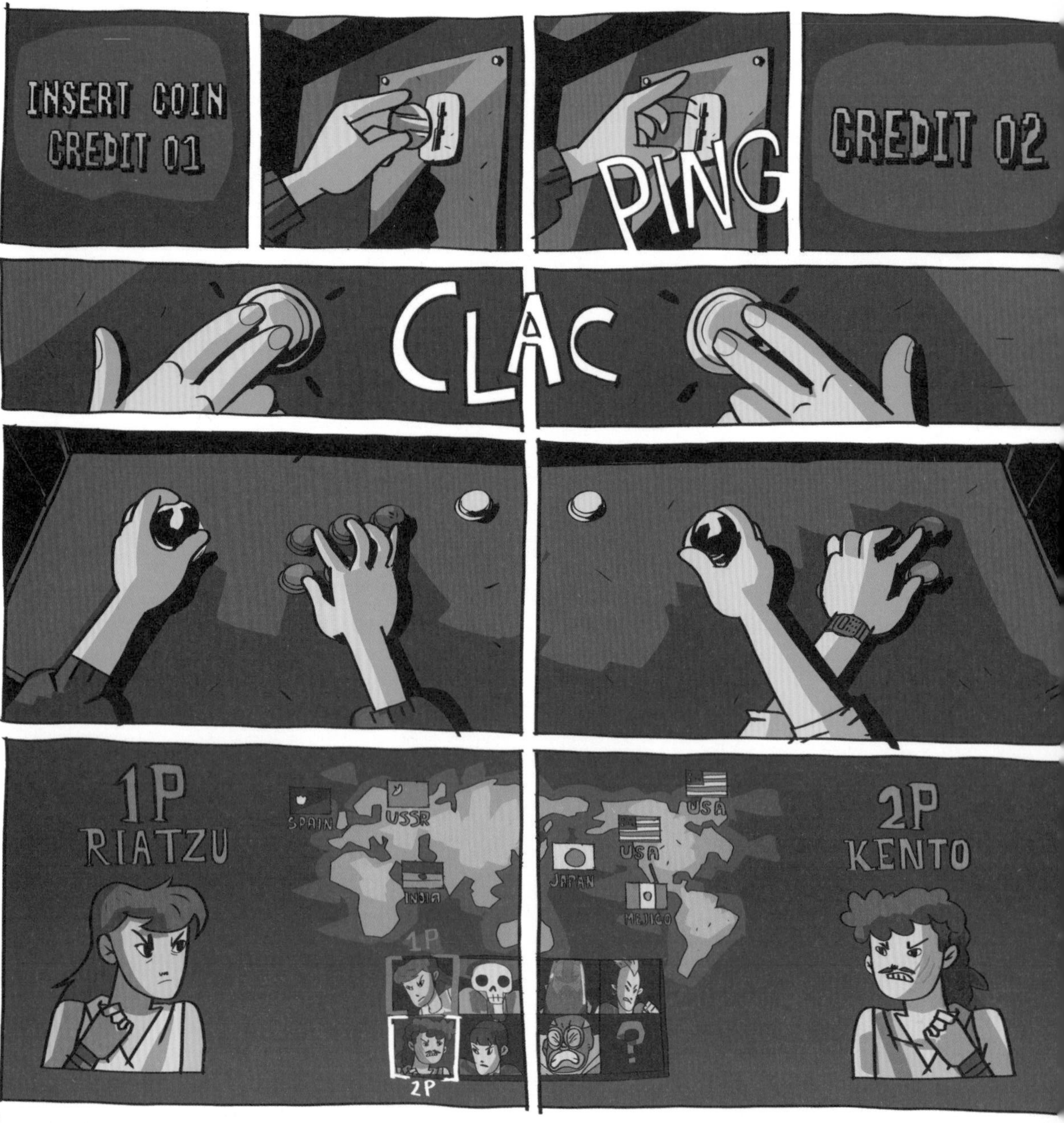
INSERT COIN
CREDIT 01
PING
CREDIT 02
CLAC
1P
RIATZU
SPAIN
USSR
INDIA
USA
USA
JAPAN
MEJICO
1P
2P
2P
KENTO

ROUND 1
READY
FIGHT!

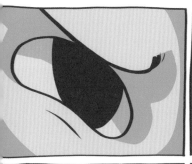

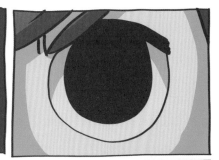

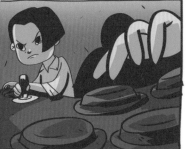

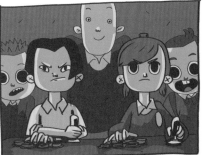

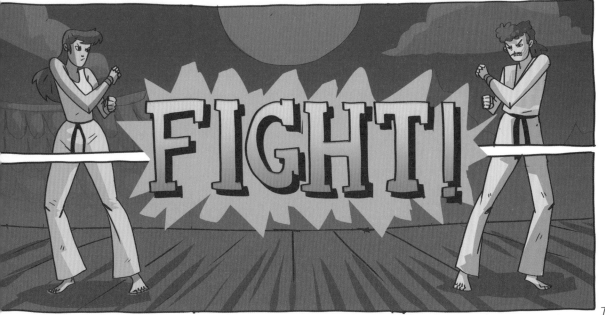

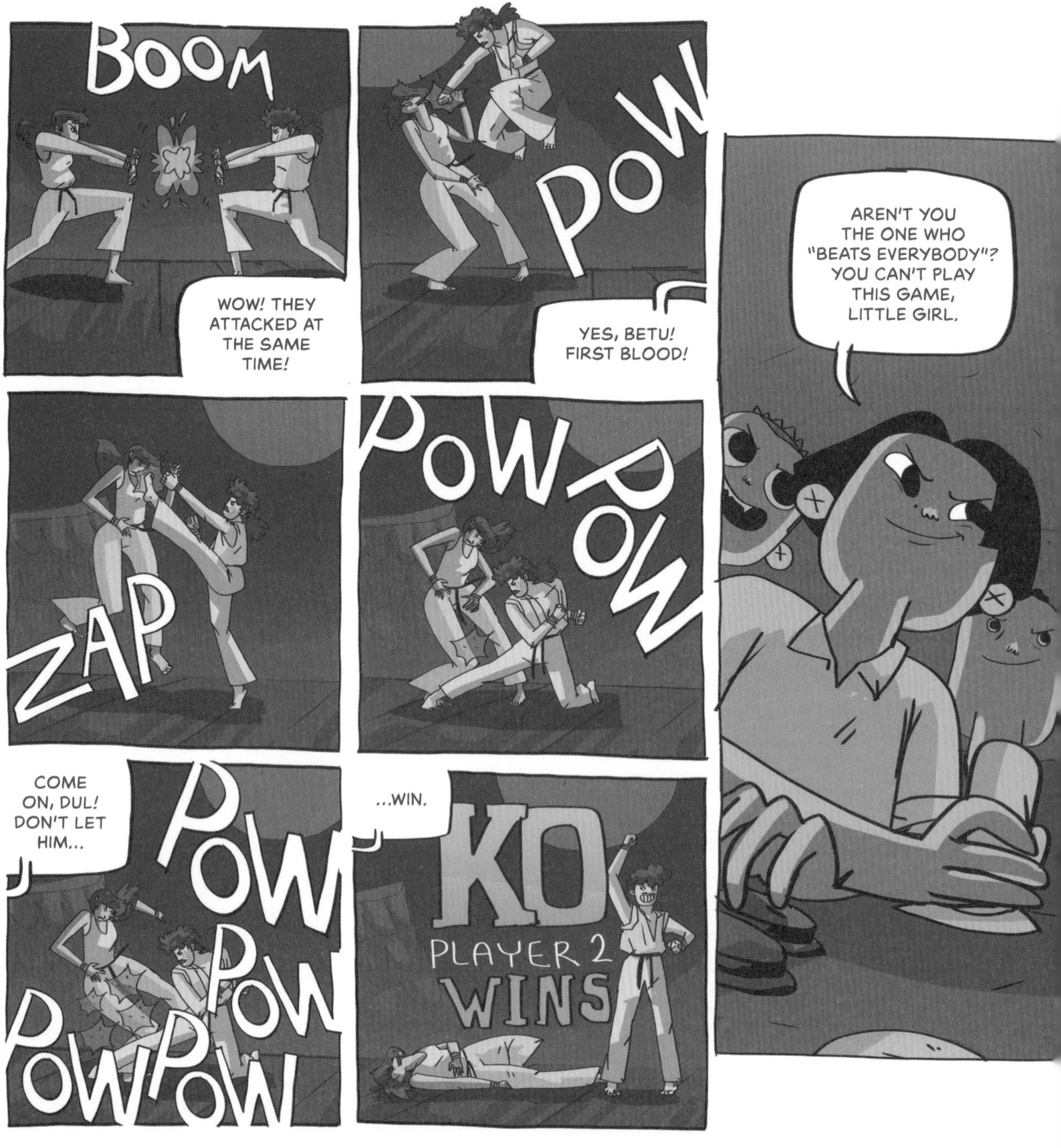
BOOM
WOW! THEY ATTACKED AT THE SAME TIME!
POW
YES, BETU! FIRST BLOOD!
ZAP
POW POW POW
ARE'NT YOU THE ONE WHO "BEATS EVERYBODY"? YOU CAN'T PLAY THIS GAME, LITTLE GIRL.
COME ON, DUL! DON'T LET HIM...
POW POW POW POW POW
...WIN.
KO
PLAYER 2 WINS

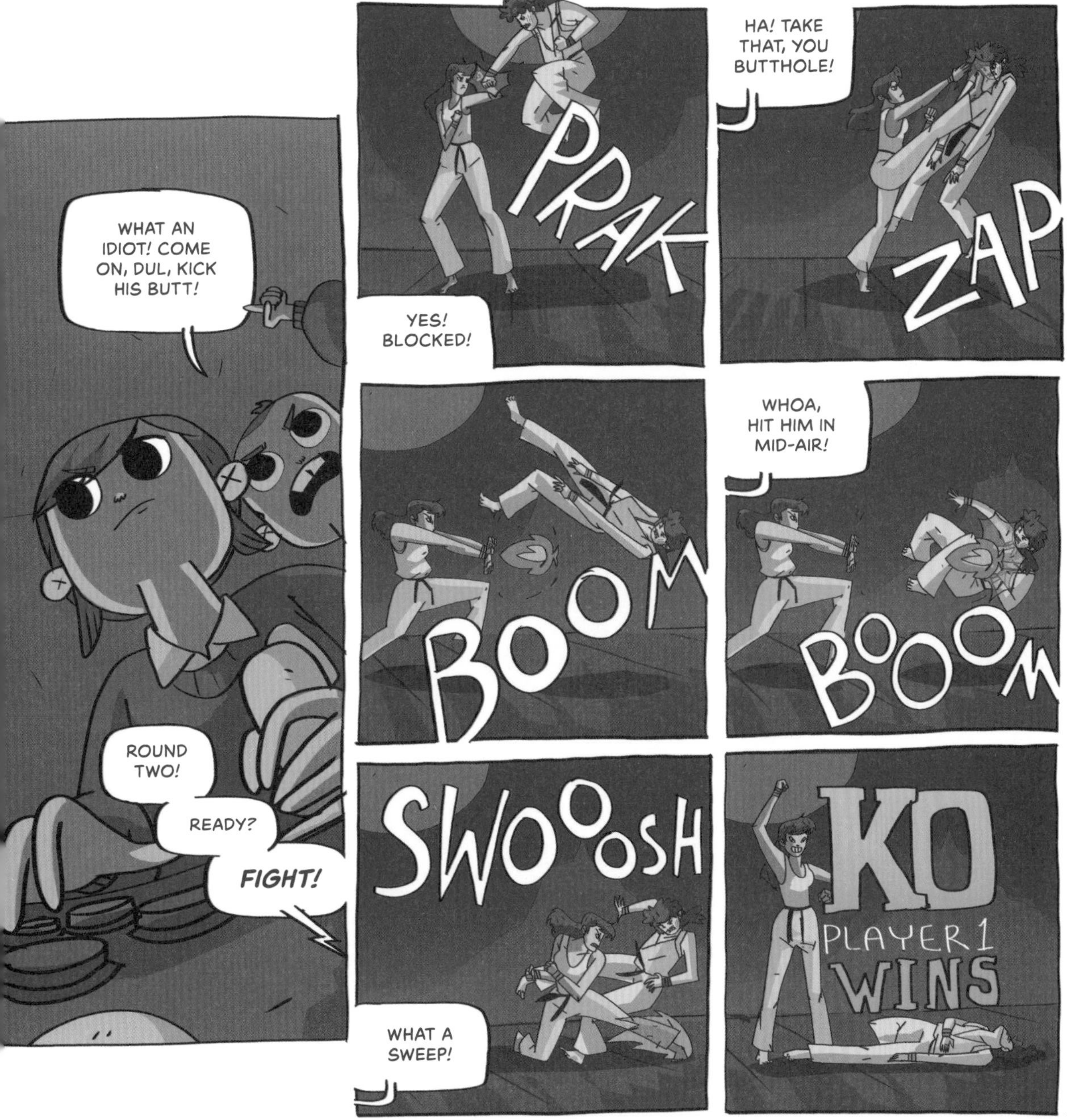

WHAT AN IDIOT! COME ON, DUL, KICK HIS BUTT!
ROUND TWO!
READY?
FIGHT!
PRAK
YES! BLOCKED!
HA! TAKE THAT, YOU BUTTHOLE!
ZAP
BOOM
WHOA, HIT HIM IN MID-AIR!
BOOOM
SWOOOSH
WHAT A SWEEP!
KO
PLAYER 1 WINS

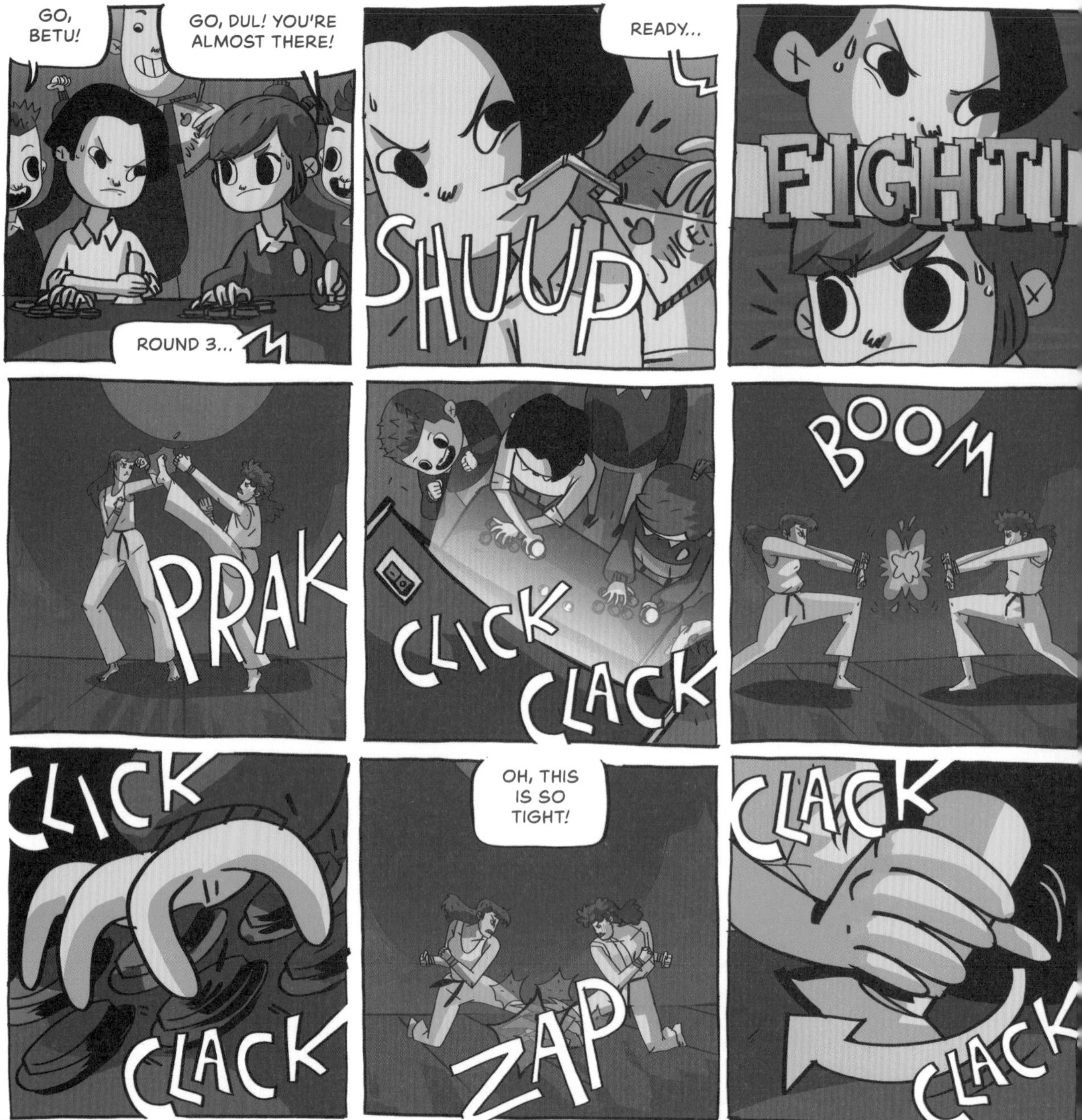
GO, BETU!
GO, DUL! YOU'RE ALMOST THERE!
ROUND 3...
READY...
SHUUP
JUICE!
FIGHT!
PRAK
CLICK
CLACK
BOOM
CLICK
CLACK
OH, THIS IS SO TIGHT!
ZAP
CLACK
CLACK

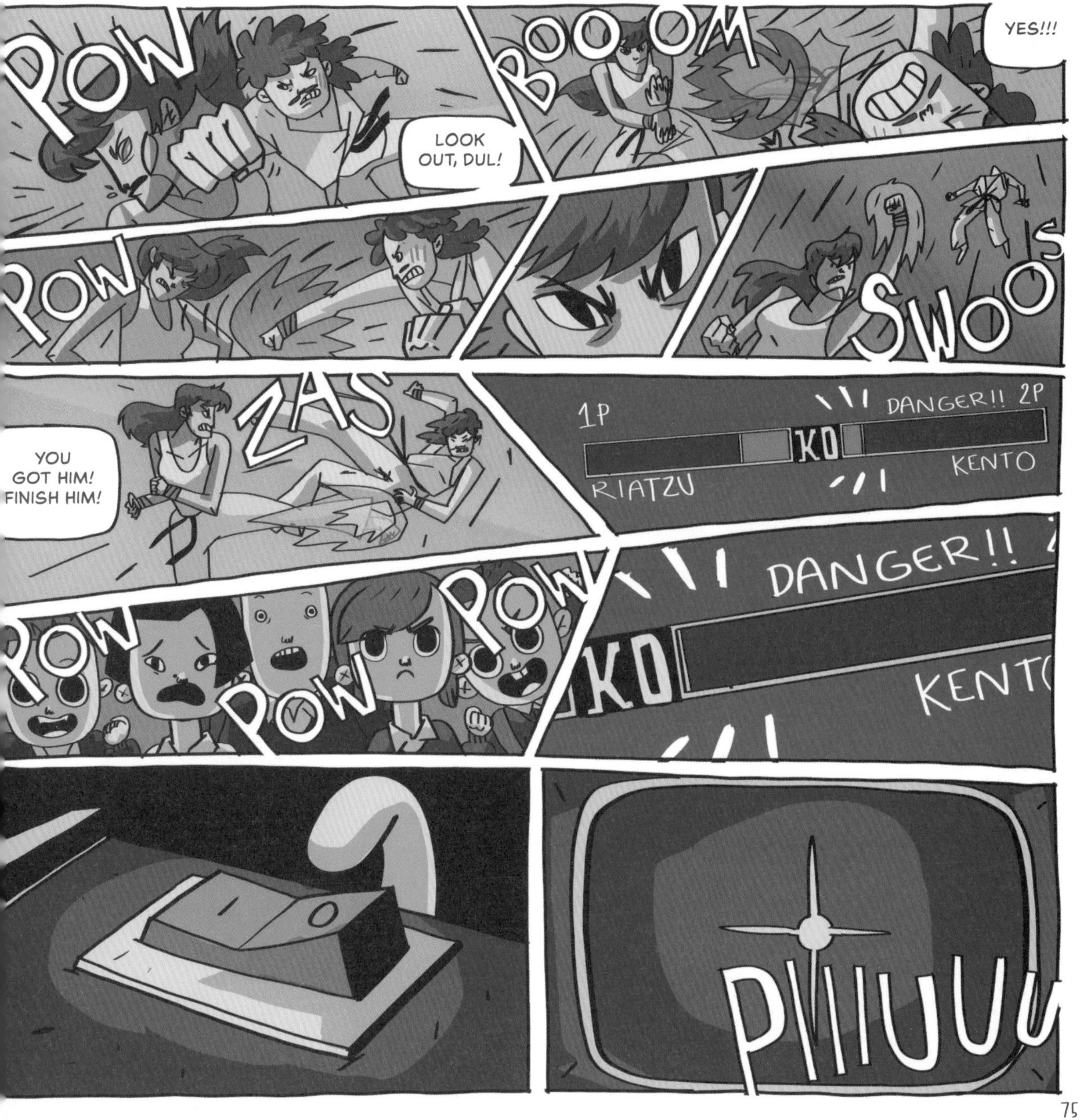
POW
LOOK OUT, DUL!
BOOOOM
YES!!!
POW
SWOOS
ZAS
YOU GOT HIM! FINISH HIM!
1P
DANGER!! 2P
KO
RIATZU
KENTO
DANGER!!
KO
KENTO
POW
POW
POW
PIIIUUU

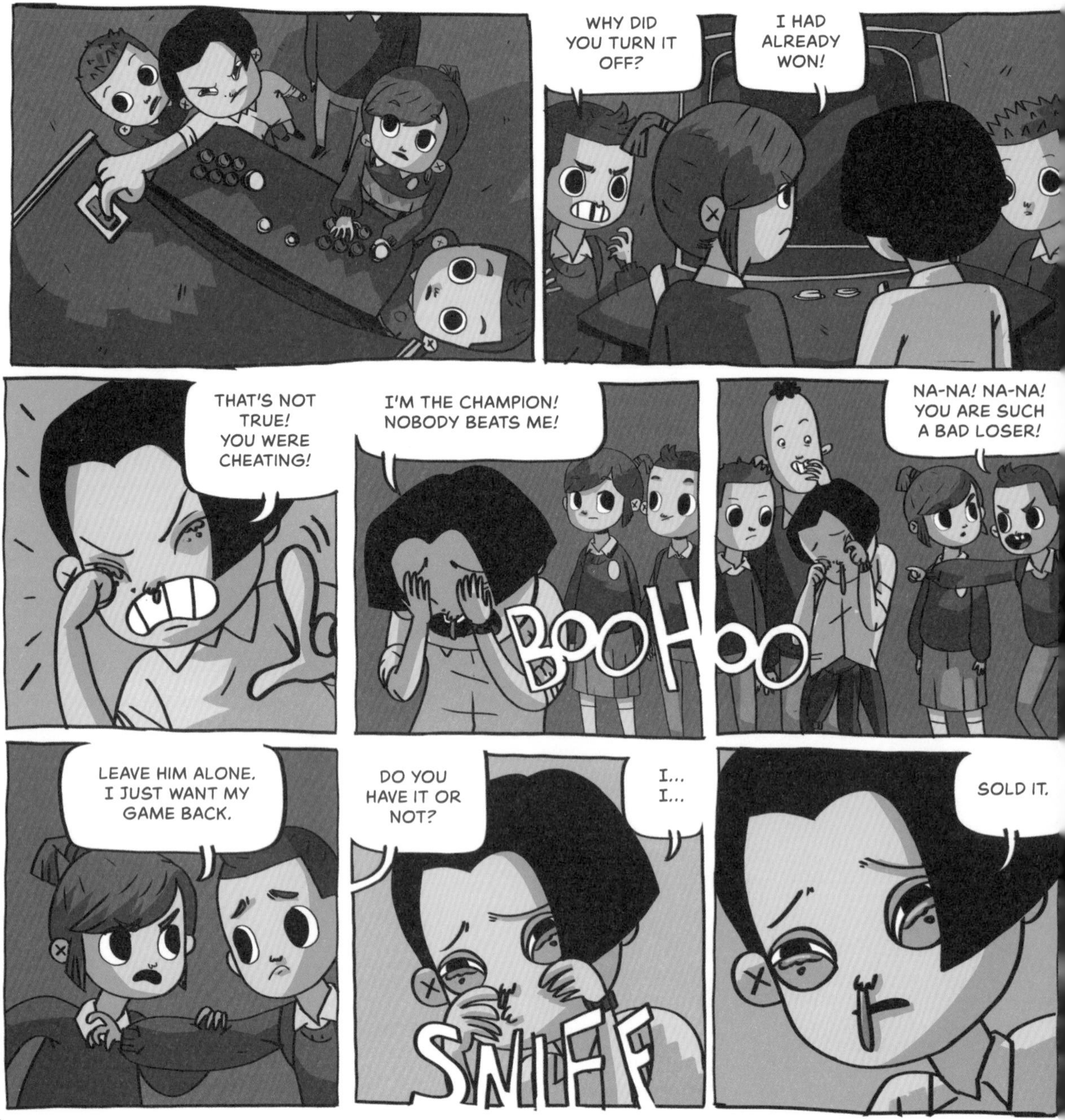

WHY DID YOU TURN IT OFF?
I HAD ALREADY WON!
THAT'S NOT TRUE! YOU WERE CHEATING!
I'M THE CHAMPION! NOBODY BEATS ME!
BOOHOO
NA-NA! NA-NA! YOU ARE SUCH A BAD LOSER!
LEAVE HIM ALONE. I JUST WANT MY GAME BACK.
DO YOU HAVE IT OR NOT?
I... I...
SNIFF
SOLD IT.

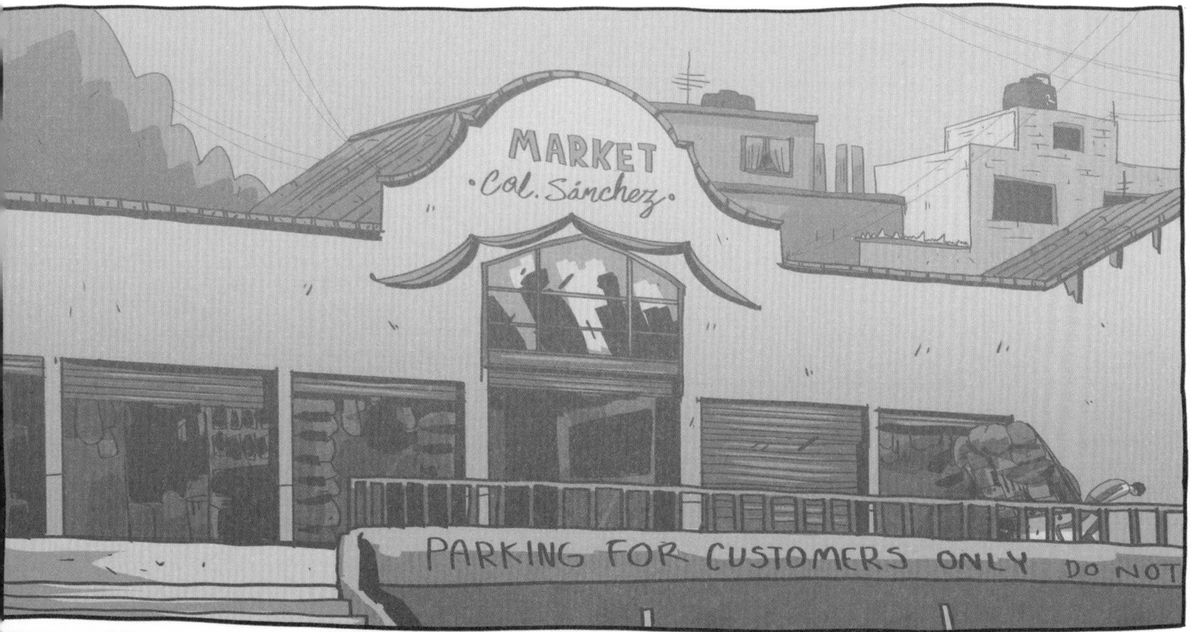
MARKET
Col. Sánchez
PARKING FOR CUSTOMERS ONLY
DO NOT

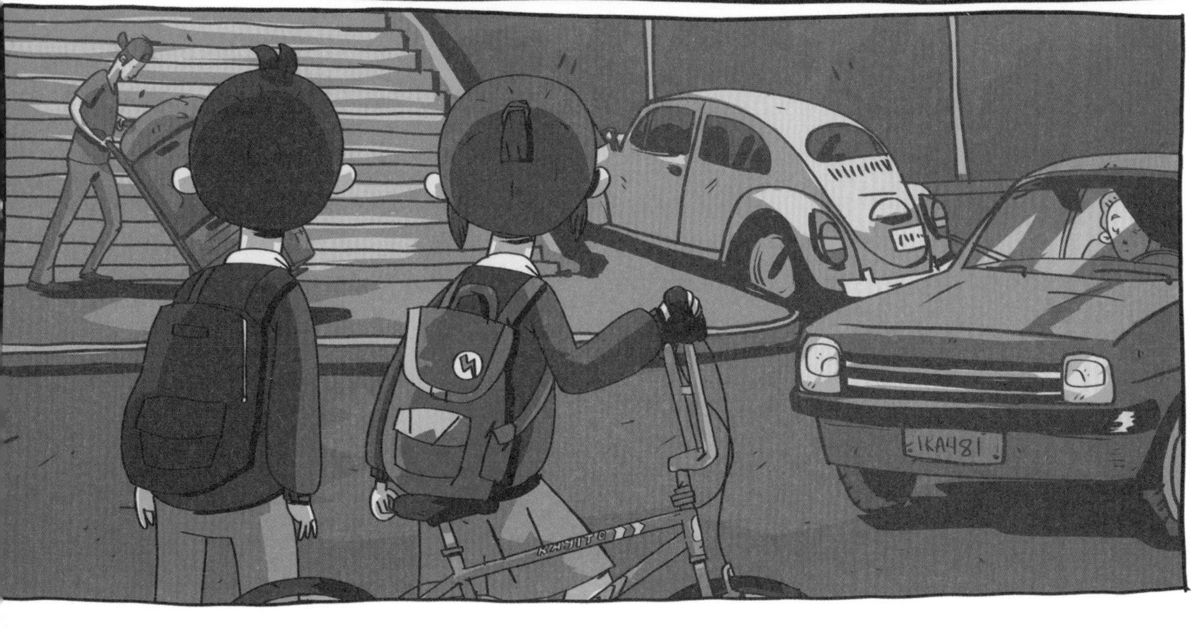
IKA481

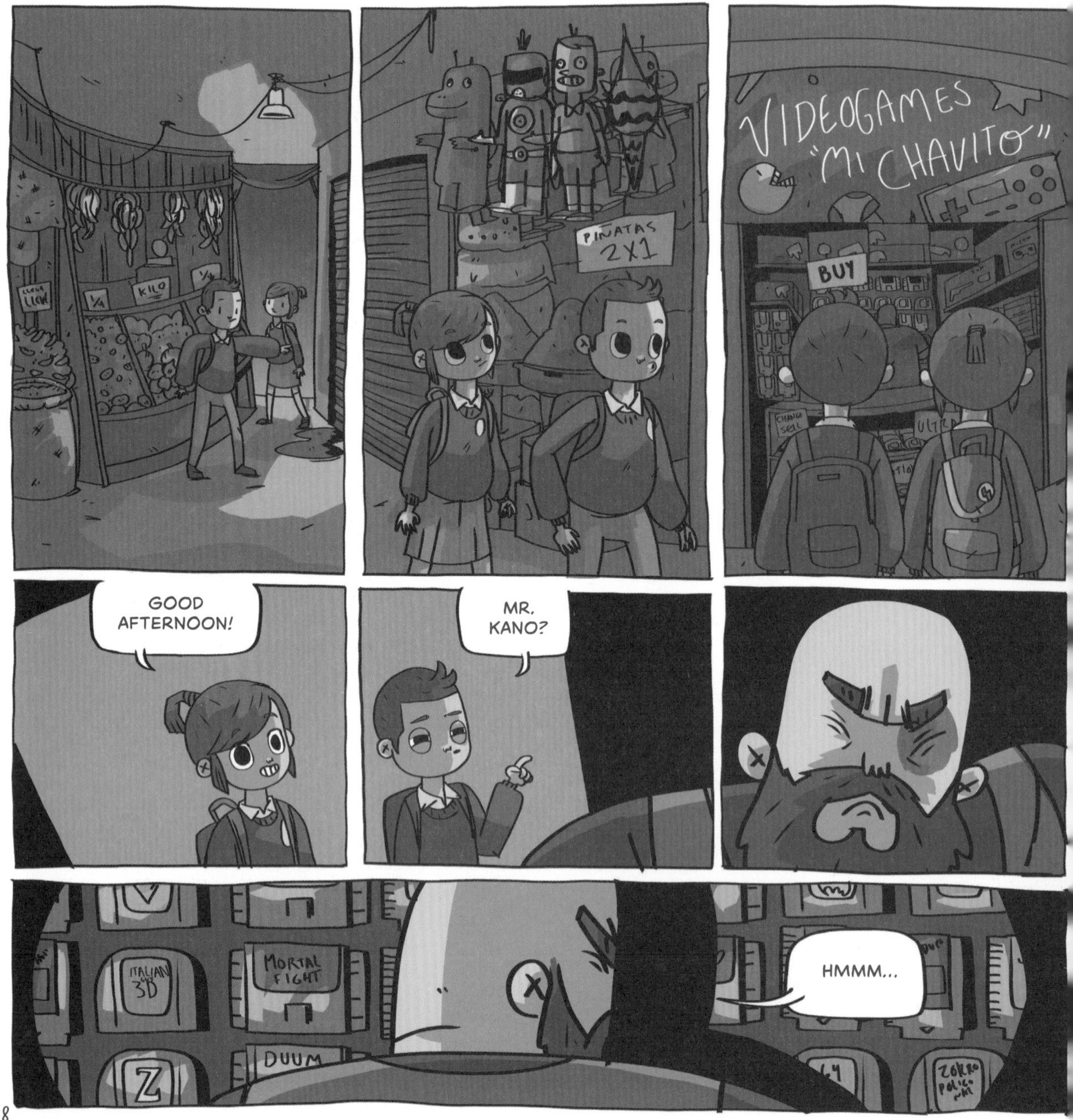
KILO
PIÑATAS 2X1
VIDEOGAMES "MI CHAVITO"
BUY
GOOD AFTERNOON!
MR. KANO?
MORTAL FIGHT
ITALIAN 3D
DUUM
HMMM...

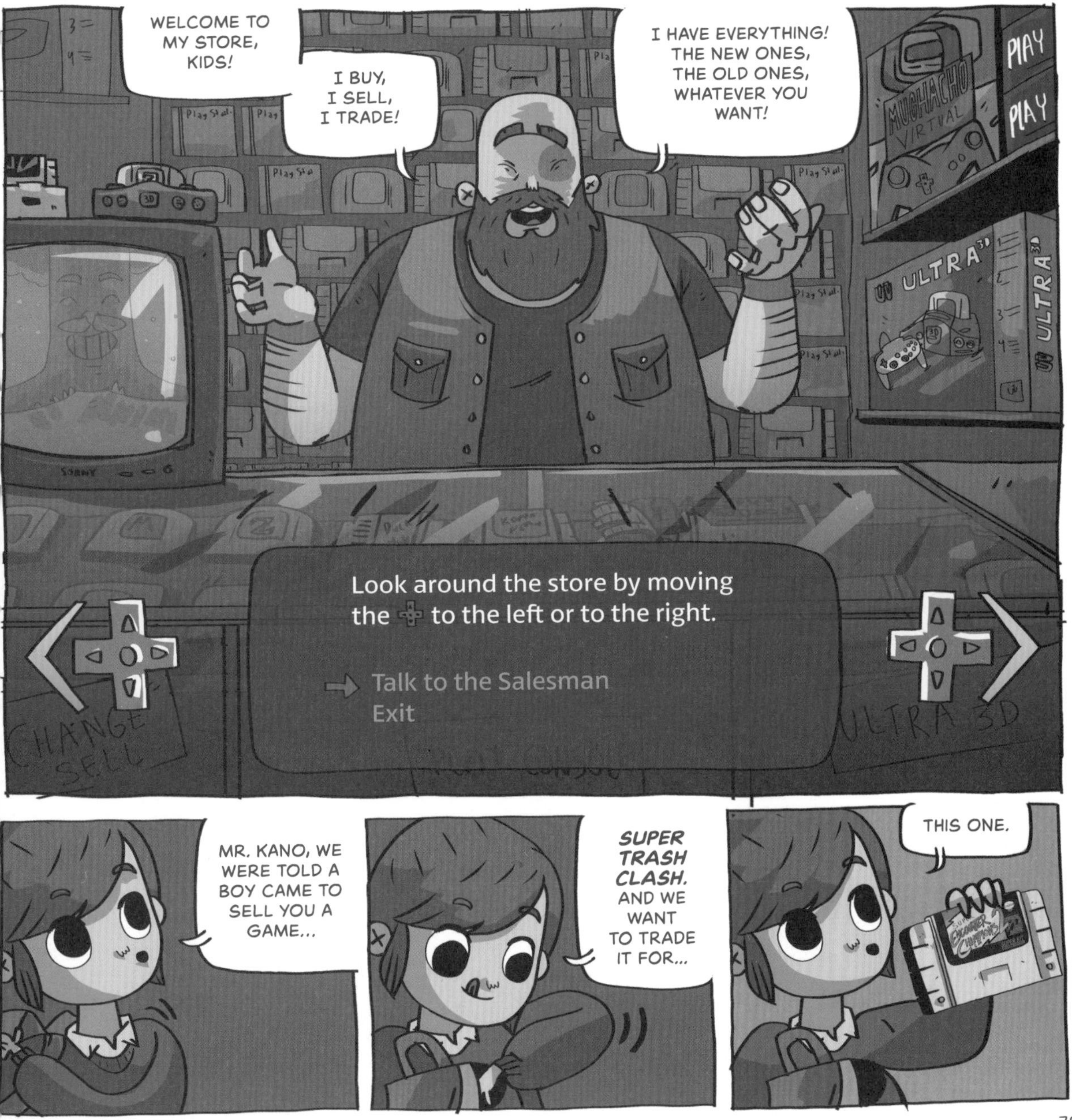
WELCOME TO MY STORE, KIDS!
I BUY, I SELL, I TRADE!
I HAVE EVERYTHING! THE NEW ONES, THE OLD ONES, WHATEVER YOU WANT!
MUCHACHO VIRTUAL
PLAY
PLAY
ULTRA 3D
ULTRA 3D
Look around the store by moving the ✚ to the left or to the right.
Talk to the Salesman
Exit
MR. KANO, WE WERE TOLD A BOY CAME TO SELL YOU A GAME...
SUPER TRASH CLASH. AND WE WANT TO TRADE IT FOR...
THIS ONE.

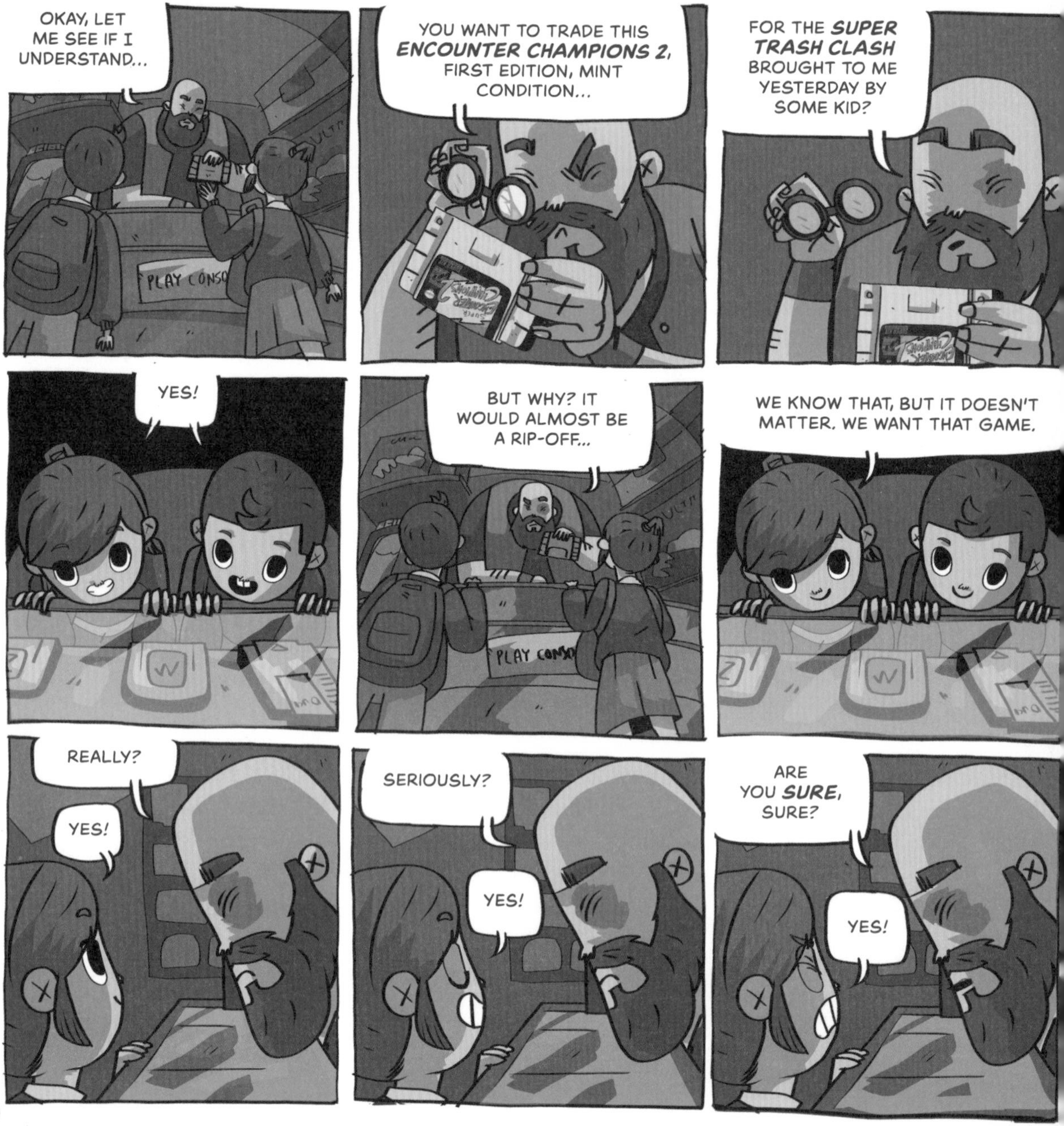
OKAY, LET ME SEE IF I UNDERSTAND...
YOU WANT TO TRADE THIS **ENCOUNTER CHAMPIONS 2**, FIRST EDITION, MINT CONDITION...
FOR THE **SUPER TRASH CLASH** BROUGHT TO ME YESTERDAY BY SOME KID?
YES!
BUT WHY? IT WOULD ALMOST BE A RIP-OFF...
WE KNOW THAT, BUT IT DOESN'T MATTER. WE WANT THAT GAME.
REALLY?
YES!
SERIOUSLY?
YES!
ARE YOU **SURE**, SURE?
YES!

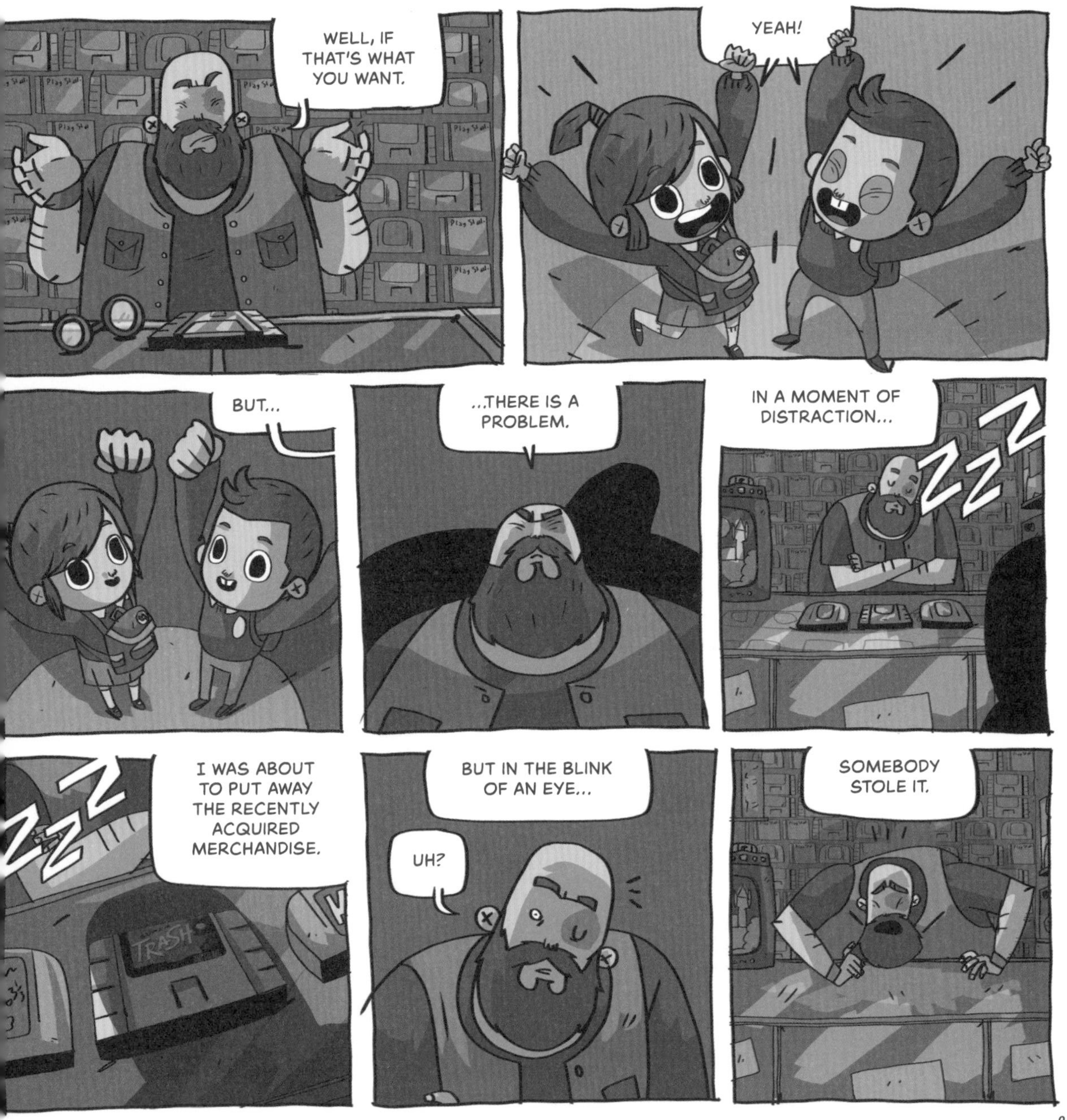
WELL, IF THAT'S WHAT YOU WANT.
YEAH!
BUT...
...THERE IS A PROBLEM.
IN A MOMENT OF DISTRACTION...
ZZZ
ZZZ
I WAS ABOUT TO PUT AWAY THE RECENTLY ACQUIRED MERCHANDISE.
TRASH
BUT IN THE BLINK OF AN EYE...
UH?
SOMEBODY STOLE IT.

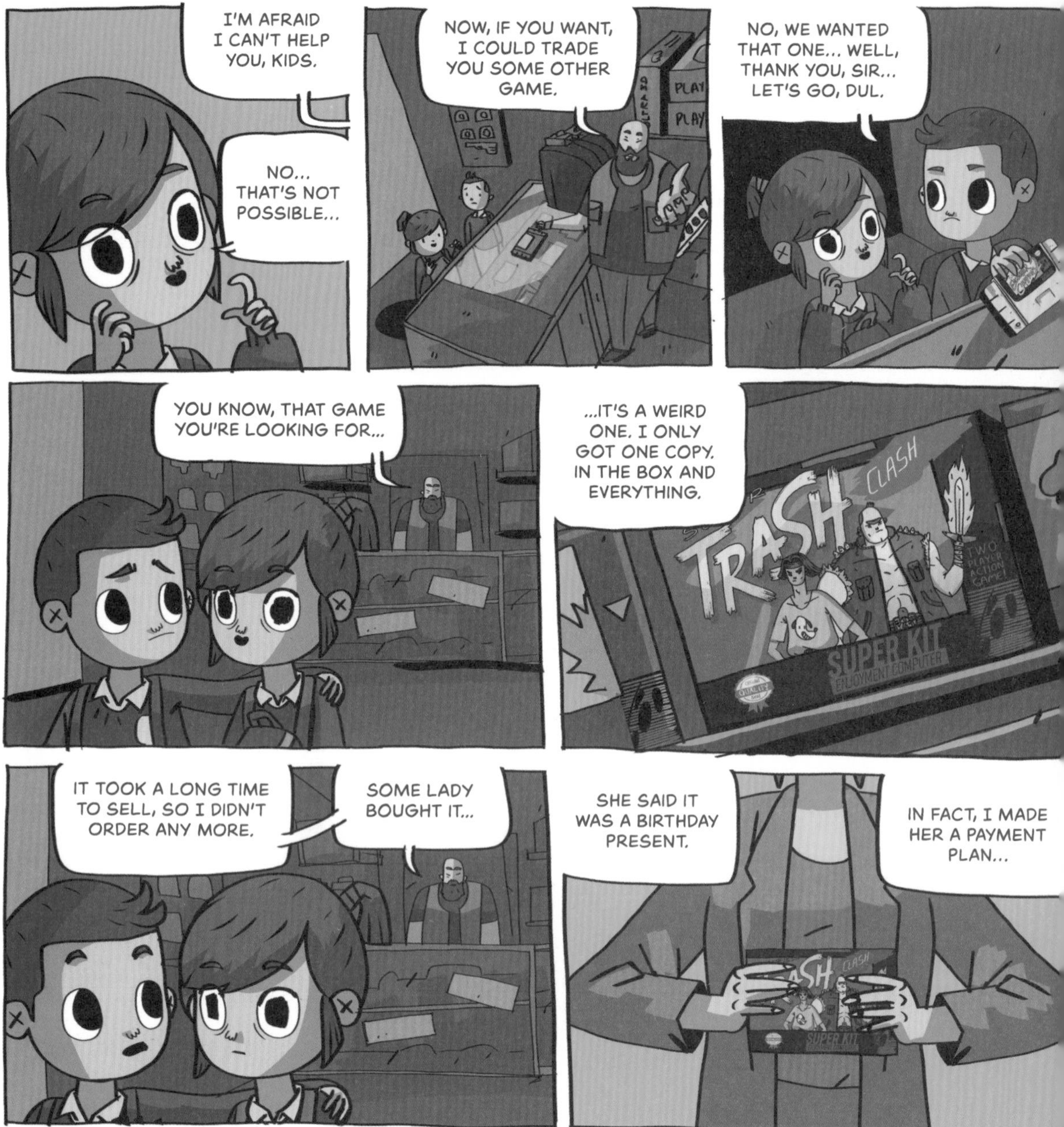
I'M AFRAID I CAN'T HELP YOU, KIDS.
NO... THAT'S NOT POSSIBLE...
NOW, IF YOU WANT, I COULD TRADE YOU SOME OTHER GAME.
NO, WE WANTED THAT ONE... WELL, THANK YOU, SIR... LET'S GO, DUL.
YOU KNOW, THAT GAME YOU'RE LOOKING FOR...
...IT'S A WEIRD ONE. I ONLY GOT ONE COPY. IN THE BOX AND EVERYTHING.
TRASH
CLASH
TWO PLAYER ACTION GAME!
SUPER KIT
ENJOYMENT COMPUTER
IT TOOK A LONG TIME TO SELL, SO I DIDN'T ORDER ANY MORE.
SOME LADY BOUGHT IT...
SHE SAID IT WAS A BIRTHDAY PRESENT.
IN FACT, I MADE HER A PAYMENT PLAN...

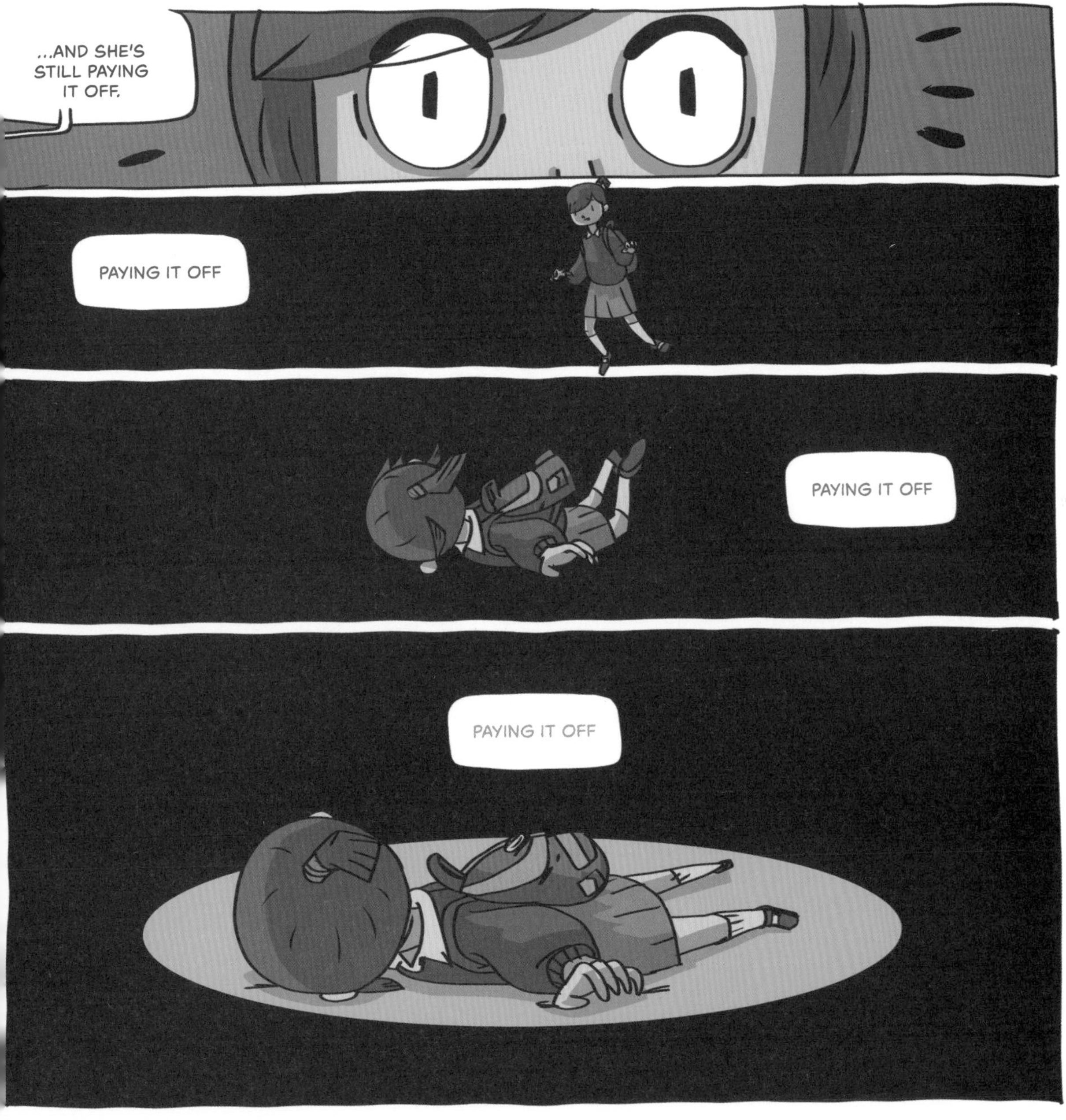
...AND SHE'S STILL PAYING IT OFF.
PAYING IT OFF
PAYING IT OFF
PAYING IT OFF

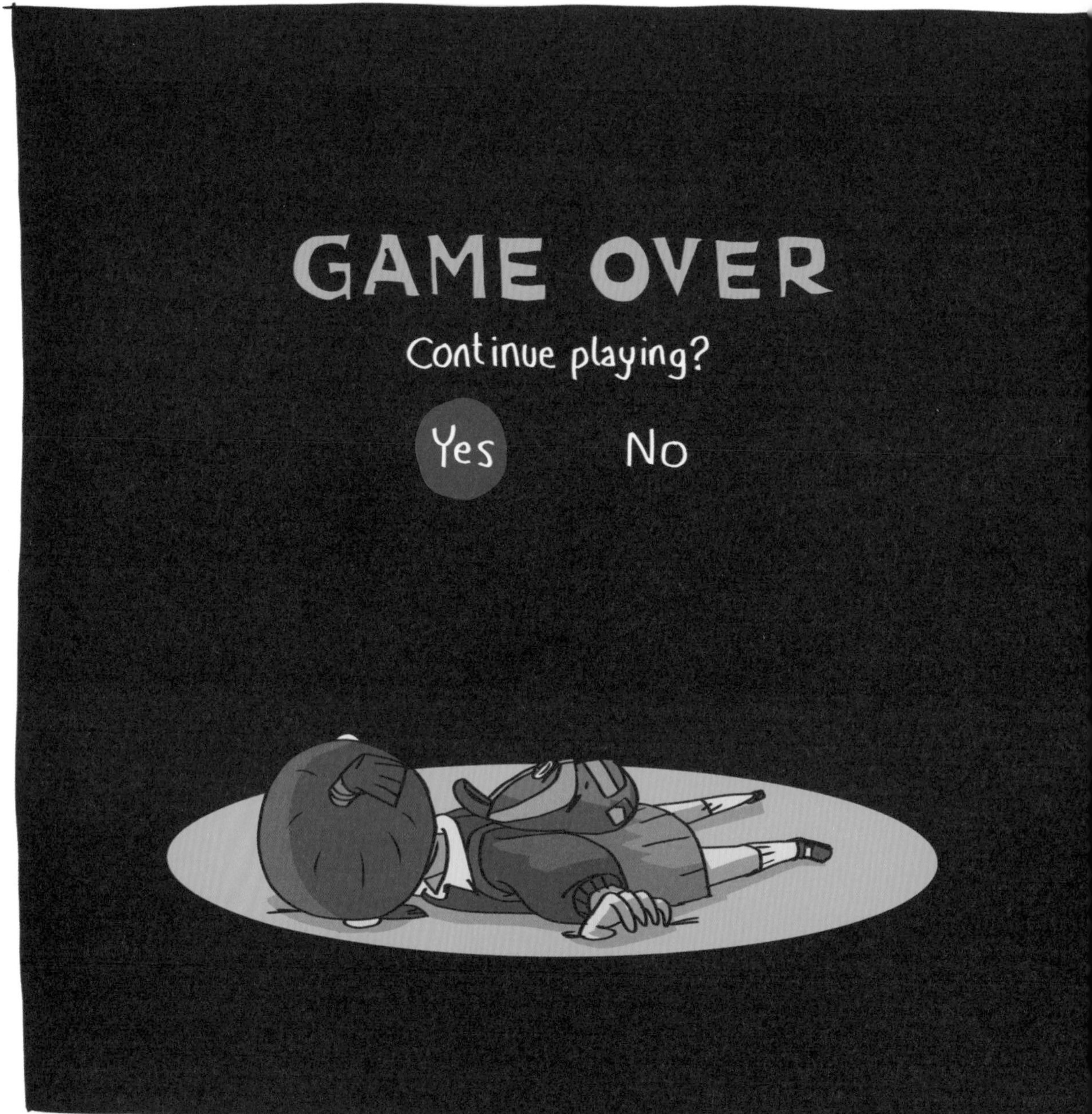
GAME OVER
Continue playing?
Yes
No

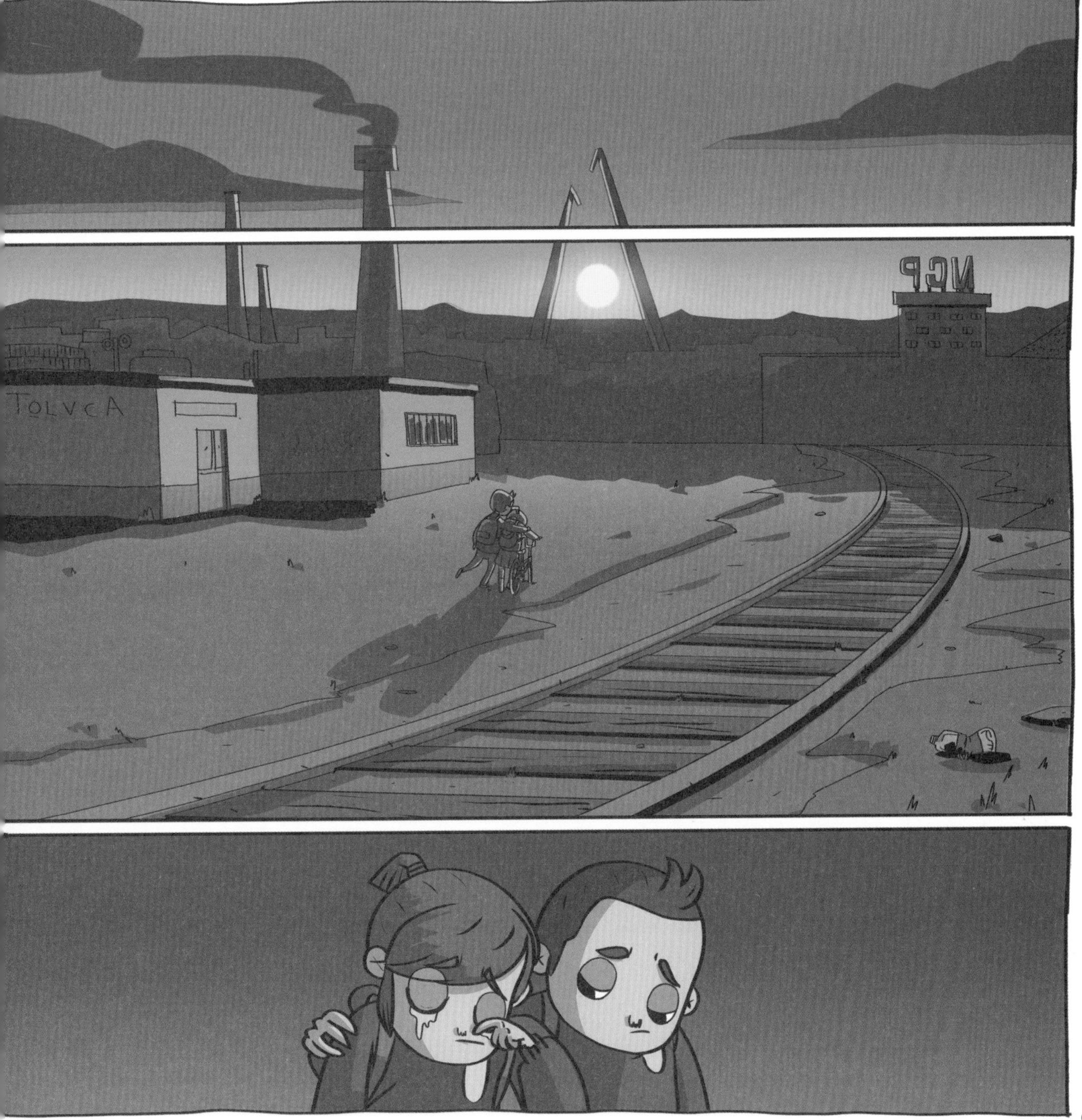
TOLUCA

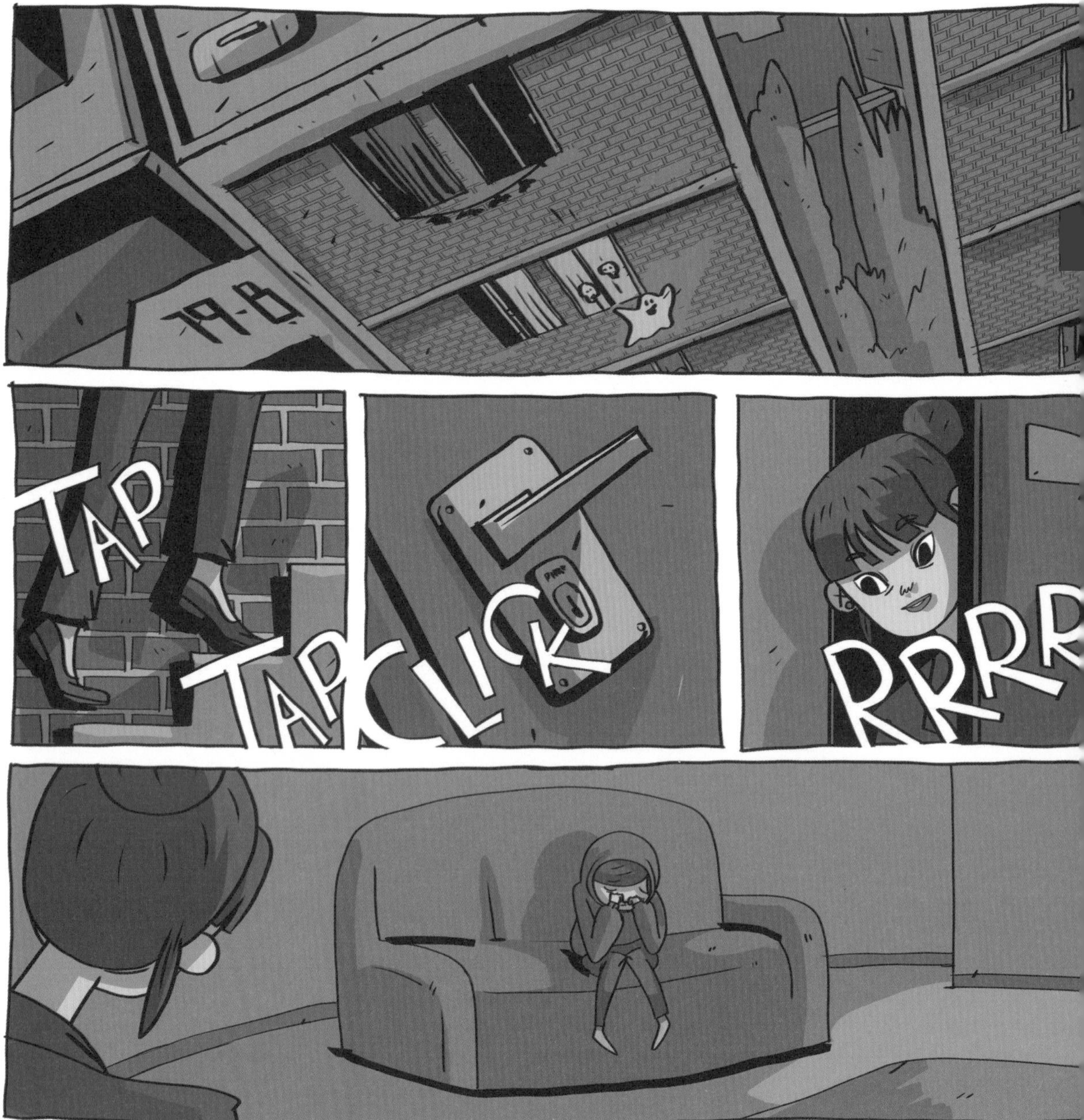
TAP
TAP
CLICK
RRRR

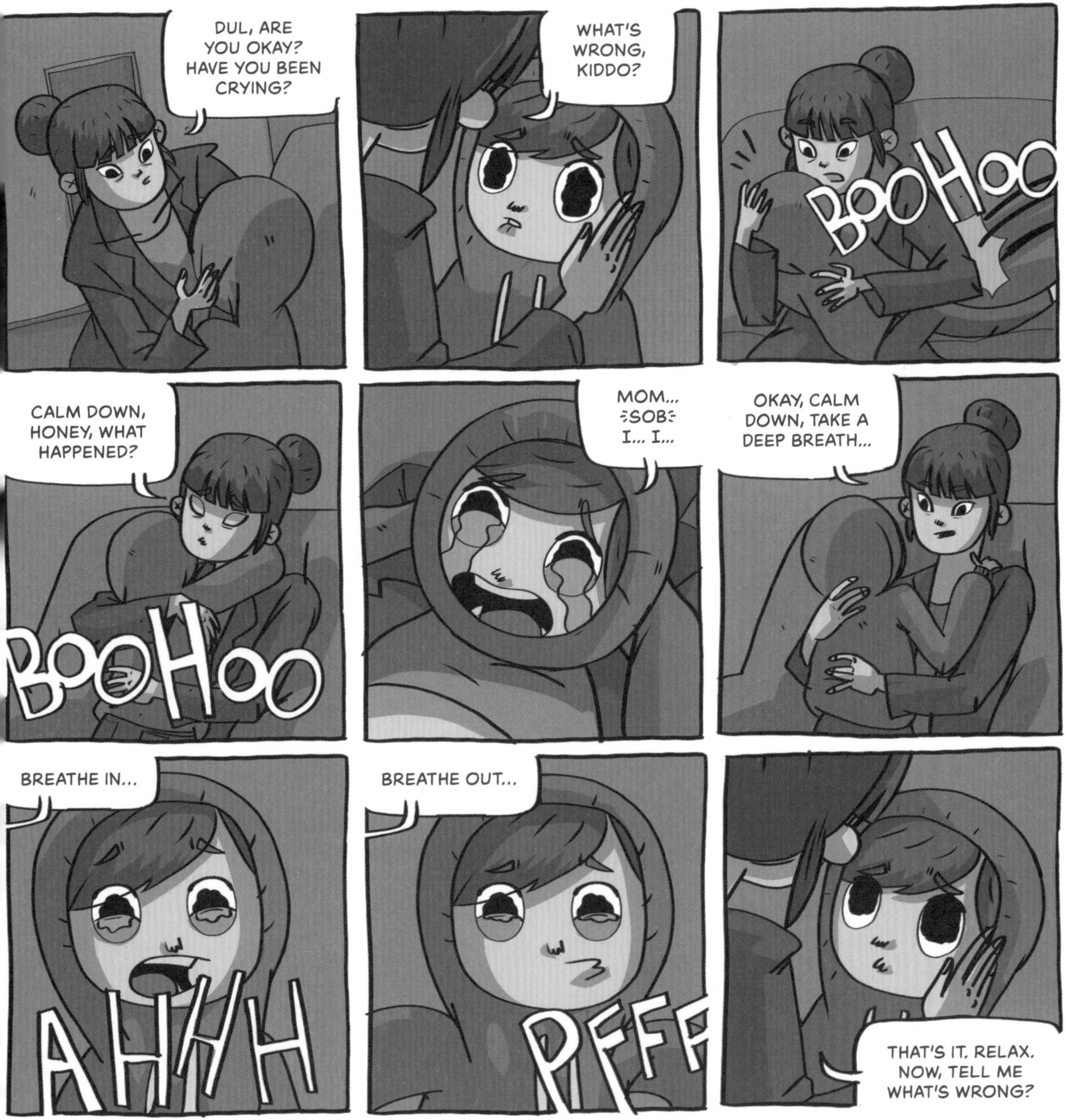

DUL, ARE YOU OKAY? HAVE YOU BEEN CRYING?
WHAT'S WRONG, KIDDO?
BOOHOO
CALM DOWN, HONEY, WHAT HAPPENED?
BOOHOO
MOM... SOB I... I...
OKAY, CALM DOWN, TAKE A DEEP BREATH...
BREATHE IN...
AHHH
BREATHE OUT...
PFFF
THAT'S IT. RELAX. NOW, TELL ME WHAT'S WRONG?

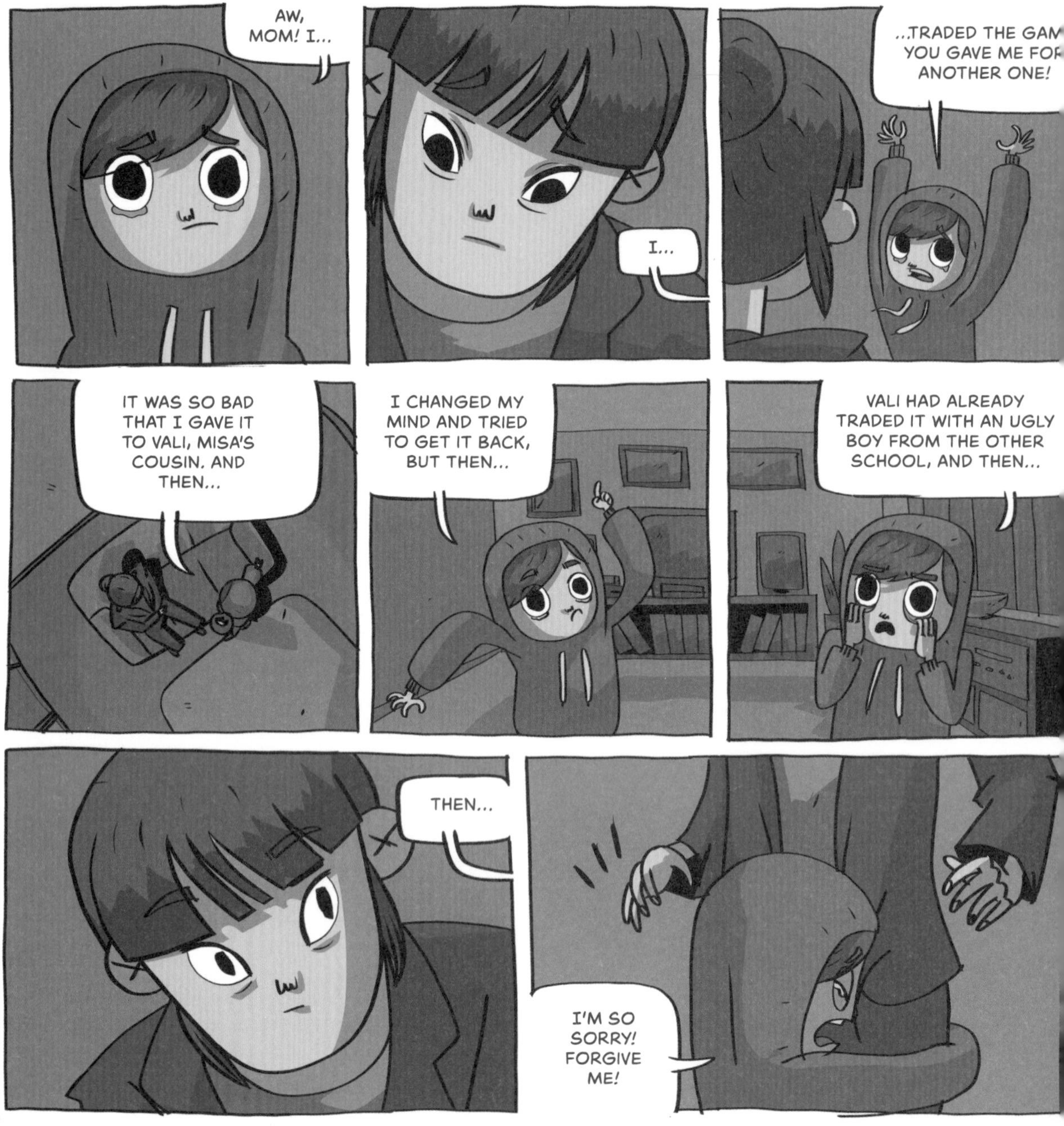
AW, MOM! I...
I...
...TRADED THE GAM
YOU GAVE ME FOR
ANOTHER ONE!
IT WAS SO BAD THAT I GAVE IT TO VALI, MISA'S COUSIN. AND THEN...
I CHANGED MY MIND AND TRIED TO GET IT BACK, BUT THEN...
VALI HAD ALREADY TRADED IT WITH AN UGLY BOY FROM THE OTHER SCHOOL, AND THEN...
THEN...
I'M SO SORRY! FORGIVE ME!

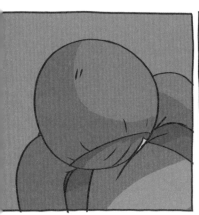

DUL, YOU HAVE BEEN A GREAT HELP LATELY AT HOME.

BETWEEN HOMEWORK AND ALL THE RESPONSIBILITIES I GIVE YOU, YOU HAVE VERY LITTLE TIME FOR YOURSELF.

AND EVEN THOUGH I DON'T LIKE THE IDEA OF YOU SPENDING TOO MUCH TIME IN FRONT OF THE TV...

I KNOW YOU ARE HAPPY PLAYING YOUR GAMES.

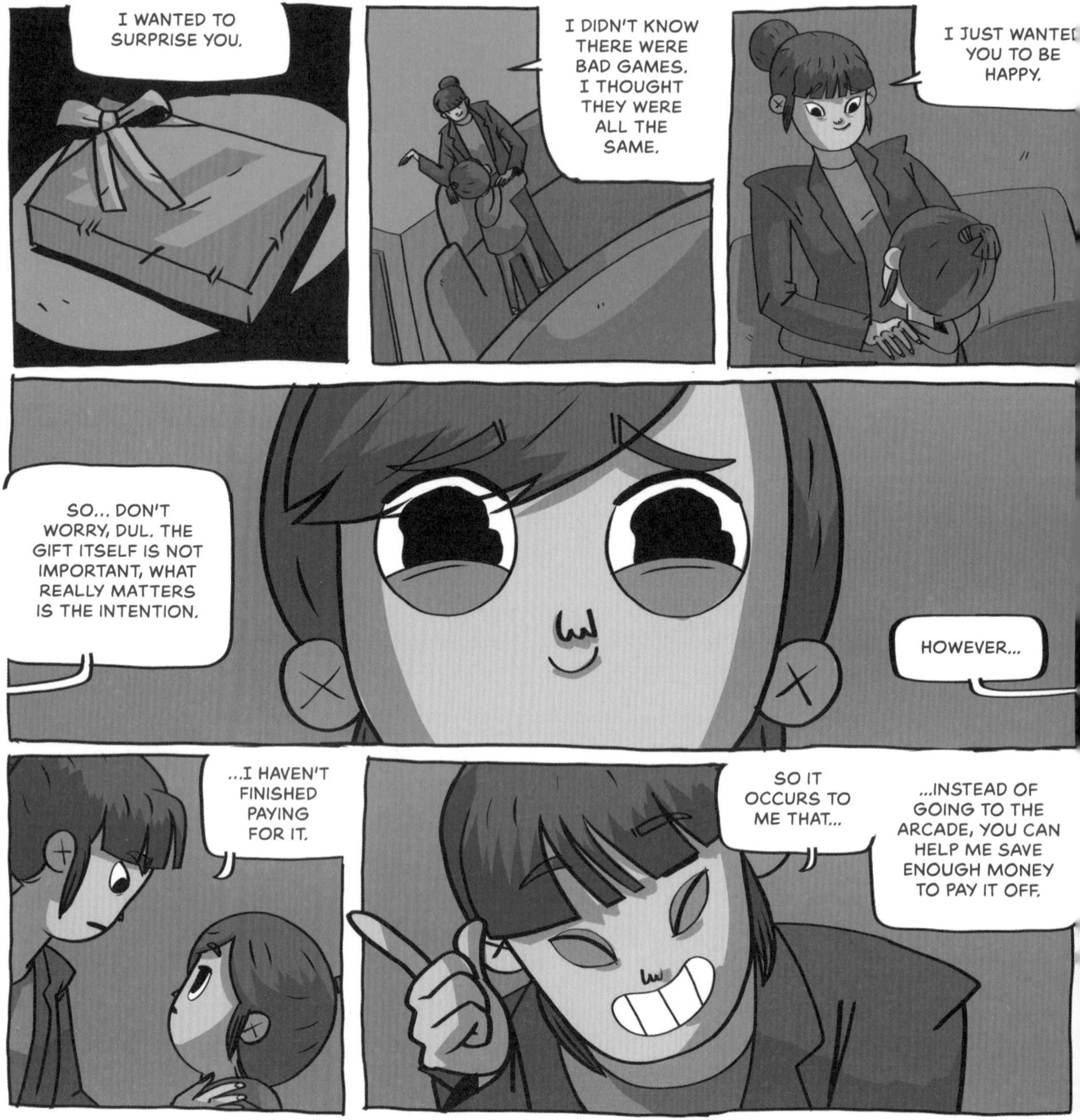
I WANTED TO SURPRISE YOU.
I DIDN'T KNOW THERE WERE BAD GAMES. I THOUGHT THEY WERE ALL THE SAME.
I JUST WANTED YOU TO BE HAPPY.
SO... DON'T WORRY, DUL. THE GIFT ITSELF IS NOT IMPORTANT, WHAT REALLY MATTERS IS THE INTENTION.
HOWEVER...
...I HAVEN'T FINISHED PAYING FOR IT.
SO IT OCCURS TO ME THAT...
...INSTEAD OF GOING TO THE ARCADE, YOU CAN HELP ME SAVE ENOUGH MONEY TO PAY IT OFF.

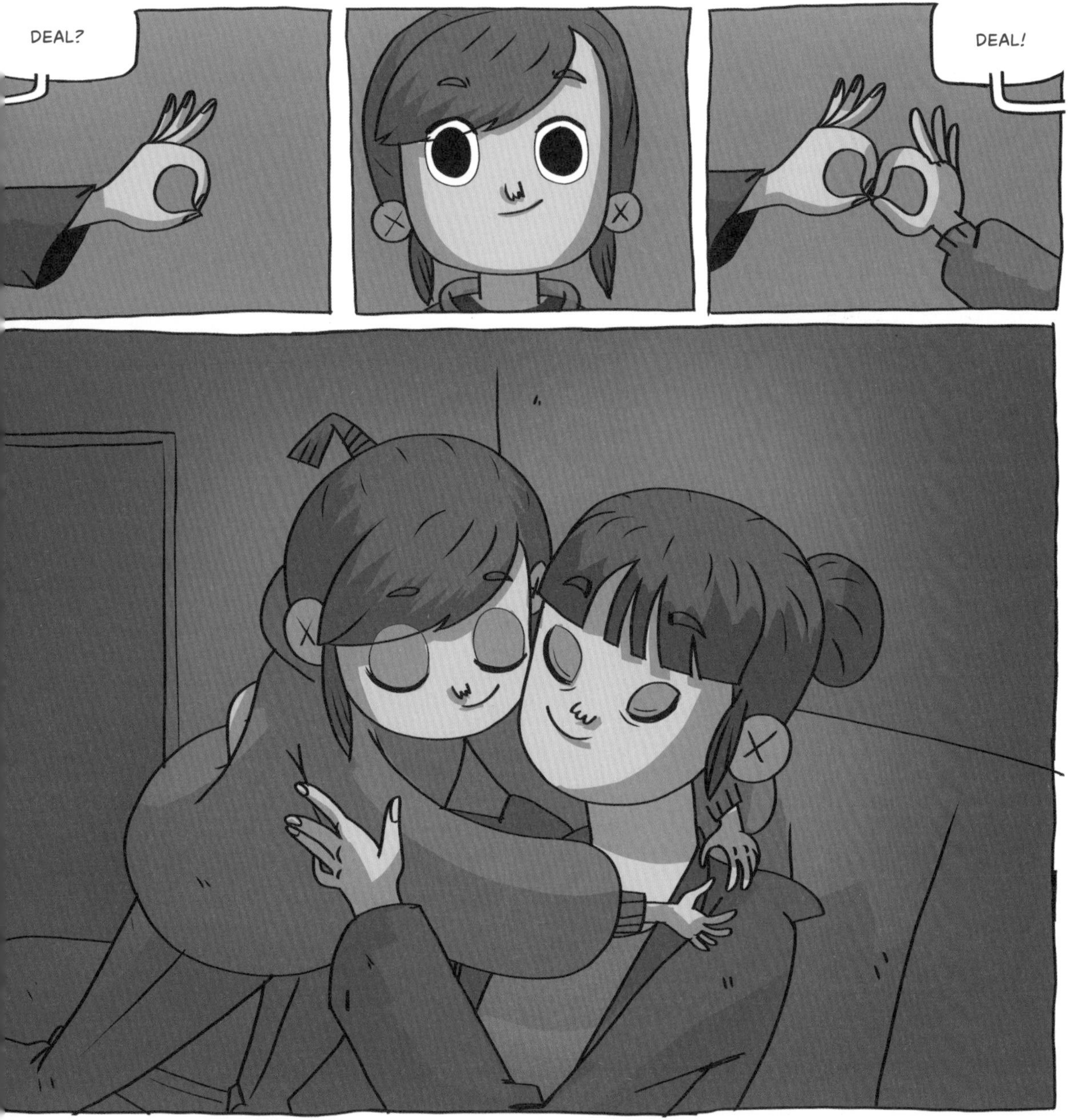
DEAL?
DEAL!

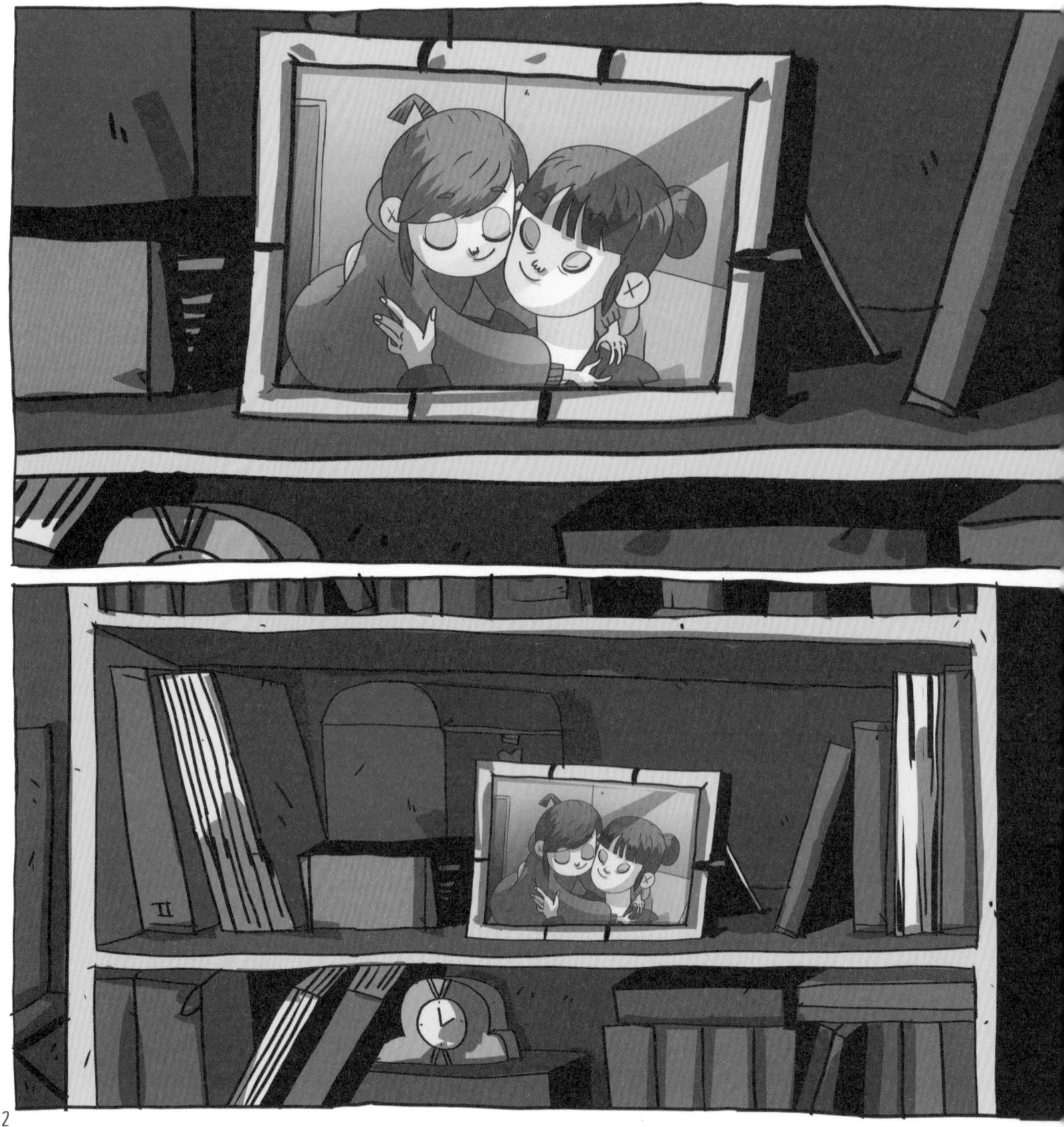
II

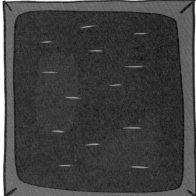

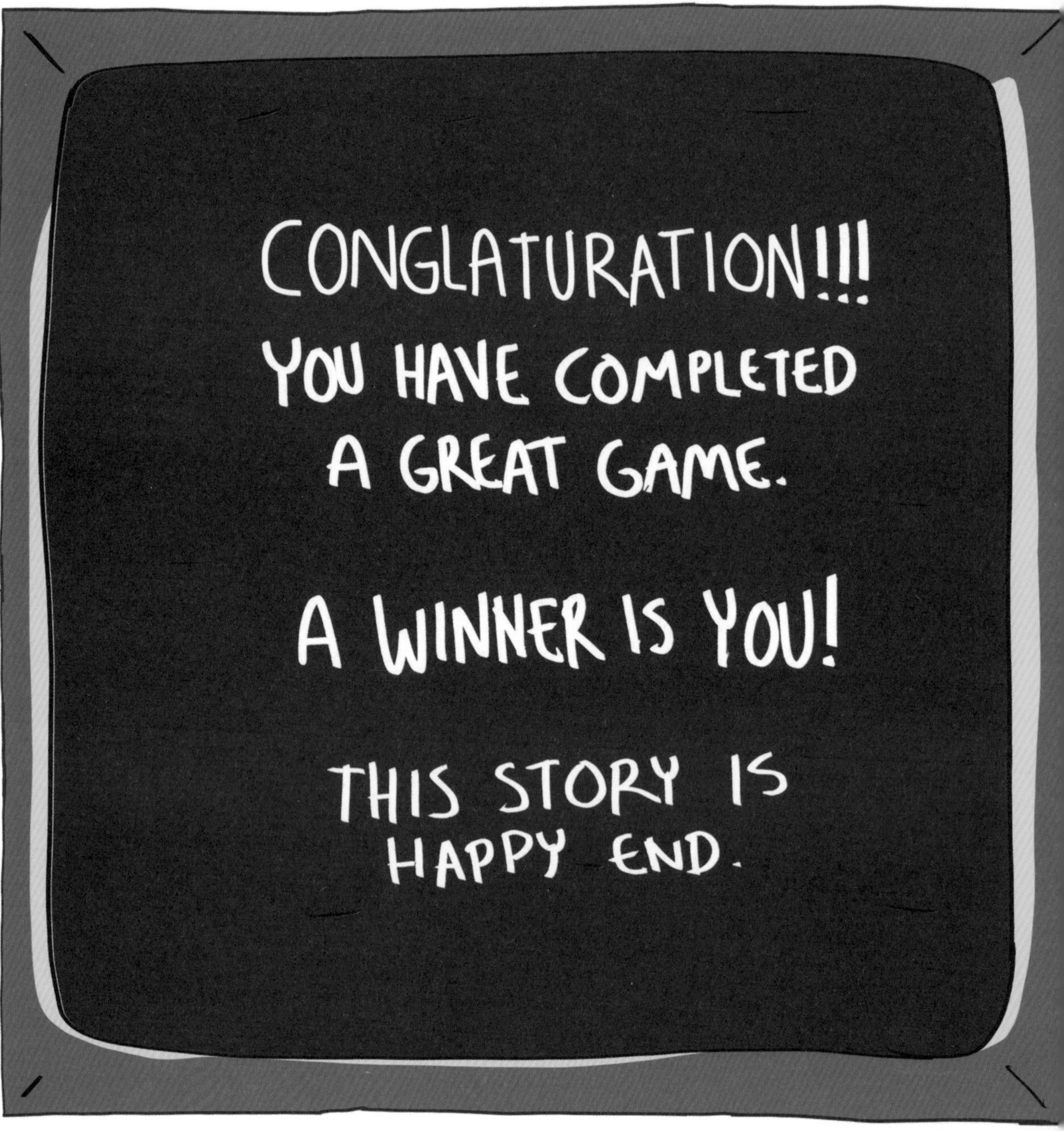
CONGLATURATION!!!
YOU HAVE COMPLETED A GREAT GAME.
A WINNER IS YOU!
THIS STORY IS HAPPY END.

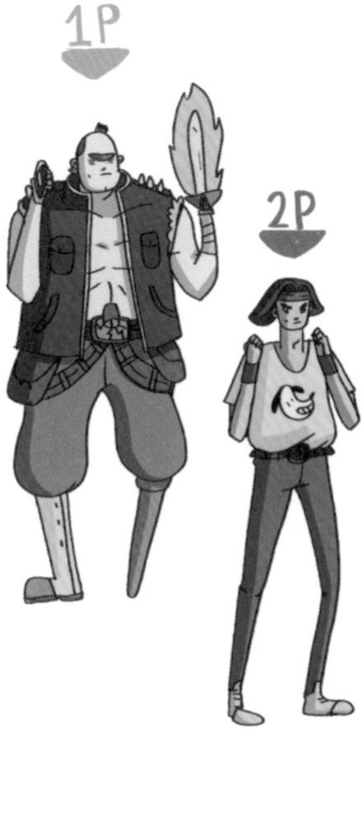
1P
2P

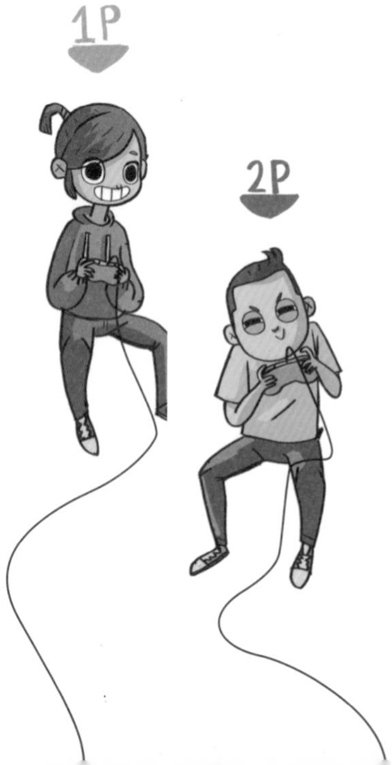
1P
2P